Ryan's Run

hunter parker price

To Alix
my own parallel star

TABLE OF CONTENTS

Chapter One
Reflection

"She's beautiful, but why give her a scar? Trying to make her look tough?"

I knew Speckler would make some dumb comment like this. When I saw him walking up behind me in the reflection of the Bean I expected it the moment he looked down at my sketchbook.

Speckler's my best friend and has been since sixth grade when we found out we both loved drawing comic book super heroes. His first name's Ralph but everyone just calls him Speckler. Even the teachers. Now we're in high school and are both in Mr. Carnofsky's Honors Art class and this is our first "Artists Field Trip" of the year. We're in Millennium Park in the Loop. It's a cool place for art lovers because it has some amazing outdoor art. It's also right next to the Art Institute, but we're not going to the museum this trip, just sticking to the park. We were told by Mr. C to spread out and find something interesting to draw.

Some of the students went over to the Frank Gehry designed concert stage. If I look over I can see them crashed out on the big lawn, their sketchbooks resting on their knees while they take in the giant ribbons of steel "blowing" in the wind. A few went over to the gardens. I saw Marty Kekner and Linda Grotlik hand in hand making a kamikaze run straight for the gardens. There are a lot of tall bushes and trees that can keep you pretty well hidden. I'm sure they have nature on their minds but it's probably not the kind that Mr. C expects. More birds and bees than flowers and trees. Most of the kids though went over to the massive water fountains—these two huge glass towers that project giant faces on the front with water spilling out of their "mouths" like some modern-day gargoyle. And even though it's late September it's still pretty warm and the fountains are still going. This is where Speckler went. Actually, he went following Amy Dierdorf, a girl he's had a crush on since Freshman year and who thinks he's as appealing as green slop regurgitated by a toad. But that hasn't stopped him from stalking her.

I'm sitting in front of the Bean. Its real name is Cloud Gate but since it's shaped like a giant steel kidney bean, everyone in Chicago just calls it "The Bean." It's the size of a city bus and has this smooth mirrored surface that curves around it. When I sat down I was going to sketch the reflection of the Chicago skyline, but then I saw the girl sitting not far behind me reading a book. She looked about my age—sixteen—and I wondered why she wasn't in school. Maybe she's home schooled. But she definitely fit the profile of "something interesting."

She's dressed in black and looks like a refugee from an apocalyptic horror movie. She's wearing a pair of old canvas hi-tops, dark gray cargo pants, and a large black jacket that could hide either an AK-47 or a chainsaw—depending on what was after her. Of course, I don't think she has either of these things, but it's just that I've seen so many horror movies it's what naturally comes to mind. She's reading a book so I don't think she's worrying about some flesh-eating mutant maniac coming after her. She has short dark hair that looks like she cut it herself, but it looks cool in an—I DON'T CARE WHAT ANYBODY THINKS ABOUT ME—kind of way. And the scar just makes her look even more like a badass. It's a thin line that comes down from her left eye—no it's her right eye—I forgot I'm looking at her reflection—down to her cheek. Her face is thin, her lips a bit pale, and moving slightly as she mouths the words as she's reading. It's her eyes though that is the most captivating. Large, round, dark—brown or green, I'm not sure which since she's not close enough—and very intense. She's concentrating hard, her eyebrows arched, chin sinking slowly as she gets to the bottom of the page.

I have most of her face sketched out and I think it looks pretty accurate. This is when Speckler came over and made the comment about her looking beautiful—except for the scar.

"I drew a scar because she has a scar," I tell him without looking up from my work. "What happened? Mr. C kicked you out of the fountain?"

He shakes his head in disgust. "Can you believe it? He says I'm not taking this serious enough."

I give him a quick glance in the reflection of the Bean. Speck's taller than me by almost a foot, skinny as a charcoal pencil, with green-streaked brown hair for that funky look he can't quite pull off.

His shoes and socks are dangling casually from one hand, his jeans are rolled up to the knee and I can see several inches of water stain on them. His sketchbook, tucked under one arm, probably has nothing on it except maybe some dried nacho cheese. Not taking this serious? Speckler? No way.

He wanders over to the concrete railing, leans over for a better view of the fountains down below at street level, then comes back looking disappointed. "He's still down there like a freaking *eunuch* guarding the harem. He obviously doesn't care one iota about true love."

"I'm sure Mr. C's job description doesn't mention giving breaks to students who think they're in love—"

"Whoa, back up buddy. *Think* Ryan? No, not think. I *believe*. You'll find that out one day when you meet your true love. Geez, if the man would just go over to the gardens to pry apart Kekner and Grotlik, then I can ninja back over to the fountains."

"You mean back over to Amy?"

He gives me a grin. "I am a man with a plan. She likes to deny that we're meant to be together. It's a little game we play. I call her a fox—she calls me a scum-sucking freakazoid. I say her lips say no but her eyes say yes—"

"And she says you need to learn how to read eyes better." I'd heard this rant before. It was funny the first hundred times. If only Speckler would get the hint, but he's too dense. Or too much in love. At least it gives him a purpose in life. Me? I'm still trying to find my purpose.

I get back to my drawing before my muse leaves. I work on her neck, which is quite lovely even if most of it is covered up by this strange necklace with these odd V designs around it. It's really more of a collar than a necklace, like a dog collar except it's made of metal. It's got great lines—the neck not the necklace. Graceful. She could be a dancer. A slam dancer. I can picture her in some punk rock club with her elbows flying lost in some hard-driving song.

Speckler is still standing over my shoulder waiting for Carnofsky to exit the fountains. He turns his attention back to me for the moment. "So what did you mean by that?" he says. I guess Mr. C isn't in any hurry to leave the harem.

"What did I mean by what?"

"You said you drew a scar because she has a scar."

"What's not to understand? And can you keep your voice down? She might hear you."

"Uh—who might hear me?" There's a blank look on his face. Can he be that completely clueless?

"Uh—the girl."

He lays a hand on my shoulder. "I think you've been out in the sun too long. Your brain is beginning to bake. I don't see any girl. Unless you mean these fat tourists from Omaha trying to squeeze out the fat tourists from Tokyo for the best angle of the Bean?"

I stop shading her neck to give him a piercing look. Speckler's a practical joker—the class clown—but sometimes he can go too far or carry a joke too long. But he's not smiling. He looks completely serious.

"You don't see the girl?" I point my pencil at her reflection. "Amy's right—you do need to learn how to read eyes better— starting with your own."

Speckler turns around and looks behind us. "I have no idea what you're pointing at, Ryan. The only people I see are a weird albino guy in a suit punching in his Blackberry like he's trying to get the last trade in before the market closes and a guy with an I heart Chicago T-shirt selling overpriced popcorn. So which of the two is your dream girl? Or maybe she's hiding in the popcorn machine. Does she pop out just for you?" His voice changes to a low sultry tone. "Hi, Ryan—you want to come pour some butter on me big boy?"

I smile despite myself. "You sound like a demented drag queen." I point emphatically at her reflection once again. "There!" I quickly lower my voice to a whisper before she hears me. "The girl sitting ten feet behind me?"

The blank look remains on his face.

"The one reading the book?"

He shakes his head.

"THE ONE DRESSED IN BLACK."

She must have heard me this time but she still has her nose in the book. Maybe she's listening to music? I can't see any ear buds but they could be some new kind, wireless and microscopic.

Again Speckler looks behind and all around. "Are you kidding me? You're joking right?"

I don't know why he's pretending not to see her. Maybe just to have some fun before he can return to Amy. "I'm not joking. You're the one that's joking."

"One of is joking and it ain't me brother. Maybe you *think* you see her. If she's not hiding in I heart's popcorn machine then maybe she's a ghost." He cups his hands around his mouth. "Hey!"

Some of the other students who are at the Bean and even some who are stretched out on the lawn look over. The group of Japanese tourists also want to see what this idiot is shouting about. Some aim their cameras at him—maybe to finally capture the elusive Jerkzilla they've heard so much about.

"Hey!" Speckler continues to yell, "Girl with the scar! Ghost girl!"

I grab him by the bottom of his Green Day hoodie. "Geez, Speckler! Shut the hell up will you!" I let go of the hoodie and take a quick look in the Bean to see her reaction. Hopefully her music's up real loud—if she's even listening to music. Could be she was just ignoring us earlier but now, even if she has Disturbed or Generation Kill cranked up full blast blowing out her ear drums there is no way she didn't hear Speckler screaming like a madman.

But no. Her head remains down. She's still reading. There's no sign she even heard him. How can this be? Then it hits me. She's deaf. She has to be deaf. How else to explain ignoring Speckler? If anything, he's almost impossible to ignore.

"See," Speckler tells me. "Your girl must be a ghost. Hey, maybe we can talk her into doing the haunted house." He's referring to the fundraiser for the Art Club. Mr. C wants to take us to New York City for Spring Break to visit the Met and the Guggenheim and some real SoHo art galleries so we've planned this elaborate haunted house for Halloween to raise money. Everyone in the club is pretty psyched about it. I think most of us are more excited about putting on a haunted house than going to New York. I know that's all Speckler can talk about—what freak monster he's going to dress up as to scare the bejesus out of little kids.

"The girl is definitely not a ghost," I tell him. "I just guessed that she's probably deaf, so it is so not cool to be joking about the handicapped."

"I wasn't joking about her being handicapped, since I just found out. But it's a stupid point we're arguing about because there is no girl. So can you cut it out and help me with Carnofsky? Go down there and distract him or something. Tell him Kekner and Grotlick are in the bushes doing the super-duper double-nasty."

"I have no idea what the 'super-duper double-nasty' is and I probably don't want to know. But the girl is no ghost. Do I have to take you over to her to prove it?"

"Yeah, you do. I want to meet this hot goth girl with the scar. Too bad she's deaf or else you could have a long conversation about art or politics or how you want to know more about the super-duper double-nasty. I'm sure she can tell you all you need—"

"Okay, funny guy. I'll prove it."

I get to my feet and turn around. I stop cold. I can't believe it. There's no one there. I look around. Nothing. *Where could she have gone?*

"I swear she was sitting right there." I point to the spot. "I was looking at her less than a minute ago. You saw me. There's no way she could've gotten up and left. No way."

"Okay, ha ha. Presto magico! Poof and she's gone. That's a good one. Look, Ryan, if you don't want to admit you were drawing your dream girl I get it. I know you haven't had a date in over a year but really? Has it gotten that lonely for you that you have to invent imaginary girls?"

I grip the front of his hoodie. "I'm not joking! How can I make this any plainer you moron? I saw her. I sat down to draw the Chicago skyline and when I looked up . . ." I turn to the Bean to show him what happened. My mouth drops open.

"There she is." I point at her reflection. "She's still sitting there. But how is that possible?" I turn around and there's no one there. I turn back to the Bean and I see her sitting cross-legged reading her book. "You see her don't you?" I continue to point at her reflection in the shiny steel surface. "You have to see her!"

He slowly untangles my fingers from the front of his hoodie and takes a step back. "Ryan, you're going too far with this. A joke's a joke."

"DO YOU SEE HER?"

"No, dammit! I see you and me and these other schlubs looking at you as if your head is on backwards. Now, cut it out will you?"

This is freaking me out. *It cannot be possible.* How can I be the only one seeing something that isn't there?

12

Suddenly the girl stops reading and looks up at me. We stare at each other's reflection. Her own eyes open wide like she can't believe what she's seeing. Maybe she's looking at me like I'm looking at her. Like we're seeing something that isn't there but is there. Our eyes are locked on to each other for a good long ten seconds—maybe the longest ten seconds of my life. Then something spooks her. She breaks the spell, her eyes dart to something ahead of her. She snaps her book shut and springs to her feet. She looks ready to break into a run but something happens to her. She freezes as if her feet are encased in cement and then her whole body suddenly convulses, shakes, and then collapses to the ground. It's like she was shocked by something, as if she'd grabbed hold of an electric cable and a thousand watts just whipped through her whole body. She's not moving. Is she dead?

"She's hurt!" I want to run to her but when I turn around she's still not there. *Where the hell is she?*

When I look back at the Bean something new has appeared. Something grotesque. I can't believe what I'm seeing, like some horror movie come to life. There's a creature standing over the girl. It's enormous, almost eight feet tall. I can't see its face because it's wearing some contraption like a gas mask. It's head is completely bald—and yellow! A sickly-looking yellow. Diseased. It's dressed in what looks like black body armor and it's holding a gun of some sort. A silver metallic rifle. He's pointing it at the girl like he intends to shoot her.

"Don't!" I yell. "Keep away from her!"

The creature doesn't hear me, just like the girl didn't hear anything that Speckler said. Maybe I'm glad there is no creature standing there. What would I do if there were? But if he's not standing there and she's not lying there, then where are they?

Speckler grabs a hold of my arm. "Ryan, if this is some kind of joke to scare me . . . well, you're doing a great job."

Then a sharp pain hits my brain like a dozen daggers stabbing into my head at once. I scream and fall to my hands and knees. I can hear Speckler yelling for Carnofsky as the pain ratchets up. I've never had headaches before but my mother gets migraines. She says it's like having a bus back over your head—slowly—and stay there.

And just like that the pain is gone.

I stand up and steady myself as everything comes back into focus. I check the reflection in the Bean. There's no girl and no creature, just me surrounded by a crowd of students and tourists. My classmates ask me how I'm doing, if I feel all right, the look of frightened concern plastered on their faces.

Speckler comes running up with Mr. C who looks pretty worried himself. This is probably way worse than catching Marty and Linda doing the super-duper double-nasty. Maybe. I'm not sure.

"Are you okay, Ryan?" Carnofsky asks. "Let's give him some room. Don't all crowd around."

"Yeah, give my bud some room!" Speckler begins to force everyone back.

Mr. C stops him. "Speckler, please. I think I can handle this. What happened, Ryan? Speckler says you saw something."

I give Speckler a look that warns him not to say anything about my visions. I don't want to have to explain what it is I saw. Everyone around, all my peers and even the Japanese tourists are looking at me like I went crazy. I tell them I'm fine. Whatever happened it's gone now. But Mr. C won't listen. He says I should go to the emergency room to get checked out. He says he has to do this, it's his job. I know he does. If something really were wrong with me then he'd be blamed for doing nothing. But *something* must be wrong with me. Maybe I'm getting migraines like my mother. But is hallucinating a symptom of migraines? I've never heard it was.

"You really had me scared," Speckler says as we wait for the ambulance to arrive. I can see the fear in his eyes. It's for real.

"Me too," I say.

I study the ground and say nothing more. I know he wants to talk about my vision, but I'm not ready yet, and not here, not now.

As the ambulance pulls up I take one last look back at the Bean. Still no girl or creature. A part of me is glad, but a part of me wishes I knew what happened to her. It's like walking out before the end of a movie. Even if they were nothing but figments of my over-active brain—a brain raised on comic books and horror movies—I still can't help wanting to know what happened. She was so real to me. I look down at my sketchbook. Her face is as real to me as all the others around me.

They take me to the emergency room and run a simple neurological exam, the lights in the eyes, the follow the finger game.

Carnofsky, after getting the rest of the students back to school, is there and so is Speckler. After awhile my mother and father show up. I hated that they called him. I knew they had to, that it was procedure, but still. I hate that they called him to leave work and come down for nothing. They do more extensive tests but find nothing wrong with me. That's what makes it worse.

Chapter Two
The Magnificent Mungo

Even though they found nothing wrong with me, my father is convinced I was tripping the drug fantastic. He doesn't believe me when I tell him I'm not taking drugs. Art is my drug, as the commercial says. My mother, however, thinks it's migraines since that's what she suffers from, so she comes to my defense.

"Maybe," he says reluctantly. He would hate to admit he's wrong. If he's got it in his head I'm some kind of whacked-out drug addict then it's almost impossible to shake that perception loose. So all during the week he's watching me—looking for obvious signs of addiction. And I know he's searched my room trying to find my "secret stash" or the meth lab I've got cooking in the crawl space behind my bed. Of course not finding anything won't stop him from thinking the worse. I can only imagine what he would think if I tell him the truth about what I saw in the reflection of the Bean. He thought I was on drugs without my revealing to him any of my visions. What would he think if I told him I saw an eight-foot tall yellow-headed monster threatening a girl with a laser gun?

My dad is not a bad guy though, even if we're not very close. I was never his favorite son. If it's any conciliation I like to think that I was his second favorite son—out of two sons. His first son, my brother Jack, died in Afghanistan. This was a year ago and my father still hasn't gotten over it yet. Well, none of us have. Jack was the best. He was handsome and smart and a great athlete. He played power forward on the basketball team and catcher on the baseball team. He was fearless. And when he joined the Army we thought a strong kid like him and smart—nothing will happen. And nothing did the first year he was over there. Then, one night outside Kandahar Province on a routine patrol, the Humvee he was riding in got hit by an RPG—rocket propelled grenade. It killed everyone inside. It killed my dad inside as well. He shut down and got angry. He kept it bottled up and exploded at anyone at anytime over the smallest thing. He was hurting and didn't know how to deal with it. My mom tried to get him to attend a support group for families who lost someone in the war. He wouldn't go though. He said he would heal in his own way. But he hasn't. The wound that ripped him apart is still there, under the surface. At least he's tempered his anger somewhat. Mom's the one who has really gotten involved. She helps organize care packages for soldiers and attends weekly meetings. I go sometimes when I can. These meetings are not as depressing as you might think. And it's good to talk to others who know what you're going through.

But I think the thing that hurts Dad the most, the hardest obstacle for him to get over, is the way Jack died. When my brother first enlisted Dad couldn't have been more proud. That first year it was all he could talk about, how much honor his son was showing this great country. He thought of Jack as some kind of super soldier. A real American hero. Then he died suddenly just riding in the back of a Humvee. No heroics. No saving of anyone or attacking a machine-gun nest or leading his men through enemy fire back to safety. I think that's what bothers Dad the most. He can't even brag his son died a hero.

During the week I don't suffer any more headaches, but I can't get the girl out of my thoughts—or the creature. It's all I can think about. I've convinced myself that what I saw wasn't a hallucination. It had to have been real. But how? That's what I can't figure out. At night, instead of doing my homework, I work on sketch after sketch of the thing. I can see its face—or lack of a face since it had a mask covering it—vividly, its hulking form standing over the girl's prone body.

I work on its skin with some watercolors till I get the tint just right. It's not a bright yellow—not canary or lemon—but more duller, a brown mustardy yellow. Hairless, but its skull was not shaved. There was no indication that it had hair at all—at any time. It had a smooth almost leathery texture to it. The mask covering its face, like the suit it wore, was shiny black. There was a glass—or what looked like glass—shield where the eyes should be, but the glass was tinted almost as black as the outfit it wore. Maybe it was a computer screen ala the Terminator's eyes. Maybe the thing gets readings on it, readouts that come up in green digital displays. Threat assessments or orders. What could it have received about the girl? Obviously she was no danger to anyone. He only had three feet and two hundred pounds on her. Not to mention the weapon. She was unarmed. She was only reading a book! I can't help but get enraged when I think of the brutality of the thing—attacking her for what reason? Reading? Is that behavior so insidious that it's outlawed? I know in our past history reading certain books could be considered heretical—punishable by death. Is that what she received at the hands of that creature? Death? I can't think she's dead. I can't look into the eyes staring back at me from my sketchbook and think that one moment she was looking into my own eyes—and then the next her life was being snuffed out by that monster.

"These are so cool," Speckler says flipping through the sketches. "I wish I could've seen it."

"No you don't, believe me."

We're up in my room. It's been a week and we haven't talked much about my crazy vision. Speck's pretty much forgotten about it and has moved on to once more being consumed with Amy Dierdorf. I reach for the sketchbook but he pivots away from me. It's hard enough looking at what I've drawn, but to show them to Speckler makes it even harder. It makes the girl's death seem more probable in some way.

"But it wasn't real." He looks up from the full page drawing of the mustard-yellow monster. Mustardhead I've begun calling it. "You were imagining it, weren't you? Hallucinating?"

"I don't think so, Speck. It looked real enough to me. How could I imagine something so vivid? So strange?"

"From all the monsters you have stored in your brain." He taps the drawing as proof. "I mean, dude—you got a whole rolodex of monsters up there."

"Sure, monsters. But what about the girl? No, I can't believe it's all in my imagination. This was no movie or comic I've ever seen."

"But your headache? The two must be related somehow."

"Maybe. But the headache only lasted for a few seconds."

"Yeah, but you said it was the worst thing you ever felt—"

"Like a railroad spike being driven into my skull. Yeah, it was intense. But it came afterwards—after I saw the images. It would be different if I had the headache and then saw the girl and Mustardhead."

He flips back to the first sketch of the girl. "Okay, if they're not figments of your imagination then who do you think she is?"

"I wish I knew." I manage to take back the sketchbook and before putting it away I stare once more into those eyes. I can't help but remember the look of fear that came over her when that thing showed up. No, she can't be dead. I won't believe the life those eyes revealed can be taken away so easily. But I know personally that life is like that. Here one moment, gone the next in the blink of an eye.

The next day after school I avoid Speckler and the Art Club telling him I need to get home to help my mom box up care packages. Then I hop on the el and go down to the Loop and sit in the same spot in front of the Bean. I sit for hours hoping to see her again. A part of me even wants to see the creature, just to know I wasn't hallucinating. I want some reassurance that what I saw was real. But more than anything I want to look into those eyes—not just the eyes of a drawing—but the eyes of a real girl. There was something about her that was so strange and different, as if she wasn't a part of this world. But is Speckler right? Is she living in some unknown unseen ghost world? The hours go by and nothing emerges except the glare of the setting sun reflecting off the skyscrapers.

"I thought this is where you'd be." I don't need to look up into the Bean to know it's Speckler.

"I just want to see her again," I say.

He sits down next to me. "Listen, you're my best bud and all but you know that all this is pretty bat-shit crazy right?"

"Just as crazy as chasing after a girl for two years who thinks you're lower than fungus?"

He gives me a grin. "I may be lower than fungus but I am a *fungi*—get it? A fun guy?"

"Yeah, I get it. But I know what I saw. And the weird thing is—I know she saw me too. She looked right at me. Just before that—*thing*—showed up."

"Okay, say what you saw was real. How would you explain it?"

"I can't explain it. Maybe she was a ghost. Maybe there's a ghost world all around us with creatures and monsters that we can't see."

"That would be so awesome," Speckler says. There's a mad gleam in his eyes. He's already imagining outrageously invisible monsters walking all around us.

"But how come I only saw it in the reflection of the Bean?"

"Maybe this is some kind of weird multi-dimensional spot. A window into the ghost world." He moves his hands in the air—trying to feel some weird paranormal electro-magnetism? Or maybe he's trying to punch a hole into another universe? Hell, maybe he's trying to summon Rice Krispy—his crazy Monkey God. You never know with Speckler. After a minute he gives up and puts his hands down.

"And how come I can't see anything now? And why me and no one else? You were standing right next to me, yet you didn't see anything."

"I don't know. Maybe the window's closed and the curtains are drawn. But I do think this is so far above us that we need professional help. It'll take a bigger mind than ours to unravel this mystery."

"I don't need a psychiatrist," I tell him emphatically.

"That wasn't the professional help I was talking about, but I'll keep that idea on the back burner just in case you really dive into the deep end of the crazy pool. No, I was talking about *real professional help.*"

"You don't mean . . . ?"

"Of course I do. Who else?"

We both say it together: "Mungo."

Jerry Mungowski, or "Mungo" as he's better known, owns the city's best comic book store—Mungo's Pages of Peril. The place is a second home to me and Speckler. We often work for Mungo for free just to get first dibs on the latest copies of *X-Men* and *The Walking Dead.* Some people have their church or synagogue, Speckler and me have Mungo's.

We manage to get to Pages of Peril just before it closes.

"Looks like your classic mutant of the apocalypse," Mungo says after looking through my illustrations of the creature. "You got your gas mask so the air is probably pretty toxic. You got your freakish size so you can bash people to death. The gun for widespread terror. Yep. Classic mutant. Seen it in a thousand comic books and a gazillion bad movies. Nothing original. Sorry, Ryan. The sketches are good but you'll have to do better if you want to impress me." He slides the sketchbook back to me.

We hadn't told him the story yet, just showed him the sketches to get his reaction. "But this wasn't any movie or comic book," I tell him. "I saw this thing for real."

Mungo gazes at me skeptically. He looks nothing like the character Comic Book Guy on *The Simpsons*. Mungo's a little person, standing no taller than four feet, and looks like he could be an accountant. He wears nerdy horn-rimmed glasses, a white short sleeve shirt and a tie with a picture of Tor Johnson glaring at you from the movie *Plan 9 from Outer Space.*

Mungo gives the sketches another quick study. "Where did you see it? I know you weren't at Comic-Con in San Diego or I would have seen you." Mungo makes a yearly pilgrimage to Comic-Con, the largest comic book convention in the world and Mecca for anyone mad about sci-fi, fantasy or horror. Each year he dresses up as a different character—very elaborate—and usually very obscure. He does it as a test to see how long it takes someone to guess who he is. At a place like Comic-Con, where people live breathe eat sci-fi and horror, it usually doesn't take long. This year he tried to make it a little more fun, steering away from such popular sources as *Star Wars, Star Trek,* and the known universes of both Marvel and DC. He decided to go with Zombie Bill Murray from the movie *Zombieland,* except he had to give it an extra spin and went as the zombified character Bill Murray played in the movie *Kingpin.* Zombie Ernie McCracken, complete with bowling ball and comb over. It was pretty funny and he said a lot of people didn't get it. He didn't say it but we knew that it was mostly because of his size. Most people think of little people as childlike, and so don't see him as an adult. One girl guessed it right away though. They're having a long distance love affair. She lives in Topeka, is not vertically challenged as Mungo likes to say, and owns a tattoo shop called Topeka Ink!

"He saw it in the Bean," Speckler clarifies before I can respond.

"What bean?"

"The Bean—you know, that big shiny sculpture in Millennium Park? He saw it in the reflection." The way he says it makes it sound like I really am bat-shit crazy.

I quickly explain what happened during the field trip. When I finish I ask Mungo why the creature would be wearing a gas mask and not the girl. "If the air's toxic then it should be toxic for her too, right?"

Mungo shakes his head. "Not necessarily. You say that thinking they might be the same species, but you're not taking into consideration that they might be *two different species*."

Speckler and I look at each other and nod. Mungo the Wise. We knew we came to the right place.

"But how come Ryan only saw it in the reflection and not for real?" Speckler asks. "My theory is that he was looking through some kind of window into another world."

"Perhaps, but the question then is what exactly were you looking into? Was it a parallel universe? A window into the future? Another planet? Maybe even the past? Maybe you were seeing the Lost City of Atlantis."

"In Chicago? That sounds pretty bizarre." But then again it's no less bizarre than the other choices.

"I have to admit I don't believe that one myself. My guess is that whatever you were looking at must have been right there. You were seeing Chicago, but was it a parallel Chicago or a Chicago of the future? That's the question."

"What do you mean—a *parallel* Chicago?" I ask.

"You've heard of the multiverse theory?"

Both Speckler and I look at each other. "I've heard the term," I say.

"Me too," Speck says.

"Okay, it goes something like this. During the big bang there might have been multiple bangs creating multiple universes simultaneously—some of them mirror images of one another."

"Like a set of twins being born," I say.

"Twins, triplets, octuplets, there's no end to the number of parallel universes. And in each one there might be a duplicate of ourselves. However, each universe may not be totally alike. Remember the episode 'Mirror, Mirror' from the original *Star Trek* series?"

"Is that the one when Kirk switches with another Kirk—the evil Kirk?" Speck says.

"Exactly. His double was from a parallel universe. Might be the same thing here."

"You mean each one of us has an evil duplicate in another universe? I wonder what Evil Speckler is like?"

22

"Maybe you're the Evil Speckler and your double is actually a saint," I tell him.

He raises his eyebrows in his best evil warlord imitation. "Maybe I am the Evil Speckler—HUAHAHA!"

"It doesn't work like that," Mungo says. "I was just using the *Star Trek* episode as an example of a parallel universe. It doesn't mean that the parallel universe has an exact opposite of us, just another version. That episode was written just for more dramatic effect."

"So I don't have an evil duplicate?" Speckler seems disappointed. As if he really *wanted* to have an evil duplicate.

"Probably not," Mungo tells him. "But who knows, your duplicate—each of our duplicates if there is one—may be extremely different from us. It just depends on the circumstances of their lives and the world they live in."

"Like a world where yellow-headed monsters are chasing after them?" I say.

"Precisely."

"So in that universe, it may not be uncommon to have monsters running around?" Speckler asks.

"Well, it depends on what you mean by monsters."

"Monsters like this?" I point to the illustrations.

Mungo glances back at the sketches. "They might appear to be monsters, but they're really not. I told you I thought they were typical apocalyptic mutants. Well, they're typical because it wouldn't be unreasonable for them to exist. If they're human, then they could be the result of some kind of toxic disaster. If they're not human, then as an alien this could be their normal appearance. Of course, with the mask covering their faces we really can't tell."

"You mean they might have one eye or two mouths?" Speckler says.

"No, nothing that extreme. But the size, color, shape of their eyes might give some clue. The nose could be different. The mouth might have different sets of teeth—or no teeth at all."

"But couldn't a toxic mutant have that as well?" I say.

"It could. Sure. But like I said, without seeing the face we really don't know. Mutant or alien? It's a toss-up without more evidence."

"Or alien mutant?" Speckler says—almost hopefully.

"Yes, it could be that as well."

"I told you Mungo would know," Speckler says as if the whole thing were solved. But it's far from solved. It only creates more questions.

"Mind if I take these to study some more?" Mungo asks. I say sure and tear out some of the sketches of the creature. He sees the girl on the first page of the sketchbook and gives a low whistle. "Nice," he says. "Reminds me of Nadine. But instead of a scar she has several tattoos of tiny Hello Kitty figures—with devil horns." Nadine is his Topeka squeeze doll.

"That's the damsel in distress," Speckler says. "Every story needs one."

"This isn't a story," I tell him. This is real. "She's the girl I saw in the reflection. The one I saw before the creature showed up. She was sitting reading a book but then got spooked when she saw the creature. She tried to get out of there but then she got shocked by like a thousand volts of electricity and then collapsed to the ground."

"What's with the weird collar?" Mungo asks.

"I don't know. It's what she was wearing."

He looks at it more closely. "What are those markings on it?"

He indicates the strange V markings decorating the surface. I've drawn them as best as I can. They ring the collar in a strange pattern—sometimes the Vs are right side up, some are upside down, and some on their sides.

"They look familiar," he says after some thought. "But I can't place it." He gets a sheet of paper and copies down the pattern of Vs. "I'll let you know what I find."

"Thanks, Mungo," I say.

"You're the best," Speckler adds. "Now, do you have the new *Justice League*?"

24

Chapter Three
The Hotel Zamboni

The next few days are nerve-racking as I wait for Mungo to call. I fight the urge to go back to the Bean and instead concentrate on my schoolwork that I avoided all last week and make the Art Club meetings. Mr. C called a special meeting for today saying it was urgent we all attend.

There's about twenty of us in the club. Art geeks most of the kids at school call us. Not all of us are total geeks though as some of us are more into art than others. Some joined because their friends wanted to join. Kind of like me and Speckler. I'm way more into art than he is. He still enjoys drawing comic book heroes and cartoon figures, but as far as art goes, he wouldn't recognize an Edward Hopper painting if it jumped out and bit him—and he's been to the Art Institute umpteen million times and has seen "Nighthawks" every single one of them. He probably would have quit the club a long time ago if it wasn't for Amy.

"I hope you got us a good rate at the Plaza Hotel," Speckler says. He gives Amy a hopeful look that says something like: Me-You-Hotel-Late Night-Pure Bliss. She gives him a soul-destroying look that says: You-Me-Never Going to Happen.

"I'm afraid there's not going to be any New York," Mr. C says. After that little bomb everybody begins attacking him with questions.

He holds up his hands to quiet us all down. "The building we had secured for the haunted house fundraiser is no longer available. As you know, the building we were going to use was up for sale, but the owner said if he didn't get any serious offers by the end of October he would lend it to us free of charge for the one night. I figured the way the economy is that meant we were in. I was wrong. The owner got a good offer."

"So just get another space," Speckler says eagerly. I can see his fantasy of paying Amy a midnight rendezvous quickly vanishing.

"It's not that simple, Speckler," Mr. C says. "Getting another space that's as good as the first one with this much short notice will be nearly impossible."

"Why can't we just do it here, Mr. C?" Amy asks. "I'm sure the school will let us. We can have it in the gym."

"Yes, we could. But I'm afraid it won't get us enough money to cover the cost of the trip. No, if we do a haunted house we have to go big. Something that would attract a lot of people. I don't think we'll be able to make it now."

No one is more upset about this than Speckler. Like I said, the idea of spending three nights in New York with Amy Dierdorf paled in comparison to dressing up and scaring the hell out of people.

"We have to find some other way to make the money," he says later as we walk home to my house.

"You heard Mr. C. It has to be big or else we won't make enough money. Do you think your parents will give you five hundred dollars to go to New York?"

"My parents wouldn't give me five dollars," he says.

"My point exactly. And my dad? He's already working extra hours at the airport just to pay bills."

"At least you can get a discounted airline ticket since your dad works as a baggage handler," he says.

"Yeah, for me, but not for twenty other people."

"Maybe your dad can sneak us onto the plane? We can hide out in the baggage compartment."

"You're not serious are you?"

"No . . . of course not." I can tell by his face that he was quite serious.

As soon as we walk into my house my mother tells me I had an urgent phone call. "A man named Mingo or something called," she says.

"It's Mungo, Mom. Mungo. And what did he say?"

"He said to tell you bingo—that's why I confused his name."

"Bingo? Are you sure Mrs. Whitaker?" Speckler asks.

"I'm quite sure, Ralph." She's one of the few who actually calls Speckler by his first name. Besides his own parents of course.

"He's found something," Speckler says. There's excitement in his voice. I'm excited as well and we immediately race over to Pages of Peril.

"I knew that collar looked familiar," Mungo says. "Here, take a look." He pulls out a comic book from behind the counter. It looks very crude. Definitely not Marvel or DC or any of the other professional comic book companies. It looks homemade. I know Mungo sells several amateur comics from local artists. He believes in supporting local talent no matter how good or bad they are and rarely makes any money from them. Most of the time they're pretty awful but a few are really good and have even launched the careers of several artists and writers. Speckler and I even created our own comic book. *Nuke Fist and Kid Fantastic.* They team up to battle evil-doers of course. Basically it's a poor man's—and I mean really living-out-of-garbage-cans poor—Batman and Robin. So far we've only managed to sell one copy. And I think the guy was either drunk or stoned who bought it.

Speckler reads the title over my shoulder. *"The Other Side."*

Mungo points to the book. "About ten years ago this guy comes in with a small box of these. I paid him and told him to check back in a month to see how they sold. I didn't think they would sell at all. The art work is pretty lousy and the story wasn't very original."

"Who's the guy?" I ask.

"He went by the name Charlie Fingers."

"Charlie Fingers?" Speckler says. "Why? Because he didn't have any fingers? How did he draw it—with his feet?"

"No—he had all his fingers. Half these artists use a pen name. They didn't sell just like I thought and I didn't see the guy ever again. I threw the box down in my basement with the rest of the non-sellables. Looking at your drawings made me remember it, but it took me a while to find them. Take a look, I think you'll find it interesting."

I sit down and begin reading. The artwork is pretty crude and the writing is not much better. It tells the story of a bike messenger—I'm guessing it's this Charlie Fingers—who gets a delivery to an old abandoned hotel that sits on the south branch of the Chicago River, except he doesn't think it's abandoned. He finds a side door open, goes in, and looks around expecting to find the owner or maybe a construction crew doing demolition. The place looks condemned. He looks about, goes upstairs to the rooms and finds no one. Just before he gives up and leaves he gets a massive headache, goes over to a window to breathe some fresh air and sees people outside on the street shuffling by in large groups. All of them are wearing the same collar I saw on the girl—the one with the strange V markings on the side. They look ragged, like refugees fleeing their homes. They carry bags and suitcases and push carts or pull wagons filled with stuff. Then he sees two of the yellowheaded creatures—the Mustardheads. They look up and see him standing in the window. They break in and chase him up to the roof where he sees the city of Chicago in ruins. Skyscrapers are demolished, or broken in half. The Sears Tower is nearly destroyed. And above it all huge spaceships hover in the sky. Smaller ships are also flying about. Just as the creatures come up to get him he runs to the side and leaps into the river. When he surfaces he's back in his Chicago. No Mustardheads. No spaceships. It's just as he left it.

I hand it to Speckler to look through. A weird sensation comes over me. At least I know I'm not the only one who's seen them.

"So you don't know how I can get a hold of this Charlie Fingers?" I ask Mungo.

"Like I said he disappeared on me. He left no phone number or address. I googled the name but came up empty."

"Do you think this really happened to him?" Speckler asks. He's finished reading and hands it back to Mungo. "How do we even know this is real and not some fictional story?"

"It had to have happened," I tell him. "It can't be a coincidence. Both creatures are obviously the same. And the people with those collars on with the same V designs?"

"That's what made me remember it," Mungo says. "The creatures weren't very original. But those collars with the same markings? Very distinctive."

"But this didn't happen at the Bean but at some old hotel. The Hotel Z-something."

"It's called the Hotel Zamboni," Mungo says. "I asked one of the delivery guys—an old timer who knows the city like he knows a pastrami sandwich at Manny's Deli—very well. He remembered it as an old railroad hotel just south of the rail yards. He said it was located right on the river so it fits."

"Zamboni?" Speckler repeats the name. "Like the machine they use on hockey rinks? But what can all this be? Are we really dealing with some kind of parallel universe—one where aliens have conquered earth?"

"Just like Ryan's vision it's not clear. It could be. Could be a time portal. There's still not enough information to go on." Mungo opens the comic book to where the messenger escapes the creatures by jumping into the Chicago River. "It seems when he jumped off the building and hits the water it pulls him back to his own world."

"Pretty interesting about the headache huh?" Speckler says. "Ryan experienced the same thing."

"Really?"

"What do you think it is?" I ask.

"Maybe it's a side effect of getting to look through the magic window," Mungo says.

"But it seems like Charlie Fingers was actually in their world," I point out. "The monsters saw him and we're after him—"

"You said the goth girl saw you," Speckler reminds me.

I'm glad he's stopped calling her the scarface girl. "Yeah, but the monster didn't. And it's obvious I wasn't in her world because I never left ours."

"And she didn't hop through the looking glass into this world," Mungo says.

"No, she was just in the reflection of the Bean. And what about the city Charlie Fingers saw? It's obviously Chicago but some of the buildings were destroyed. I'm guessing by the aliens. What was it—some kind of World War III with aliens? This is all too weird. It can't be real."

"Normally I would agree," Mungo says. "But unless you and this Charlie Fingers have been planning this elaborate practical joke on me—"

"Not likely," Speckler says. "The joke would have started ten years ago when Ryan was six years old. We never even heard of you or your store until—what? About three years ago we started coming here?"

"About that," I say. "No, I have no idea who this Charlie Fingers is."

"I didn't think you did," Mungo says. "So everything points to you and Charlie experiencing something that—to my knowledge—no one has ever experienced before. At least I never heard of it happening before. Sure, there's a bunch of wing-nuts out there who may say they've been to other worlds or other dimensions but the proof is in the pudding. And this is the pudding," he says holding up my drawing and the comic book.

"So what do I do now?" I say. "I want to know if this girl is okay. But I went back to the Bean and saw nothing. Maybe I'll never get another glimpse again." The thought of this is depressing. That brief connection with the girl just before the creature showed up was powerful. Like this girl and I had some strange connection.

Mungo gives me a reassuring nod. "Find Charlie Fingers and maybe you'll get your chance. Maybe you can find out what both of you have in common that gave you access to this other world."

"There's only one problem with that," I say. "There's no way to find him. You said so yourself that he just disappeared."

"Start here." Mungo points to the building in the comic book. The Hotel Zamboni.

"Did your delivery guy give you an address?"

"No, but I did a quick search. It wasn't hard to find." He slides a piece of paper across to me with an address written on it.

I glance back at the comic book. "This happened ten years ago. What if the building's been torn down?"

"Only one way to find out," Mungo says.

I look at Speckler. "Up for a little adventure?"

He smiles. "Nuke Fist and Kid Fantastic!"

We gleefully fist bump each other and end with the obligatory explosive sound effects. I just hope the whole escapade doesn't blow up in our faces.

Chapter Four
The Other Side

We begin our search the next day. I looked up the address that Mungo gave me and found the best way to get there was to take the Red Line to Chinatown and then walk west towards the river. It wasn't very far from there.

When we arrive at our stop Speckler wants to stop at one of the restaurants in Chinatown Square and get some egg rolls but I tell him we don't have time. I'm anxious to see if the hotel is still there and don't want to waste time sightseeing and eating.

"Sorry if I'm hungry," Speckler says. "You know it's Soylent Green Wednesday." Every Wednesday the school serves a stew with this mystery meat we nicknamed "Soylent Green" in honor of the sci-fi movie of the same name. At the end of the movie Charlton Heston finds out what their new food source is really made of—Soylent Green is people. If a teacher is absent on Wednesday and has a sub in his or her place Speckler and I usually look at each other, nod, and say: "Soylent Green." It's one of our little in-jokes.

"If we find the building I'll treat you to a whole Chinese barbecued duck," I tell him. "But this is kind of important."

"Okay, but I'm going to hold you to that duck."

We head west until we reach the south branch of the Chicago River. From the bridge that spans the river I can see several old buildings along the west bank, but from this vantage point we can only see the back of the buildings. I can't tell if any of them are the Hotel Zamboni or not. I don't see any sign but all of them are old and look empty.

"Do you think it's one of those buildings over there?" Speckler asks.

"Let's go find out."

We cross the bridge and head down the side street the buildings are on. It's a pretty rundown area of the city. A lot of old warehouses and old train tracks that probably haven't seen an actual train on them since Al Capone was shooting it out with Elliot Ness.

I start checking the address on the first building but Speckler grabs my arm and shouts, "There it is!"

I see a faded sign that says H T E L   Z   B   N I on the front of one of the buildings. My heart beats faster. I motion for Speckler to follow me as I run across the street to the front door but soon find it chained and padlocked. The front windows are boarded up just like they were in Charlie Fingers's comic book. The side door, the one Charlie was able to enter through, is likewise locked up. There's an old fire escape on the front of the building but it doesn't go all the way down to the street. I have a thought that maybe if Speckler boosted me up I could reach it.

"Place hasn't been open in years," a voice calls out to us. A man looks at us from the other side of the street. He's wearing a dirty white apron and leaning in the doorway of a small diner called the Whistlestop. He's a chubby, unshaven guy in his mid-thirties, with long greasy hair and a cigarette tucked behind one ear. Except for him and us the street is deserted.

"Do you know anything about this hotel?" I ask him.

"Sure I do," he says. "The place was an old railroad flop house for all the workers coming into town. Rail yard's not far from here." He jerks his thumb in a northerly direction.

"When did it close?" Speckler asks.

"Back in the early eighties I guess. Wasn't much need for it anymore. Why are you two so interested in an old hotel for?"

"School project," I tell him before Speckler starts talking about aliens and spaceships.

"Uh-huh," the man says.

"Yeah, we're investigating old buildings that have reputations of being haunted," Speckler adds. "We heard this place has some weird things going on."

I turn and look at Speckler. It's a pretty good excuse and I'm actually amazed he thought of it. By the look on his face I think he's amazed he thought of it, too.

"Yeah, I don't know anything about that. I never heard anything about it being haunted."

"So no one else has been around investigating?" I ask.

"Like who? Those guys on that cable show who go to all those haunted places?"

"Sure, or anyone else. Could be anybody. A guy on a bike . . ."

He looks at me closer. "A guy on a bike huh? Any special guy on a bike? You think Lance Armstrong's been investigating?"

"No. Just . . . well . . . just anybody."

"Uh-huh. Nope. Ain't seen nobody investigating. Specially no guy on a bike." He goes back into the diner but I get the feeling he's still watching us from inside. There's something about the guy that doesn't seem right.

"What do we do now?" Speckler says.

"I don't know." I look back at the building. "I wonder why it's still here. It's been unoccupied a long time. I'm surprised someone hasn't bought it and torn it down already."

"Yeah, it looks pretty spooky too. I would bet it probably is haunted."

We head back to the train station. Speckler wants to talk about how his dream date with Amy would have gone if we'd been able to go to New York but I'm only half paying attention. He'd already told me half a dozen different versions of his dream date before. They all end the same with him saving Amy from a wild gang of hoodlums and her falling madly in love with him. I'm glad he's sticking to the PG rated version. The R rated version gets a little embarrassing.

"Are you listening to me?" he asks halfway through the story.

"Of course I am." But I'm too busy thinking about the Hotel Zamboni. The fire escape wasn't too far above the street if someone had a ladder or a rope. And those windows didn't look too secure. Just maybe . . . .

I don't tell Speckler what I'm thinking. One reason is that I'm not sure he'd be able to keep his mouth shut. Another, I think he would try to talk me out of it and I don't want to be talked out of it. So that night, after my parents have long gone to bed, I get some rope and a flashlight out of the garage and sneak out of the house. I stuff everything in my backpack and decide it'd be better if I took my bike instead of the train. It wouldn't look good for a sixteen year-old kid getting on the train at one o'clock in the morning with a coil of rope and a flashlight. Then my dad would really think I'm on drugs.

When I get there the street is dark and empty and the Whistlestop Diner is closed for the night. The Hotel Zamboni is a just another dilapidated building sitting in a row of equally dilapidated buildings. Dark, empty, with a sinister appearance at night. Speckler was right—it does look haunted. I have a moment's hesitation, thinking this might not have been the best idea. What if I find an eight-foot tall alien with a laser gun waiting for me inside?

I shake off the feeling and decide that I didn't come all this way to give up and go home. I take the rope out of the backpack. I tie a small weight to the end so that I can get it hooked around the bottom of the fire escape. It's only about twenty feet up so I don't have far to toss it. Even though I've never been the athlete my brother was I'm in pretty good shape so that the climb is not very difficult. I pull the rope up behind me. I try the first window I come to. It's locked. I climb up and try another window on a different floor. I wish now I'd brought a crow bar. I guess if they're all locked I can always break a window. Luckily the next window opens and I don't have to destroy anyone's private property. The window is so old that I can barely get it open all the way, but at least it opens enough for me to squeeze in.

I turn on the flashlight. I'm in a small room. One of the hotel rooms I guess, though there's no furniture. It's completely empty. I'm glad. It would be creepy to walk in and see the place with a bed and dresser. I would think someone was probably sleeping on the bed or maybe in the bathroom washing up. I wish now I'd never seen the movie *The Shining*. I can't help thinking about Jack Nicholson wandering around the Overlook Hotel.

I sweep the light around. I don't know exactly what I'm looking for so after a few minutes I leave the room. The place looks pretty much how Charlie Fingers drew it even if it was kind of basic. The center of the hotel is built around an atrium with a cracked and broken skylight at the top. I can hear the sounds of pigeons cooing softly up above, the only guests that now stay at the Hotel Zamboni. What used to be the lobby is down below. I shine my light on it. Nothing but more garbage and dust.

I look around and wander from room to room. There are no doors to any of the rooms and were probably sold off with the other fixtures because I notice the bathrooms don't have any sinks or toilets either.

It's a small hotel, only about six floors, not counting the lobby. There's an old elevator at one end. I don't bother with it. It probably doesn't work and I don't want to find out if it does. There's nothing scarier than the sound of an old elevator in an empty hotel at night.

The Hotel Zamboni is not exactly the Plaza. I don't think Speckler and Amy would be having a romantic rendezvous in this place.

"This is stupid," I say out loud after checking several more rooms. What did I expect? I would find the girl walking the halls? Reading her book in one of the rooms?

Still, I can't bring myself to leave just yet. I drift to the stairwell and head up one more flight to the third floor. But I only find the same—empty rooms, garbage, dust, and pigeons that fly out when I walk in. Not exactly a glimpse into another world.

I think back to the comic book. Charlie Fingers was standing at one of the windows at the front of the building looking down onto the street when he saw the people with the collars and the creatures. I go into one of the rooms at the front and cross over to the window. The glass is so grimy I can't see anything. I pick up a tattered newspaper and wipe away some of the dirt. It's dark outside. The street is still empty. Maybe the window into the other world only opens in the daytime. Maybe it's closed at night. I saw it during the day and so did Charlie Fingers. It makes as much sense as any of this—which is all pretty senseless.

Just as I've considered it a bust and decide to leave, I hear a noise from downstairs. A chain rattles. A door opens. Footsteps. Could it be the creatures? Did they see me at the window? I certainly didn't see any of them. My heart races and I immediately shut off the flashlight so I don't give myself away.

I hear the footsteps shuffling across the lobby and then coming up the stairs. I dart out of the room trying not to make any noise. I'm not sure where to go. There's only one stairwell and the elevator. But then I remember the way I came in. The fire escape is on the outside of the building. But the window I opened is one floor below me.

I head back into the room and try the window. It won't budge. I think about breaking it. If it were those creatures I'd rather risk breaking a window than being caught. But what if it's not? Maybe it's a cop or the owner? Someone who obviously has a key to get in. And the footsteps weren't the sound an eight-foot tall monster in body armor makes. But should I give myself away? Be arrested for trespassing? This would make my dad even angrier and I'd be grounded for life. Or at least until I turn eighteen. I can't decide what to do and stand there frozen in place. The footsteps reach this floor and I see a light shining as it sweeps around like a lighthouse warning ships to be wary of rocks and death.

It has the same effect on me. I duck into the bathroom hoping the person didn't see me head into this room. If I wait maybe he'll go away then I can make my escape. My heart keeps beating a mile a minute. I begin to sweat and tighten my grip on the flashlight unless it slips out of my hand and falls to the floor.

I wait and listen. I can't hear anything. No footsteps or breathing. Maybe he's gone. I wait a few minutes longer, listening. Still no sound. I feel safe and begin breathing a little easier. My heart begins to slow as well. I exit the bathroom and when I do a light immediately hits me. I practically jump out of my skin.

"What are you doing here?" a familiar voice demands. It's the guy from the diner.

"You?"

"I thought you'd be back here." He points the light down at the floor. "Looking for ghosts?"

"I'm looking for a guy named Charlie Fingers," I tell him.

"Well, you found him."

"You're Charlie Fingers?"

He nods. "I haven't heard that name in years. I expect you want to know about *The Other Side*?"

"I've seen it," I say.

A slow smile comes across his face. "I've been waiting a long time to hear that," he says. "I guess me and you got some talking to do."

We go across the street to the diner where he unlocks the door. He tells me he owns the diner and the Hotel Zamboni as well. I take a seat at the counter. He pours a couple of Cokes and asks if I want a piece of pie. "My chef, Sam, makes the best damn rhubarb pie you've ever had."

"No thanks, this is fine." I sip the Coke and look around the place. There's a calendar on the wall with a picture of a beach somewhere. It's not the right year. Besides an old clock with a layer of grease covering its plastic face there is nothing else on the walls. I ask him if he still goes by Charlie Fingers.

"Charlie Lunsford's my real name." He tells me a little of his story. His father was a lawyer and when he died he left Charlie a lot of money. Charlie bought both the diner and the building. "After having my *other-worldly* experience," he says.

When he saw me and Speck earlier he didn't think anything about it. Just a couple of kids looking around. It was the comment about the bike that got him curious. He knew then that I must have read the comic book. He told me he created it because he had to tell his story and it was the only way he knew of to get the images across that were burned in his head. He had no art training, which was obvious, but like me, he was always into comic books and was always drawing. Anyway, he sat all night in the diner waiting to see if I'd come back. That's when he saw me climbing up the fire escape.

"You looked pretty determined," he says. "I guess that whatever happened to you must have been as extraordinary as what happened to me."

"It was, though judging from your comic book I don't think it was as exciting as yours—just weird."

"Weird sums it up pretty good. Major weird. But go on—what happened?"

I tell him the story—the Bean, the girl, the creature, the mind-shattering headache. He nods the whole time.

"I thought my skull was going to explode," he says.

"What is it—some kind of side effect to crossing over?"

"I guess, but it sounds like you didn't really cross over. You only saw the girl and the creature in the reflection, right?"

"Yeah, for only a few minutes. It wasn't like your experience. You were over in their world."

"For a long time I thought I was crazy. I came back to the building over and over again. At first I just stood outside staring up at it. I was afraid to go in. Afraid I might see one of those creatures again. But eventually I got up the courage. I just couldn't stand it to think that what happened might not have been real. I wanted to know for sure that what I experienced really happened."

"The same as me. I went back to the Bean and stared into it for hours—"

"Did you see them again?"

"No. Nothing. When the girl and I looked at each other it was only for a few seconds. I don't know how, but our eyes locked onto each other. That was just before Mustardhead showed up--"

"Mustardhead?"

"That's what I call the creatures."

"Yeah, they did look a little mustardy."

"The girl must have seen it approaching because she got scared and tried to get away but she got—*shocked*—or something. I don't know what happened, but that thing had some weird rifle with it. I thought it was going to kill her."

"Just like the creatures that were after me. Same thing. I thought they were going to blast a hole in me. You know, like with some kind of laser beam or something. But then I thought about the people I saw. They all had on these collars around their necks—"

"So did the girl. I wish I had my sketchbook so that I could show you."

"Yeah, well, I think those collars are how the creatures control them. Maybe those rifles shoot some kind of a pulse at the collar that shocks them."

"That makes sense," I say. "Like controlling animals with electric cattle prods."

"Right."

"But you said you came back and you never saw them again. You never crossed back over?"

"No. For ten years I've been wandering that old building but so far nothing."

"Do you know why or how you crossed over the first time?"

"Not at all. I've been searching the Internet for years trying to find someone with the same experience. Everyone I've contacted who says they've had similar stories all turned out to be a bunch of crackpots. None of them saw what I did. Until now." He smiles at me.

"Do you have any idea who they were?" I ask. "I only saw the girl and one creature. You were there."

"It was Chicago, I know that. But a different Chicago. Much of the city was destroyed but there was enough left for me to recognize. It looked like some kind of alien invasion because there were these enormous spaceships hovering in the sky and smaller black ships flying around."

"Mungo thinks it's either a parallel universe or you time traveled to the future."

"Mungo? The dwarf who owns the comic book store?"

"Yeah, he's pretty smart about stuff like this."

"It wasn't the future I can tell you that."

"How do you know?"

"My father was a corporate lawyer for one of the largest developers in the city. They built a lot of these skyscrapers you see and my dad would often bring me to these buildings as they were going up. Something about him wanting me to get a sense of how capitalism works by seeing the gears of industry. You know, the architects—the visionaries—the builders, and then the corporation people who move into these buildings. I remember one of these places being built—this was a couple of years before I had my experience and crossed over. A little more than ten years ago. I think my dad was hoping I'd get the capitalism bug and quit slacking off, quit being a bike messenger and enroll in Harvard or Yale. Maybe join the rowing team and Skull and Bones—"

"What's that?"

"It's a secret organization run by the sons of all the movers and shakers. But I didn't want that kind of life. To be honest, I didn't know what I wanted. But he took me on a tour anyway of one of the big new glass skyscrapers that was just being built—you can't miss it. However, two years later, when I had my experience and I crossed over into that other Chicago, I saw that same building and it was still not fully built yet. Just as it was then. So it had to be the same time. It had to be when they made their invasion."

"So what do we do?" I ask. "I've been hoping to get another glimpse, but you've been trying for ten years. What if that's all it was? What if it was just that one time and we'll never get another glimpse again?"

"I don't want to think about that," Charlie says.

He looks determined, as if he won't ever stop trying to get another look. Kind of like Ahab going after the white whale except his white whale are a bunch of freaky aliens in another universe. I can't blame him though. A large part of me wants to sign on as first mate to his mad hunt just to be able to see the girl again and know she's safe. I don't want to think about the other option.

Chapter Five
The Haunted Hotel

The next day at lunchtime I recount my late night adventure to Speckler and explain my plan to head straight to the Hotel Zamboni after school. Charlie promised to show me exactly where he was when he crossed over and I told him I'd show him the sketches I drew. "So you can come with me," I tell Speck, "or you can chase Amy around until she maces you or Tasers you or whatever she does to get rid of you."

"She's not doing any of those things," he says, "which is just another sign that she really secretly loves me." Then he shrugs his shoulders. "But are you sure you want me to go with you? It seems you didn't need me last night." He's a bit annoyed that I didn't call him up and get him to commit breaking and entering with me. "We're supposed to be the new dynamic duo, aren't we? Nuke Fist and Kid Fantastic. What would you have done if it really were those creatures? You need someone to cover your back."

"If those creatures had showed up I don't think you being there would have made any difference except maybe to shield my body with yours as I escape."

"What? Why do I have to shield you—why can't you shield me? I have so much more to live for."

"Like Amy? Who has told you repeatedly that she wants you to die."

"A minor technicality. Still, you should have called me."

"I told you, I didn't finally decide to go until it was late. What did you want me to do—call you up at midnight? Wake up your whole house? Besides, would you have really gone with me or try to talk me out of it?"

"I'm hurt you'd even suggest that. We're a team aren't we? Like Batman and Robin. Luke Skywalker and Han Solo. Ben and Jerry."

"Okay. You're right. I'm sorry I didn't tell you."

"What would you have done if you'd crossed over to their world like Charlie Fingers did?"

"His real name's Charlie Lunsford. I don't know. It doesn't matter now. I didn't cross over and probably never will. Charlie hasn't crossed back over and he's been trying for ten years."

"Yeah, but he doesn't have the secret mojo that you have."

"What secret mojo do I have?"

"I don't know what it is but for some reason you seem to have it. How else were you able to see the girl in the Bean when no one else could?"

"I'm sure it wasn't through some secret mojo."

"You never know. You may have some kind of power inside you you're not even aware of."

"Like the Force? I'm no Luke Skywalker, Speck. No matter how many times we played *Star Wars* and battled it out with our light sabers."

"We'll see. I'll keep to my mojo theory until something better comes along. Who knows, maybe this Charlie *Lunsford* is really your Obi-wan Kenobi."

"Or he could just be a guy who runs a dirty diner and owns an abandoned building."

Speck does his best Yoda impression: "Learn the secrets of the deep fryer you will."

We both laugh. "All right," he says in his normal voice. "I'll go with you, but only because you need someone objective with you to sort out all the crazy."

An hour after school we enter the Whistlestop Diner. A lone customer sits at the end of the counter sipping a cup of coffee and reading the *Sun Times*. He's grumbling about how badly the Bears are doing even though the season just started. Charlie's behind the counter with an older black man standing at the grill in a white cook's apron and a spatula in one hand, a hamburger patty sizzling away.

Charlie introduces us. "This is Sam, head chef of the Whistlestop."

"*Chef?*" Sam says. "Is that what I am now? I have to ask for a raise then. And here I thought I was just an ordinary greasy fry cook." He smiles humorously. He's middle aged, thin, with a long Rastafarian ponytail. He looks like an ex-hippie. He points the spatula at me. "This the kid who also saw the creature feature?"

"Yeah, this is Ryan Whitaker."

I look at Charlie. "Don't worry about Sam," he reassures me. "He knows everything. He's been with me ever since I bought the Whistlestop."

"When I was younger," Sam tells us, "people would drop acid and see all sorts of crazy stuff. Spiders coming out their noses and their fingers turning into snakes."

"I don't do drugs," I tell him.

"Uh-huh," he says. He turns back to the grill and gives the burger a flip, then plops a square of yellow cheese on top of it.

"Sam is a bit skeptical on this whole other world theory," Charlie says as we walk across the street to the Hotel Zamboni.

Speckler is staring at his hand. "I wish my fingers would turn into snakes."

"Don't mind him," I say. "He was dropped several times on his head as a baby."

"Not just as a baby," Speck says.

Charlie takes out his keys and unlocks the big padlock and removes the chain from the front entrance. We go inside. The lobby of the hotel is small and dusty. The front desk is still there where people check in. Behind the counter there's a wall with small cubbyholes in it for mail or room keys. The cubbyholes are all empty except for spider webs and more dust.

There's some light coming in from the skylight above but not much. But it's bright enough that we don't need flashlights. Pigeons fly around when we enter. Speckler goes to the atrium and looks up craning his neck all around. "Wow, this is pretty cool. Does the elevator work?" He tries to open the gate but it's locked shut.

"Not in years," Charlie says. "We'll take the stairs. When I came in that first time I didn't see anyone, so I came up here thinking maybe there was someone in one of the upstairs rooms doing some work. I called out but there was no answer."

"Where have I heard this story before?" Speckler asks then snaps his fingers. "Oh, I know. In this comic book. *The Other Side*. Ever hear of it?"

I shake my head at his poor attempt at humor.

"What?"

Charlie leads us up to the next floor and into one of the rooms where he crosses over to the window. "It was here I first saw them. I felt this overwhelming headache like someone had just drilled into my brain. I didn't know what the hell it was but it scared me pretty good. I thought I was getting a brain tumor. Anyway, I walked over to the window and looked out. That's where I saw the people and then those creatures."

"What were the people doing?" I ask.

"Just going about their business. Walking down the street. Except they all looked like they'd been kicked out of their houses. They were wearing old dirty clothes. Rags mostly. I thought there was a soup kitchen nearby. And talk about a bad hair day. And no makeup on any of the women." I thought about the girl I saw. Her hair was cut short and was definitely in the category of bad hair day but at the time I thought it was done purposely, not thinking she might be some kind of survivor to an alien invasion. I guess going to the hair salon is the least of their worries.

Charlie continues: "It was then I noticed the weird collars they were all wearing. Because of that I didn't think they were homeless."

"The ones with the V markings—like this?" I open up my sketchbook and show him the drawing of the girl.

"That's it exactly," Charlie says. "And then of course came the creatures with those guns. They were acting like guards or something. The people didn't even look at them. They had their heads down and just shuffled along on their way. They were used to them, I guess—and pretty scared. That was obvious." Just like the girl. I remember the scared look on her face as she tried to leave. Just before she got shocked and collapsed.

"Is that when the creatures saw you?" I ask him.

"Yeah. One of them looks up and sees me standing in the window. He starts pointing at me and then another one stops and looks. I couldn't see their faces because of the masks they had on but they seemed surprised, as if I was somewhere I wasn't supposed to be. So I'm standing there freaking out, thinking this has got to be a movie being filmed you know? Like Wes Craven is down there filming a horror movie. But it's no horror movie. It's real. Because the next thing these two creatures come crashing into the hotel down stairs. Then I really freak out. It's bad enough seeing a couple of monster aliens, but when they start coming after you it's a whole different hockey game. I had to escape and up seemed the only place to go, so I ran up the stairs as quick as I could until I got to the roof. That's when I really freak out. Half of Chicago looked like it'd been through World War III. Buildings were destroyed. Half the Sears Tower was gone—"

"It's called the Willis Tower now," Speckler interrupts.

Charlie scowls at him. It's the most frequent look Speck gets so he's used to it. "Ten years ago it was still the Sears Tower. And everywhere up in the sky were ships. Huge, enormous saucer-like ships you would see in science fiction movies. Really scary looking. And a lot of these smaller black ships were flying in and out of them as well. I couldn't believe what I was seeing. Then I notice one of the smaller ships coming my way. Maybe the creatures radioed in about me, asking for reinforcements, or a ship to take me to one of the motherships. You know, to take me to their leader."

I nod like I understand, which of course I do having seen a hundred science fiction movies and almost every episode of the *X-Files*.

"What about the creatures chasing you?" Speck asks.

"I'm getting to that. So I'm standing there watching this unbelievable scene and then I hear the creatures coming up the stairs, getting closer. There's nowhere to run. I'm trapped. Almost. I have only one choice to make, so I run over to the edge of the building. I remember the hotel is right on the Chicago River. It's pretty high up but with a good jump I'm sure I can make it. They burst through the door, their rifles pointing right at me, and I jump."

I'm impressed. Looking at the long-haired slacker in front of me with his goatee and beer belly you wouldn't think he had it in him. "And that's when you crossed back?"

Charlie nods. "I think the water must have had some effect on me. When I came up to the surface I looked up but didn't see the creatures on the roof. I was expecting shots to be fired at me but there was nothing. I swam over and climbed out and it was the old Chicago—this Chicago."

"When did you buy the building?"

"A year later. My father died suddenly—heart attack. He left me quite a bit of money. The building was still on the market so I bought it. Then I bought the diner. I figured it was the best way to keep an eye on my investment."

"It's a pretty cool building," Speckler says. "It's also pretty spooky—you know, like a haunted house." He gives me a look and I can see the gears turning inside his head.

"I guess it's like a haunted house," Charlie says.

"A haunted *hotel*," Speckler says. "Which is even better."

"Better than what?" Charlie asks, but I know where Speck is going with this.

"No way," I say. "This will never work."

"It's perfect," Speckler says. "Mr. C said we have to go big to make enough money—and what could be bigger than this?"

"Do you mind telling me what you two are talking about? Who's this Mr. C?"

Speckler turns to Charlie and says eagerly: "Lend us your hotel. Just for one night." Then, without waiting for Charlie to respond, he launches into a rapid recital of all the reasons why we need to have his hotel for our fundraiser including, most of all, his need to get Amy Dierdorf to New York City where he can woo her in style. His exact words: "Woo her in style." I've seen Speckler's style. There is nothing woo-worthy about it.

"I don't know," Charlie says once Speck is finished with his sales pitch. "What if the same thing happens and someone crosses over?"

"You said so yourself that it hasn't happened again in ten years. I doubt it'll happen on just this one night. Come on, it's for a great cause."

"It would mean a lot to us," I say, giving my support to Speckler. It's really not a bad idea at all once I think about it. The place is crazy spooky.

Charlie considers this for a moment, and then relents. "All right. Just for the one night. And you have to make sure the place is cleaned up afterwards."

"Absolutely," Speckler says. "It'll be cleaner than when we found it. Which won't be too hard since it's a freaking mess right now. I can't wait to tell Mr. C."

We conclude our tour of the Hotel Zamboni. Charlie takes us to the roof to point out what he saw and the location of the ships. There's an excellent view of the Loop with all the famous skyscrapers. I can't imagine how it would look if a race of aliens came in and destroyed it. Like the end of the world I guess.

We go over to edge and look at the river below. It's a long drop.

"Would you jump from this height to save your life?" Speck asks me.

"I guess if a gang of Mustardheads were after me I'd do it." I turn to Charlie. "You said the people you saw on the street were walking around on their own, that they weren't being forced."

"True. I guess that once the aliens conquered earth—or at least Chicago—then that was enough. Maybe they were more like an occupying army—kind of like the Germans in Paris during WWII."

"But the Germans were also rounding people up to put into concentration camps. Or just killing them outright."

I look back one last time at the Loop before we leave. The City of Big Shoulders a poet once called Chicago. I can see what he was talking about in those downtown buildings, both the old and the new. There's a kind of strength to them, a kind of power and beauty. I'd hate to see those monuments turn into tombstones.

The following day after school we make the announcement to the Art Club. Everyone is just as excited as Speckler.

Carnofsky is less enthused. "I'd need to see this place first."

"You'll love it, Mr. C," Speckler tells him. "You couldn't get more haunted than this place. It oozes fright from the walls. It's the kind of place where blood-curling screams were born."

"And who did you say it belongs to?"

"Friend of ours," I say. "We met him down at the comic book store. He's a fellow artist."

"And he's just willing to let us have it for free?"

Speckler nods vigorously. "When he heard about our desire to go to New York he practically begged us to use his hotel."

"Okay, Speckler. It sounds too good to be true, but I'll still need to see this place first before I can sign off on it."

"You won't regret it, Mr. C. You'll love the place. New York City here we come! The Big Apple! City of Lights!"

"That's Paris, idiot," Amy says.

"But both are the City of Love." He gives her a wink of his eye that's supposed to be sexy.

"Don't even," she warns him.

"Don't even what? I'm just saying there's nothing more romantic than being in a strange new city for the first time."

"All right, Casanova. Put a sock in it," Mr. C tells him. "Remember this is a cultural trip. Art and only art. I don't want to hear of any impropriety going on."

"Mr. Carnofsky, you're always telling us that art has the ability to inspire all kinds of emotions. Isn't love one of them?"

"Of course it is, Speckler. But just don't use that as an excuse to turn into some sex-crazed maniac."

"I think you're too late," Amy says and we all laugh. Speck fakes being hurt but I know he likes the attention, especially if it gets Amy to acknowledge his existence.

The next day is Saturday and Speck and I meet Mr. C at school. A half hour later we're parking in Mr C's environmentally friendly electric car in front of the diner. He meets Charlie, tours the building, and is satisfied that it will work. The whole time Speckler is giving him all kinds of ideas, pointing out how each floor can have its own theme. "Vampires! Zombies! Werewolves! Mutant experiments gone wrong!" His brain his racing a mile a minute. He can't control himself and we all get caught up in his grand schemes.

Carnofsky laughs. "Okay, Dr. Frankenstein. You sold me."

I pat Speck on the back and give him a thumbs up. He paints such a vivid picture that we can almost see the zombies patrolling the floor looking for brains, delicious brains!

When the club meets at the hotel the following weekend to begin planning they also get caught up in Speckler's grand plans. Soon everyone, including Amy (to Speckler's immense delight), is excited and begins shouting out ideas. We decide the first floor would be the Vampire's Lair full of coffins. Then the Mad Mutant Experiments on the second floor with lab tables covered with various Frankenstein monsters. Werewolves will be on the third floor howling at the moon and growling savagely and the final floor zombies will be caged up, hands extending out for fresh blood and brains.

Speckler volunteers to head up the Mad Mutants. I get volunteered to be in charge of the Zombie Cage and the other kids start signing up for their groups. Speckler tries to pressure Amy to be a mad scientist who helps create the Mad Mutants. "You can be my creator," he tells her.

"I'd rather be your destroyer," she says. "No thanks, I have an awesome vampire costume I wore last year. Very sexy."

At the mention of the word "sexy" Speckler gives in. "Okay," he says. "But if I go mad and run wild you might have to stop me by sucking my blood." He extends his neck to her. "You might want to start practicing."

I pull him away before he further embarrasses himself.

The following week we begin selling tickets and decide that since this is going to be a bigger better haunted house than before we increase the price. They begin selling fast and we all start seeing our trip to New York City as a done deal. There's no way this can fail and the money we plan on making will cover almost the entire trip. Sell a few more boxes of chocolates and maybe some cool T-shirts and a car wash or two and we're there.

As Halloween approaches I keep asking Speckler what his costume will be but he won't tell me, just that I'll see it when the time comes. As far as my costume goes—routine zombie. White face with black around the eyes. Bloody teeth from chewing raw body parts. Ragged suit of clothes. I use the zombie brother in the classic *Night of the Living Dead* as my inspiration. They're coming for you Baaaarbara!

I get so caught up in the planning of the Haunted Hotel, thoughts of the girl and alien become fewer and fewer. I no longer have the urge to return to the Bean to stare for hours into the curving metal surface hoping for another glimpse of either one. Though the urge has left, the desire to be reunited with the girl remains. So during the day I let Speckler's wild enthusiasm get a hold of me, and at night, just before falling asleep, I remember a pair of dark eyes looking with wonder into my own.

"This is awesome," Speckler says surveying all the work done at the hotel. It's the last day of getting everything in place. The day before Halloween. The whole Art Club is here and we're exhausted from all the last minute blood, spider webs, and scattered body parts. All the rooms are done and ready to go.

"I hate to say it, but it does look pretty cool," Amy says. "You did a good job, Speckler." She punches him lightly on the arm. The other kids agree. I have to agree as well. It does look amazingly scary.

For once Speckler is speechless. His mouth falls open and he turns red. I'm sure for him getting punched in the arm by Amy Dierdorf is akin to being blessed by an angel.

I step in to save him. "By that he means you're welcome."

"Yes . . . but it was a group effort," he stammers then takes a bite of pepperoni pizza to hide his embarrassment.

Mr. Carnofsky bought pizzas and we're sitting around the lobby joking and relaxing. I look at Speckler and we both smile. This is one of those perfect moments. I feel really good. It's been a long time since I've had a perfect day like this—not since my brother Jack died. A whole year. I can't believe it's been that long. It seems like only yesterday the government car stopped in front of the house. My mother was the one who saw it first. She was clearing the breakfast table, had a plate in her hand, but when she saw the car and the men in uniform step out she dropped the plate. It shattered all over the floor and my father yelled "What the holy Moses!" I can still hear him yell. Then he looked to where my mother was staring through the living room window, at the men walking up to our front door. The next thing I hear my father say is "No." Just that. A soft but defiant "No." But he couldn't stop what was going to happen. The knock on the door. The news of Jack's death. But no amount of wishing and no amount of denial can undo what has already happened.

Charlie gave me the key to the lock. So when we leave I replace the chain and lock. Speckler has his mother's minivan, the Mommy Machine he calls it. It's an old beat up Dodge Caravan that's carried us to plenty of soccer games and movies.

He drops me off at my house and says he'll pick me up tomorrow—*early.* He stresses early because he wants to be the first one there to set up. He acts like he's Alfred Hitchcock about to direct *Psycho* or *The Birds.*

My father is sitting in the living room drinking a beer and watching one of those new crime shows when I walk in. *CSI: Chattanooga* or something. "Why are you home so late?"

"I was with the Art Club setting up the Haunted Hotel. I told Mom."

"Well, she didn't tell me."

"Is she here?"

"Went to her support meeting. You want dinner you're going to have to make it yourself."

"We had pizzas," I say.

"So what's this hotel thing?" he asks. There's a commercial on the TV. An actor looking manly and rugged is hawking boner pills. I guess it's supposed to be worse if you're some kind of man's man and your tinker doesn't work.

I had told my dad about the haunted house fundraiser but he wasn't paying attention. He rarely pays attention to anything I tell him these days. I tell him again.

"Aren't you a little old to be playing Halloween?" he says.

"It's a fundraiser Dad. It's so we can get money to go to New York. I told you all about it."

He gives me a cold look that says I better watch my tone. But then all he says is: "You're in front of the TV."

I move out of the way. I tell him that I'll probably be home late tomorrow. "We have to clean up afterwards and some of us might go out—"

He stops me. "Shows on," he says.

I start to head to my room but then stop at the fireplace. On the mantle are several family photos. My parents still have pictures of Jack around the house. Neither of them could bring themselves to take them down. There are pictures of Jack from high school making a layup on the basketball court and one with him and this hot girl he took to the prom. He's wearing a spiffy black tuxedo and already has his hair in a crew cut. He was already planning on going into the Army by then. Next to these is a formal photo of him in his dress uniform right after boot camp. Another of him in Afghanistan. He's smiling and laughing with his arms around his buddies. It's the last photo we have of him. He was killed less than a week after the photo was taken. I pick it up and study it. The smile on his face tells me he didn't worry about dying. Why should he? He was always a cocky kid who thought he was invincible. How could he know Death was just around the corner waiting for him?

I look over and see Dad staring at me. I don't know what he's thinking. Maybe how he wishes things could be different. We all do. Maybe he wishes it were me instead of Jack.

"I always looked up to him," I tell Dad. "He was always a hero to me."

Dad says nothing but turns back to watch the TV in silence. I wish I could say more. I wish I could tell him how I think Jack was a hero no matter what he did or how he died. I carefully replace the photo back on the mantle. I don't say anything more and just go up to my room. I'm tired. I need sleep.

Chapter Six
Hallows Eve

"So what do you think?"

Speckler is showing me his costume for the Haunted Hotel. He's dressed in a black sweater covered with his own homemade "body armor," a black gas mask covers most of his face which makes it almost impossible to hear him. To top it off, literally, he has a balding yellow head he converted from a normal bald cap painted to look alien and diseased. But the most tripped out part of his costume is his size. He's standing nearly eight feet tall and holds a rifle he modified from a kid's toy. He looks an accurate picture of the creature from my drawing. It's pretty amazing.

"What are you standing on?"

He lifts up the bottom of his pants to reveal a pair of painter's stilts strapped to his legs. His father owns a house painting business.

"Can you even walk in those? What if you trip and fall on one of the little kids?"

He walks about the room. He moves pretty well for a guy who always got picked last on the playground. I'm impressed. "Not bad," I tell him. "I think you'll be the hit of the whole Haunted Hotel." He does look pretty scary. It makes me immediately think of the *real* creatures. Speckler is playing make-believe, but those things are real, and they're out there. Somewhere.

He says something but it's so muffled I can't make it out. "Take that thing off, I can't hear you."

"I said what about your costume?"

"Nothing much to do, put on some white paint, fake blood, gnaw on a severed arm and that's about it."

"All right, let's get going." He's eager to get started, even though it's hours away from opening.

"You're not going to drive in that are you?"

"Hmm, it would scare the hell out of people wouldn't it?"

"Don't even think about it."

Naturally, we're the first ones to arrive. We stop in at the Whistlestop Diner to tell Charlie we're going to set up.

"If you're hungry, come get a sandwich. Sam makes a mean Reuben."

"Old family recipe," Sam tells us. "Instead of sauerkraut I use spicy Jamaican cabbage. Gives it a little bite."

"That sounds good. If you don't mind a zombie and mutant eating in your diner?"

Sam laughs. "Zombie and mutant? That's a typical Saturday night in here."

We go through the hotel putting up some finishing touches. We add more fake cobwebs, more blood on the walls that spell HELP ME and GET OUT. It's still a couple of hours before sunset when we open to the public. We've sold out of our tickets and expect to sell more at the door. We've littered neighborhoods with flyers and got everyone to text kids in other schools to spread the word, so we expect to be quite busy up until about eleven o'clock when we shut down.

The other kids from the Art Club along with Mr. Carnofsky arrive an hour later. Mr. C is dressed as the Murdered Bellhop with a red uniform the kind a hotel bellboy used to wear fifty years ago. His throat is cut with fake blood pouring out. He's to serve as one of the guides for the groups that come through. They'll lead them up through the different floors and the different rooms we've got set up. Then we come out of coffins or break loose from our chains or jump up from gurneys where some will be covered in sheets pretending to be the newly dead—then the newly risen dead.

Mr. C gives a speech about how proud he is of all of us. I look around feeling pretty satisfied. This was a lot of hard work, but it was worth it. We have vampires and mutants and zombies and murdering psychos and werewolves. It's awesome, and I know Speckler is anxious to get started. He's even forgotten to harass Amy, who does look quite sexy as a vampire.

"You look great, Ryan," Nancy Caldwell tells me after Mr. C finishes his speech. We're heading up to our stations. She's a fellow zombie, and volunteered right after I was given the task of being in charge of the Zombie Cage.

"Um, thanks Nancy," I say feeling a bit awkward. "You look great too. Break a leg." *Break a leg*? I can't believe I said that. But it's always been awkward with Nancy. Speckler once told me she has a crush on me, which I didn't believe. She's Amy's best friend and I never really noticed her before. She's not bad looking—not a knockout like Amy Dierdorf—but she's cute, even if she's a little tall and kind of clumsy. Speckler keeps trying to get us to double date. I tell him you actually need *two* girls for a double date. He thinks that by dating Nancy the two of us can help win over Amy. I always saw it as just another one of his grand plans. But I've begun to notice how much attention Nancy pays me. She always laughs at my jokes—even the stupid ones.

Once up in the room I take a quick look outside the window. Families are starting to line up. I recognize a lot of kids from school and see many more I don't recognize. It's early but already a good crowd is forming.

We open and the first groups come in. You can hear the screams from kids and even adults from the lower floors as they're led through the various stations. My station is quite simple. We're in one of the rooms with a fake cage where the door used to be. We're all huddled around a fresh corpse and are busy devouring his entrails and other severed body parts. The guides all have flashlights and when they approach they shine their light on us. We look up from our grisly meal, toss aside the arms and intestines we were eating and attack the new food source. Except we don't actually attack anyone, since we're caged up. We reach through the bars at the kids while screaming and moaning. It's pretty cool and we all have a great time. I can only imagine how much fun Speckler is having being a mutant alien. Judging from the sound of the screams coming from his floor, I'd bet he's having a pretty good time.

The night goes by fast. Group after group are led up and we frighten the hell out of each one. Even adults who probably don't think they'd be scared are pretty scared. Later on I catch a glimpse of Mungo. He's not in any full costume (he usually saves the cosplay for Comic-con), just a T-shirt splattered with fake gore and a tiny alien trying to claw its way out of his innards. He gives me a thumbs up to show his approval though I don't think any of it scared him—he's just not the type. I think when you grow up being no taller than four feet there's not a lot that life hasn't already thrown at you, so I think he's probably developed a pretty tough skin. It would take a lot to rattle Mungo. Maybe real eight-foot aliens would do it, but that's about it.

We're kept busy with the show up to about closing time when the groups become smaller and smaller. Finally the last group comes through and the Haunted Hotel is officially closed for business.

I'm exhausted. Who knew being a flesh-eating zombie would be so much work?

I start picking up some of the body parts, putting them in a large trash bag.

"Need some help, Ryan?" Nancy asks.

"No thanks, Nancy. I'm just going to clean up a little here. Tomorrow we'll get the rest."

She wants to say more but Linda Grotlik says, "You were awesome, Ryan. This was so much fun. You want us to help you?" Her boyfriend, Marty Kekner, is by her side looking anxious to leave. I heard they had a party to go to afterwards.

"No, you guys can take off. It's not much. We can get most of it tomorrow but I just want to pick up a few things tonight."

I say goodbye. Nancy seems reluctant but she leaves with Linda and Marty. Wally Hathaway shouts "Zombies Rule!" and gives me a high five before leaving. I don't know about that. I'm sure Speckler's mutants would probably have something to say in that regards. I know Speckler is still waiting around for me. Maybe finally getting his chance to go after a certain sexy vampire. I hear people down below leaving, saying goodbye, saying how great everyone was. Their voices and laughter float up through the atrium as testimony what a huge success this was. It'll probably go down in school history as BEST. FUNDRAISER. EVER.

I start laughing to myself as I scoop the fake body parts into the garbage bag. It's pretty dark since Charlie's never paid an electric bill since owning the place. We did string some small lights out in the halls so that the groups can at least partly see where they're going, but the rooms are in almost total darkness except for the little light coming in through the window from the street lamps down below.

I finish cleaning up, eager to get downstairs to ask Speckler how things went. I must really be exhausted because my head starts hurting. I get a real blinding headache. It comes on so quickly and then it's gone. It must be all those screams from the kids finally working on me.

I hear someone coming down the hall. Someone heavy by the sound of the pounding footsteps. I turn around and see a dark shape filling the entire doorway. There's heavy breathing coming through a gas mask. It's Speckler. He's got the toy rifle in his hands and he points it at me.

"Very funny." I toss him the garbage bag. "Help me with this, will you?"

He knocks the bag aside and body parts go flying out.

"Hey! What's the idea? I'm not picking those up again."

He switches on a light on the rifle and shines it in my face. I didn't know his toy rifle even had a light on it. I shield my eyes. "Cut the light off, Speck!"

He says nothing, just stands there making the heavy breathing sound through the gas mask.

"What are you doing? Fun time's over. I know you wish you could be a real alien mutant but I want to get home and climb into bed and sleep for about twelve hours. So can you stop playing around?" I take a step toward him and he backs out into the hallway. I still have my hand up shielding my eyes from the light he has aimed at my face. When I step out into the hall there are no lights. Who took them down? I didn't hear anyone. In fact I can't hear anything. The whole place is as quiet as a tomb. All the conversations I was hearing before have stopped. Has everyone left already? It seems impossible. It's only been a few minutes. Then I hear a loud noise down below. I lean out over the rail and see another creature dressed like Speckler—dressed exactly like one of those creatures—standing down in the lobby looking up. When he sees me he shines a similar light from a similar rifle right at me. This is completely strange. Speckler was the only one dressed like that. No one in the club even knew about the creature. I think maybe it's Charlie, but he doesn't seem the type to get dressed up for Halloween—especially as one of the creatures that tried to kill him.

I look back at Speckler. He leans over the rail and calls out to the person below. It's a language I don't recognize, and not because the gas mask makes it hard to understand. The language actually comes out clear, but it's one I've never heard before. I don't know who or what that thing is but I'm positive of one thing—*it's not Speckler*.

Then a chill runs through my entire body like a bucket of ice water thrown on me. It's not someone in the costume of one of those creatures—IT IS THE CREATURE. I crossed over, just as Charlie did. I'm in the other Chicago! I remember the sudden headache. *How could I be so damn stupid not to make the connection?*

The creature is still shining the light in my face. It probably doesn't know what to make of me. I'm still wearing the zombie makeup—white face, black around the eyes and on my lips. Fake blood dripping from my mouth. I must look as strange to it as he does to me. I'm not like any human he's ever seen before, I'm sure of it, unless for some reason people still go out trick-or-treating, which I doubt.

I need to get away. I can hear the other Mustardhead coming up the stairs to help subdue me—or kill me—so I can't go down, unless I leap over the railing, which would probably break at least half the bones in my body. I could try for the fire escape but I'm sure the creature would reach me before I get a window open. And what if the window is locked? That idea is out. The only way out is up. I remember Charlie's experience trying to escape the creatures. What I have to do sinks into me. I don't like it but I have no other choice. It's the only thing that might save me and get me back to my world. So I turn and run for the stairs and race up to the top floor till I get to the door marked ROOF. I only pray it's not locked.

It isn't.

I yank it open and rush up the stairs and out onto the roof. The sight—the sight I wasn't prepared for and that nobody in my world can be prepared for—hits me full in the face like a freight train at top speed. Seeing it in a badly drawn comic book is one thing, but seeing it for real is something else. The city is in a blackout. No lights. But there's a full moon shining which gives it an even more eerie appearance. Charlie described it as a war zone. He wasn't too far off. It's more like the aftermath of a war. I remember seeing photos of Europe after WWII. The devastation left by Allied bombings. Places like Dresden, Berlin, Hiroshima. This is what I'm looking at. Most of the buildings are destroyed. What was once the Sears Tower is cut in half. And above all the destruction is an enormous spaceship hovering silently over the city. Then I notice smaller ships flying to and from the larger ship. They're flying low over the city with bright searchlights aimed below them. They remind me of lions searching for prey, or vultures circling above a decaying carcass.

I don't have much time to think about this strange new world. I can hear the creatures coming up the stairs behind me. I run to the edge of the building and do the thing I didn't want to do. The thing I didn't think I could do, given that I'm no athlete like my brother Jack was, or brave like he was. He was always the fearless one. I'm just a comic book geek. But I do it anyway. I have to in order to save myself, and to bring me back to my world. I leap off the edge of the building, into the night, and down into blackness. I can't even see the river below me. I hope it's not a dry riverbed. If it is then it's my grave I'm leaping into.

The river isn't dry.

I plunge into deep water. Even though the Indian summer has kept the weather warm, the water's frigid. I surface and swim quickly to the far side and pull myself out. I can't wait to find Speckler and tell him what happened.

But something's not right. There should be streetlights and traffic noise, but it's still dark. A light shines on me from above. I look up and see the two creatures standing at the edge of the building shining their lights down. I also see the ships in the sky with their searchlights blazing. I haven't crossed back. I'm still in the other Chicago!

Chapter Seven
Chinatown

This isn't good. I have no idea what happened. Maybe I didn't land in the right spot in the river—if there is a right spot. But I have no time to think about it. I only know I have to get away, especially with those creatures lighting me up like a deer in headlights for every eight-foot Mustardhead around to use as target practice.

So I run.

I don't know where to go but I know I need to put as much distance between those creatures and me as possible. I run east towards Chinatown. At least it's towards what I think is Chinatown. Who knows what it is here?

I come to an overpass that's been destroyed causing me to slow down as I climb over the rubble. Once over this obstacle I continue running until I reach Chinatown where I finally stop to catch my breath and get a plan together.

It looks like the Chinatown in my Chicago, but just barely. The place is dead, not a soul around. Every building is blacked out. Not a light anywhere. No sign of life at all, not even a stray cat running the streets in chase of a midnight snack. I wonder if all of Chicago is like this. Is there anyone left at all? Did the creatures take them all—or kill them all? Could I be the only human left in this city?

But I know I'm not. The girl is here. She was reading a book when I saw her in the reflection so it didn't seem like she was the only one left alive. And Charlie said he saw people out the window of the hotel when he crossed over, so I know there are people here. I just have to find them and hope they'll help me.

I wonder if I should try to make my way to the Bean. Maybe the girl lives close by—in one of the downtown condos or maybe even in one of the hotels along Michigan Avenue. But not now. It would be better in daylight. As the only human on the street I stand out, and already I can see more of the smaller ships coming in my direction. I need a place to hide out for the night. Maybe in the morning things are different. Maybe there are people here but they don't come out at night. Or they're not allowed. Are they watching me from their windows? Wondering why this idiot is out on the street? Thinking that if I get killed by the Mustardheads then surely I deserve it.

Just ahead of me is Chinatown Square with its mall of restaurants and shops covering two floors. I figure I can hide somewhere in there for the night. Plus I need to get out of the cold wind. The temp has dropped significantly. I'm soaking wet and freezing and it'll be the worst of ironies if I survive those creatures only to get hyperthermia.

There's broken glass and debris everywhere inside the corridor of restaurants and shops. I duck into one of the restaurants, climbing in through the broken front window and ripping my pants. I feel the glass cut into my leg but I don't feel any pain. I guess it's the endorphins taking over. I hope these creatures are not some alien humanoid-bloodhound hybrid that can smell blood.

I head through the restaurant to the kitchen in the back. It's as big a disaster as the rest of the place but I find a discarded tablecloth on the floor and scoop it up. It'll make a nice blanket. There's an empty pantry, which gives me a hiding place. I crouch down into the dark space, wrap the tablecloth around my shivering body and wait. My heart is beating at the speed of a NASCAR race. Forget the blood, it's the sound of my heart and chattering teeth that'll give me away.

I sit and wait and soon begin to breathe normally again as the shivering eventually stops. I use the tablecloth to dry myself as much as possible. I remember I still have on the zombie makeup. The river didn't totally wash it all off. I wipe at it and get the rest. I imagine trying to walk down the street asking for help looking like a zombie. They'd probably immediately turn me over to the creatures—or kill me themselves.

An hour passes with no sign of a Mustardhead. The place is eerily quiet. I begin to think about my predicament. If they search the square I'm a perfect sitting duck. A sitting Peking duck Speckler would probably say. Speckler! I forgot all about him. I wonder what he thought when I disappeared. Did he think I crossed over? Or just ditched him and went home? And what if he says something to my parents? Or to Mr. C? Or the students at school? I can picture him spilling his guts to Amy in order to pull her into this whole bizarre mess. It's too much to think about. I have more pressing concerns at the moment so I drive those thoughts away and concentrate on my present situation.

I decide to move to another location, at least one that gives me a better chance of escape if I see them coming. I make my way back out of the restaurant, careful not to make too much noise as I tread over all the broken glass.

In the outside corridor there's a set of stairs just to my right leading up to the second floor of shops. I figure it would make a better hiding place. One advantage is it'll give me a lookout so I can see if anyone approaches.

I don't have much time to consider this. A metallic humming noise draws my attention to something in the sky. It's one of the smaller ships coming down. Maybe they spotted me! I head up the stairs and crouch down behind the railing.

The ship lands in an open area of the square about a hundred feet away. A door opens and six of the eight-foot Mustardheads come out looking just as lethal as before. Black body armor, gas masks, rifles at the ready. They each have the lights on and they begin to fan out shining their lights all around. It's obvious they don't know where I'm hiding by the way they scattered, but just being here means they have a pretty good guess I'm somewhere around. I don't think they'll give up until they find me. To make things worse the ship takes off but doesn't leave. It hovers just above the square with its own light shining everywhere.

I stay crouched as I peer below me through the iron railing. Now I am a sitting target. Maybe the restaurant was the better hiding place after all. My heart begins to race again and sweat beads down my face, my underarms, even my crotch. I've never been this afraid in my life.

Below me the creatures search steadily inside one restaurant after the other. I can hear glass crunching loudly beneath heavy boots. They're not afraid of making any noise. Why should they? What harm could I possibly do to them? Toss a large bit of broken brick at their heads? It'd probably feel like a spitball. And each crackle of glass and each sweep of a light only brings more fear until I feel like I'm going to choke on it.

I flatten myself down as much as possible as one of the creatures hunts just below me. I can hear him pause beside the stairs. If he comes up I'm doomed. He does! I can hear his heavy feet on the stairs.

I have to move, overcome my fear and move! Even if he sees me and shoots me I'll die on my feet and not cowering in fear. But just as I'm about to make a run for it one of the creatures calls out in its alien tongue. From the direction of the sound I guess he's on the northern side of the square, quite a distance away. The others leave where they were searching to join him, including the one on the stairs. The ship moves over in that direction as well.

This is my chance. I spring to my feet and bolt to the far end of the balcony, practically leap down the other set of stairs and race across the open square where the ship originally landed. I don't stop running but head across the street and as far away from the creatures as I can get. I don't hesitate to even look over my shoulder but just keep running.

There's no one in pursuit. Whatever they saw or heard is obviously still keeping them busy which gives me a chance to put more distance between us. I make it to Wentworth Avenue, the main street in Chinatown that runs south, and sprint under the huge red Chinatown sign, which now hangs down blocking half the street. Good, maybe it will help shield me from any alien eyes.

Wentworth Avenue is much the same as Chinatown Square. A ghost town. Darkness and destruction. Just as before there are no lights or any sign of life. The few cars left on the street are nothing but burnt-out wrecks, hunks of metal that still have the charred human remains—ghastly skeletons sitting in their seats, their skeletal fingers still grip the steering wheels, all left as a reminder that this world is full of death. On my right is the familiar brick building of Chinatown with its pagoda-like roof. It now lies in a crumbling pile along the street.

I can't stop to stare at any of it. I have to keep running.

Soon my side is killing me and it feels like my lungs are once more about to explode. I stop for a short rest to get my breath back and take a moment to check behind me. The ship is still hovering over Chinatown Square with its searchlight criss-crossing the area so I think I'm safe for the time being. But for how long?

It doesn't take long to answer that. The ship now starts moving towards my location and probably the aliens on the ground as well. Whatever it was that distracted them, a rat or maybe a mad dog, obviously didn't prove to be me so now they've taken up the search once again.

Out in the open like this it's only a matter of time before they spot me. Then what will they do? Kill me? Experiment on me? I only have the movies and comic books to go by, and none of them are very helpful as I imagine the worst possible scenarios, my body lying on an operating table. My chest sliced open. Heart, lungs, liver lying in cold metallic bowls for study.

I shake the image out of my head. It's time to start running again, so I head down the next side street thinking to get into the alleys and possibly find an open door. Maybe I'll just keep running south until I reach Cellular Field where the White Sox play. If the ballpark is still there. It might be a great place to hide—big enough at least. But it's also farther south of the Bean. Maybe those creatures are just trying to drive me south away from the Loop. I get the image of cows being herded. Maybe they're herding me into a certain location where I'll be trapped—like a dumb cow in a holding pen heading for the slaughterhouse.

Suddenly, I see a door on the side of a building open several inches while a face peers out. A human face! They see me and instantly the door closes shut. But now that I know someone is there I don't hesitate. I run to the door and pound on it. "Hey! Open up! I know you're—"

The door opens. A hand whips out and grabs me and pulls me inside. I'm shoved back up against a wall, my head smacks it hard but at least I'm off the street and safe. *But am I safe?* Three faces in the dark look at me. I can't see much but I sense the hostility and the wariness. The one who grabbed me has his hand tight around my throat.

"You better start talking," he orders me.

"I will if you stop choking me," I gasp.

The hand loosens its grip. I breathe better and my eyes become somewhat more accustomed to the darkness. We're in a small space, a room or hallway.

"I was running . . . " I say.

"I saw that. Who from? Bruzers? Scavengers?"

"What are Bruzers? You mean the Mustardheads?"

The hand instantly tightens back around my throat. "How the hell you don't know what a Bruzer is?"

"Let's take him up to Tolliver," one of his companions says. *Yes, take me up to Tolliver! Whoever the hell he is. Because it has to be better than standing here getting choked to death.*

"All right," the man says.

He pushes me ahead, up a set of stairs into a larger room. There's a small light ahead and a group of people huddled together. There's the sound of an argument but when we appear they quiet down and turn towards us.

"Hey, Tolliver! I caught this kid running from some Bruzers," the man who had me in a Darth Vader choke says. "But he claims he don't know what a Bruzer even is."

A tall, thin but strongly-built man with a bald head and a burn mark on the side of his face steps forward. Someone has a lantern— this is the light source— and shoves it forward so they can all get a good look at me. The bald man studies me along with everyone else. There appears to be about a dozen in the group. They look real rag-tag, like they've been living on the street. Their clothes are dirty, tattered, mismatched. Mismatched is what you can call the group as well. They're old, young, black, white, Asian. They're all thin, malnourished. They're all survivors I guess. But what did they survive? And how did they survive?

"What are you doing out after curfew?" the bald man, Tolliver, asks. He seems like the group leader. He definitely has the command factor going for him, like a drill instructor ready to break a new recruit.

I mutter a pathetic: "I need help." I can't think of anything else. I don't know what to tell them. I can't tell them the truth. That I'm from a different Chicago where it's Halloween and we were hosting a Haunted Hotel to raise money for our school's Art Club. I don't think they would understand.

"How did you get here? Did you follow us?" Tolliver demands. "Anybody know this kid?"

There's a pause as the group scrutinizes me. Heads shake. I'm a stranger to them. Then a voice speaks up from the back. "I know him, Uncle Tolliver." The voice is soft, surprised. A girl's voice.

The group stands aside and she steps forward. She comes out of the darkness and into the half-light of the lantern. I can't believe it! It's the girl I saw in the Bean. The girl in my drawing. She's real and she's alive!

Chapter Eight
Violet

The moment is surreal. I'm in a state of shock, even more than looking at a devastated Chicago. The girl stands before me, ten feet away. The girl whose haunted me ever since I saw her in the reflection of the Bean. The eyes that have been staring at me from my sketchbook now look at me for real.

"He's a ghost," she says.

This little revelation stuns everyone—including myself. I remember what Speckler called her that day at the Bean. Ghost Girl. Maybe she thought the same thing when she saw my reflection. I guess that makes me Ghost Boy.

The tall man, Tolliver, turns to her. "What do you mean he's a ghost, Violet?"

I hardly listen to her explanation. I keep staring at her. She has on the similar black jacket and gray cargo pants. Her hair hasn't changed. Why should it? It's only been a few weeks. The scar is still prominent. A thin white line running down the side of her right cheek.

"I saw his reflection in the War Memorial. But he wasn't there. I thought I was seeing things. It was just before that Bruzer showed up and stunned me so the memory of it was a little hazy at the time. But he's real enough." She looks at me, studies my face like I'm studying hers. I'm glad I got rid of the zombie makeup. Still, I don't look my best since my clothes are still wet and I'm dressed to scare.

Tolliver fixes me with a hard look. "It's clear he's no ghost. Who are you then? What are you doing out here after curfew? And why the hell are you all wet?"

I weigh the option of telling them the truth. *I come from a different Chicago.* It sounds crazy just thinking it. Instead I decide to tell them as much as I can. "My name's Ryan. The . . . things . . . Bruzers . . . were chasing me. They were after me. I jumped and swam across the river to escape and then ran down here. That's when I saw your door open. I only wanted to escape those things."

"Of course the Bruzers were after you. It's after curfew and this is a Forbidden Zone. But you should know this."

"Maybe he's a Scavenger," someone says.

"He's no stinking Scav," the man who first grabbed me and pulled me inside says. He's young, with short spiky red hair and a pale, gaunt face. "He's got to be a Red Coat! He must have followed one of us here."

"Why would he go through the trouble of jumping in the river then, Brody?" Tolliver says to him. "That doesn't make sense. Plus, he's plenty scared. We can all see that."

"Look, he's got no collar." An older woman points at me. Several hands reach out and pull roughly at my coat and shirt to reveal that there's nothing around my neck. I can see that all of them are wearing identical collars—the ones with those strange V markings on them. It doesn't look like they can take them off.

"Where's your collar?" Tolliver asks me.

"I don't have one," I say.

"That's impossible. Everyone has a collar. Only the dead don't have collars and despite what my niece Violet says—you don't look dead to me."

"Not yet," Brody says through clenched teeth. He suddenly pulls out a knife, a huge Crocodile Dundee croc killer. It's long and sharp and I take an instant dislike to it and to the man holding it. "I say we cut his throat. He's got to be a Red Coat. No collar—he's sure as shit working for the Zs!"

An old Chinese man with wisps of white hair steps forward. "Do I have to remind you that this is still a house of God? There will be no violence here." Then I notice we're standing in a church. The pews are gone but I can see the large stained-glass windows, most of them broken, all around the room with images of a suffering Christ on them. Christ bearing the cross. Christ being crucified. *No violence here? We're surrounded by violence!*

The red-headed psycho, Brody, is not persuaded though. He doesn't lower the knife.

I look at the girl. Violet. Her name is Violet. She stares back at me. Her eyes soften. She doesn't look at me the way the others do. I don't think she wants to kill me. At least I hope she doesn't want to kill me.

"I don't think he's a Red Coat," she says. "There's something strange about him. Like he doesn't belong here."

"Why should we listen to you, Violet?" Brody says. "Because you're Tolliver's blood?"

She turns on him. Her voice changes to steel, sharp like a razor. "You'll listen to me because I have a voice at this council same as anyone. I've been fighting Bruzers and Zs since I could walk. I got the marks to prove it. I earned a voice here through blood and suffering. What have you ever done except talk big and piss yourself whenever a Bruzer walked by?"

There's a tense moment and Brody takes a step toward her. He's seething with anger and looks like he'll attack despite being in a church. If he'll attack one of his own, a girl, what's to stop him from slicing me up? But Violet doesn't back down. In fact, she steps forward to meet his challenge despite his being armed with a knife while her hands are empty. But somehow I think she has the advantage. She looks cool and calm. There's no fear in her face at all. But both her uncle and the Chinese man step between the two.

"That's enough, Brody!" Tolliver shouts. "Don't ever raise a knife to anyone here again! Do you hear me? That's exactly what those bastards want us to do—fight amongst ourselves. It's just another way they beat us. Besides, you know Violet's got a voice here, blood or no blood. And you better listen to her if you want good council."

Brody backs down, lowers the knife but doesn't put it away. He gives them a black look, like he wants nothing better than to cut someone up. He's dangerous, like an enraged mongoose facing off against a nest of cobras. I make a mental note to watch myself around him.

But it's not just Brody I need to be careful with. I look at the faces around me. I don't have any friends here. They all look like they want to do what Brody suggested and cut my throat. Then I see a face I recognize. I can't believe it. He's standing in the back in the shadows but he's still tall enough to be recognized. "Sam? How did you get here? How did you cross over? Is Charlie here?" I look around expecting to see Charlie, but he's not here.

They all look to Sam. How is it he's one of them? Maybe he's always been one of them.

He looks completely surprised by this. "Kid, I never seen you before in my life," he says. "How do you know who I am?"

"What do you mean? I was in your diner this afternoon. I had your world famous Reuben sandwich."

"I haven't worked as a cook for years. I don't know who told you about that."

Then it hits me. Damn, I should've known! He's not the Sam I know—he's the duplicate Sam. Mungo was right—this is a parallel Chicago, a whole parallel universe I've crossed over into. There are duplicates then of all of us. Somewhere in this city is a duplicate of myself, my parents, Speckler, Mungo, maybe even my brother Jack.

"I told you he's a collaborator," Brody says, the anger quickly boiling over again. "He probably knows all our names." This time he has supporters as several of them shout in agreement. They look scared. It's easy believing the worse about me—and safer.

Tolliver raises a hand to quiet them down. "How do you know him?" he asks me.

"I . . . thought he was someone else." It sounds lame the moment I say it but I can't think of anything else.

"But you called him Sam. You know his name. You have information on him. You're going to have to start explaining yourself or else I won't be able to help you."

They're all waiting on me, including Violet, to tell them all I know. And if I don't tell them? If I give them some other awful excuse I'm sure they'll turn me over to Brody and his cronies to start carving me up like a Sunday roast. I decide to tell them everything. What's the worst that can happen? Besides, I don't know how long I'm stuck here. What if it's forever? Better they know the truth; at least Violet can corroborate some of it. She can tell how she saw my reflection in the Bean when I wasn't standing there at all, so maybe it won't be as bad as I think it will be. But she didn't call it the Bean—what did she call it? The War Memorial?

I hesitate, not sure how to answer them. The old man puts his hand gently on my shoulder. "Son, it's time for a confession. I promise if you tell us the truth and have nothing to hide then you won't be hurt."

His eyes are kind. I believe him. "I—" But that's as far as I get. A warning is shouted: "Bruzers!" It comes from the direction of the door followed by a loud blast. The side of the church explodes sending debris and dust flying everywhere. Everyone is suddenly in a panic. They pick up the ones thrown by the blast and all scramble to escape.

"Quick, this way!" The old man guides all of us away from the blast to an exit down by the altar. We head down a small flight of stairs to a back room where a door leads to the alley.

Everyone races out the door to safety. I move to follow but Brody turns on me and grabs me by the arm. "This is your doing! You brought them here, didn't you?"

"We don't have time for this," Tolliver says. He pulls Brody away from me. "We need to get moving!"

"You're dead!" Brody promises before following the rest of them out the door.

I stand frozen. I'm not eager to follow Brody into a dark alley and get a knife shoved into me. But then Violet, who sees me standing there, comes back and grabs my hand. "Come on! We got to move!" She pulls me after her and I start running.

Tolliver is in the alley directing people where to go. Some run in one direction, some in another. "Keep running," he tells everyone. "You know where to go. Split up and keep to the side streets. Watch out for Ravens!"

"Follow me," Violet says. She takes off to the right and then left down another alley. I do my best to keep up. She's obviously in better shape than I am and knows her way in the darkness. I make a silent promise to give up junk food as I dart after her, but it's like a two-toed sloth trying to keep up with a gazelle.

She breaks from the alley and sprints across Wentworth before heading north on the opposite side of the street towards Chinatown Square. "We can't go that way," I call to her. "I just came from there. The place is swarming with them!"

"Trust me," she says over her shoulder. Instead of running straight north though she ducks down another side alley on her right. A small fence is in front of us but she clears it easily. I try my best but I'm slowed down. Ahead of me she crouches low, puts up her fist to warn me to stop and keep down, then checks to see if it's clear. Satisfied that there are no Mustardheads—Bruzers I guess they call them—she sprints across the wide street towards the elevated train station. In the moonlight the Red Line is half-destroyed. Great slabs of concrete and long twisting sections of track lay in the street.

"I don't think the trains are running," I tell her when I catch up to her.

She ignores me and keeps running. She doesn't go up the stairs to the station but follows the broken train line farther north. We run along side the line hiding in its shadow. More sections of the track lay in broken pieces. We skirt these sections but continue our escape northward.

"Where are we going?" I call out.

"I know a place—it's not far."

Luckily none of the Bruzers or the ships is following us. I pause to cast a quick look towards where we were and see that the lone black ship—the Raven—has now been joined by two other small ships, their searchlights shining down on the streets trying to spot anyone in the dark. If this were my Chinatown in my Chicago all the neon lights on the restaurants and shops would be lit up brighter than the Fourth of July. No one would stand a chance. I guess I'm grateful it's not my Chicago.

Then, what looks like some kind of rocket comes bursting down from one of the small ships and one of the buildings explodes. Then another building on another street explodes from a similar blast from the other ship.

"They're firing!" I tell Violet.

"Of course they are, it's what they do!" she says sharply.

I decide not to make any more dumb comments—at least for the time being. I follow her as we continue along the train line, the sound of more explosions echoing in my ears. Up ahead I can see a twisted row of train cars snaked out in tall weeds. It must have fallen from the tracks when it was destroyed. It looks like it's been lying there for years, much like the burnt-out cars along the streets. I hope these are not full of corpses as well.

Violet leads me into one of the sections of the train. We squeeze through the half-open doors and duck down. I don't see any human remains, but it's plenty dark.

She watches through one of the broken windows. "We should be safe here," she says after a few minutes. "I don't see any of them." Then, just as I'm about to thank her for saving my life, she spins around and before I know it has me flat on my face with my arm twisted behind me. She jerks it up and it feels like it's going to break. She can't weigh more than a hundred pounds but it feels like I'm being handled by Xena, Warrior Princess.

"What the hell are you doing?" I yell at her.

"I don't believe you're a collaborator," she says in my ear, "but that doesn't mean I trust you. Start telling me why you don't know anything about the Bruzers or the Zs."

"I'll tell you everything, but first can you please stop breaking my arm? You can trust me, I swear it."

She releases the hold on my arm and slides off my back. I turn over straightening out my arm and rotating my sore shoulder.

Violet looks at me suspiciously, then softens slightly. "Sorry, I didn't mean to hurt you. But I have to be careful. I've seen too many people die because of their own stupid carelessness. I want to believe you're not a Red Coat, but you'll have to convince me."

"Red Coat? I don't even know what that is."

Even in the darkness she must sense the perplexed look on my face. "You're not kidding are you? You really don't know? A Red Coat is a collaborator. A traitor. They work with the Zs to keep us in line in order to get special treatment."

"Who are the Zs?" I ask.

She gives me another probing look before responding. I must seem like some weird species she's never seen before. "How is it possible you don't know any of this? Bruzers? Zs? Red Coats? Why did I see your reflection in the War Memorial when you weren't there?"

"What War Memorial? You mean the Bean?"

Now it's her turn to look confused. "That's where I saw you," I tell her. "In the Cloud Gate sculpture at Millennium Park. Listen—Violet—I want you to trust me, even though what I'm going to tell you is completely crazy. I was on a field trip with my class at Millennium Park. I was going to draw the Chicago skyline when I saw your reflection in the Bean—the Cloud Gate sculpture."

She stops me with a wave of her hand. "You're not making any sense. School? There are no schools. And Millennium Park hasn't been finished yet. They just started it when the Zs attacked. I go there sometimes just to read and think. Usually the Bruzers don't patrol that area. There's a Blackhawk helicopter that crashed there. We call it the War Memorial in honor of everyone who died in that first assault. When I looked up from my book I saw your reflection in the glass—but you weren't there—"

"That was before the Bruzer showed up and zapped you—"

"Yeah. But when I came to you were gone. So tell me Ryan, how do you not know what's going on? Why don't you wear a collar?"

The moment of truth. "I'm not from here. I mean . . . I'm from here . . . from Chicago, but a different Chicago."

"I don't understand," she says. "How can it be different?"

"The Chicago I'm from doesn't have creatures running around shocking people. There are no alien ships up in the sky. We're out celebrating Halloween tonight and gorging ourselves on mini Snickers bars and Reese's Peanut Butter Cups."

"Halloween? I've heard of this. My cousin Jimmy told me about it. He was eight during the invasion."

"When was the invasion? Who are these aliens? Where do they come from?"

Even though it's dark our eyes are now accustomed to it and we can both see each other's faces. "You really don't know do you?"

"No. I don't. Look, Violet. My name is Ryan Whitaker. I'm sixteen years old. I'm a high school junior and my best friend is Ralph Speckler. My dad works at O'Hare Airport as a baggage handler. He hates his job, thinks it sucks, but who doesn't hate their job? Anyway, I know all this sounds weird, but you have to believe me. I'm really not from this world. I'm from a different world. My friend Mungo thinks it's a parallel universe and I believe him because there's a man named Sam who lives in my world who works as a cook in a diner called the Whistlestop and it's the same Sam who you know but of course he has no idea who I am or who Charlie is and probably has never heard of the Whistlestop Diner.

"I don't know how I got to this world or how the hell I'm going to get back. And I'm definitely not a Red Coat. You have to believe that. I wouldn't turn you in for anything. None of you. You can tell that to that Brody guy. And I'm not just saying that because I don't want him to cut my throat—well, I mean, of course I don't want the guy cutting my throat—who would? But I'm telling the truth—"

"Okay, shut up. I believe you, even though what you're telling me is the craziest thing I ever heard in my life. But when your planet is attacked by killer aliens I guess anything's possible." She smiles and I feel a thousand times better. I don't know if it was the possibility her thinking I was a traitor or not believing my story, but it doesn't matter. I just like seeing her smile.

"Let me tell you about my world then. It was about twelve years ago when the Zs—the Zoktari—first arrived. I was just a few years old when it happened and barely even remember it. I just remember there was a lot of confusion and fear. With good reason. There were no negotiations when they arrived. They don't negotiate. We found that out quickly. It was just kill and destroy—"

"Shock and awe."

"What's that?"

"Nothing—something we discussed in history class. Sorry, go on."

"They had ships by the thousands. Big ships—bigger even than the one you see now. It was over quickly. Most of us don't even know the full extent of it. Communication was the first thing that went. TVs, radios, phones, computers. All our satellites were destroyed. Just owning a handmade radio is enough to get you killed. We think the whole eastern seaboard has been wiped out—from Florida up to Maine. All the cities along the coast are gone. Detroit is gone, Cleveland, we know that. We don't know about the West Coast. We can only imagine it's the same."

"And these creatures you call Bruzers—they're not the others who first attacked you—the Zoktari?"

"No—they're the guard dogs of the Zoktari. Dumb brutes who can only take orders and dish out punishment. We have a saying—the Zs are the brains and the Bruzers are the muscle. Once the Zoktari had us defeated they brought the Bruzers in to keep us in line."

"The Bruzers where gas masks—is it because they can't breathe our air?"

"They can, but only barely. They need their own mix of air to breathe normally."

"So what's their purpose? Why did they come? What do they want with you?"

"We don't know for sure. There're a lot of rumors and no one knows exactly. Slave labor. Experiments. Some even believe they take us to their home world and put us in zoos. All we know is that no one returns who've been taken. But it's been less and less. A year ago the motherships started leaving. No one knows why. The whole city was once in shadow with the number of ships blocking out the sun. And we assumed it was like that everywhere. They had the city locked up tight for years. Those left alive—the ones not killed or taken—were herded into camps in the north part of the city."

"Is that why Chinatown is empty and looks like a war zone?"

"The whole city's a war zone, Ryan. But yeah, the south, west side and far north of the city are all closed off—Forbidden Zones they're called. It means death if you're found in these areas."

"Where do you live? There can't be enough housing for everyone?"

"There's not a whole lot of us left. Mass amounts of people were killed during the initial invasion. Since then a series of purges have taken thousands more. The Zs forced us out of our homes. Red Coats get real housing. The rest of us make do with what we can. What was once Lincoln Park is now a tent city. Food is scarce. A lot of people complain—say there are too many mouths to feed. That it's only a matter of time before all the food runs out and we die of starvation. They turn Red Coat just to save themselves and their families. It's easier than starving to death. Others wish they'd just take more or kill more. They don't say it out loud but they think it. You can see it in their eyes when the Bruzers come in and round people up. They're secretly glad. It means there's now more for the rest of us."

"But why risk your lives coming out here?"

"It's not as dangerous as it looks. There's not many Bruzers patrolling the city so we can pretty much come and go as we please. It's the Red Coats you have to look out for. They're constantly looking for the Resistance. They must get something extra if they turn us in. So the camp is the most dangerous place to meet. You never know who's watching and listening. That's why we sneak out, meet in places where no one can eavesdrop. But yes, there is a risk. Going into a Forbidden Zone can get you killed. But we're smart. We know where to hide, places we can easily slip through the barriers. They don't have enough Bruzers to watch all of us. Not enough patrol ships. We call them Ravens because of their black color and wide wings. But ravens are birds of warning—these are birds of prey. You saw what they did in Chinatown. They don't hesitate to kill."

"And I ruined everything," I tell her. "If it wasn't for me, the Bruzers would never have arrived."

"It wasn't on purpose. How could you know? You're from another world, remember?" The smile again. Playful yet reassuring. I smile in return. The guilt quickly disappears.

"It sounded like all of you were arguing when Brody dragged me in."

"Yeah, we were. The Zs are leaving. We think it's only a matter of time before they all leave for good."

"Why are they leaving?"

"No one knows for sure. Maybe they found another planet to destroy. Maybe it's too costly being an invading force. Who knows? But we know it'll be over one day."

"Then what?"

"What any nation does when a war is over and the victors finally leave. Rebuild. Start putting our lives back together. Take care of our wounded, teach our children. Get even with the Red Coats." There's a hint of malice in her voice. A seething tone just below the surface.

"You mean—kill them?"

"Of course. They're traitors, they deserve nothing less."

"And could you do that—kill someone I mean?"

"I would. I haven't yet but I would. Uncle Tolliver has tried to keep my hands clean. He says once you go down that road you can't go back. He says it eats up a little bit of your soul each time you kill someone—even if it's a Z or Bruzer. It's why he keeps me away from the raids. But I keep telling him I'm as strong as any of my older cousins and as strong as anyone in the Resistance. And even though I've never killed anyone, I'd kill a Z or a Bruzer if I had to. I'm ready. I've been in several scrapes already with them."

"Is that how you got the scar?" I say.

"Yes—my war wound, Uncle Toll calls it. I was only seven when I stood up to a Bruzer who was harassing me and another girl my age. I guess I'm lucky they didn't kill me—just slashed at me with its shocker."

"It's shocker? The rifle? You mean with the collar?"

"Yes, it's how they control us. Everyone is forced to wear them—even the Red Coats. Which is why I know you can't be a collaborator. But they only work when they're close. Plus we're working on how to get them off. If we can slip them we can attack them with a large force instead of these little surprise attacks we do."

"Is that why you were meeting—to plan an attack?"

"No. We sent a group out a year ago. Out to the east coast to try and survey the damage—maybe make contact with any survivors—form a coalition of Resistance fighters. Some of us just think the Midwest is all that's left. We haven't heard from our group. No one's come back yet. We want to send another group out to try to reach them. Or at least try to find out what happened. Maybe they were captured. It's the not knowing that's so frustrating. But some in the group think it's too dangerous. They believe the reason we haven't heard anything is that they failed. They're dead or captured. They don't want to risk sending anymore."

"Where do you stand on this?"

"I believe the same as Uncle Tolliver that we need to go. In fact, I volunteered to be one of the ones to leave. That's what we were arguing about before you arrived. Uncle Toll doesn't want me to go. He doesn't think I'm ready yet."

"What about your parents? What do they say?"

"My parents are gone. They were taken in one of the first purges by the Zs. I was five then. Been raised by my aunt and uncle ever since."

"I'm sorry," I tell her.

"Nothing to be sorry about," she says matter-of-fact. "It's just the way it is. Some have had whole families taken with no one left to care for them. They live on the street, scrape by like rats. Scavengers we call them. I've got it better than most, not as good as some others. You can't change what's been done, you just have to try to change what is and what may be."

"What if you could change it—I mean, with what's been done?"

"What are you talking about? You can't change the past."

"I don't mean change it exactly. I'm not sure what I mean. But where I come from none of this has happened. Maybe it never will. I hope it doesn't. And just like I crossed over to your world, maybe you can cross over into mine. You can escape the Zoktari and the Bruzers. You have no idea what life is like without a bunch of aliens around."

"But how, Ryan? How did you cross over into our world?"

"I told you, I don't know. I really don't. Maybe it has something to do with the building I was in. I wasn't the first one to cross over. A guy named Charlie crossed over first—years ago, but it was only for a few minutes. He was also chased by the Bruzers, except when he jumped into the river he crossed back over to our Chicago. For some reason I didn't. Maybe I need to get back to the same building and see if I can find out what makes us cross over. Maybe I can return. And if I can cross back maybe you can cross as well. You'll be safe."

"That sounds great. Perfect even. Who wouldn't want a life without Bruzers and Zs? But I can't abandon my family, my friends. Like it or not this is my world. I have to do what I can to make it better. Others depend on me. I can't just run away."

"You're right. What was I thinking?"

"You were thinking of doing something good. Of saving someone you don't even know. Your heart's in the right place, it's just I have to see this thing through to the end."

I admire her guts and determination. She reminds me of Jack. If she were in my world I could easily picture her in the Army or marines. A jarhead with her head shaved. G.I. Violet. Then I think what would happen if I never get back to my world.

"Violet?"

"Yes?"

"What if I can't get back to my Chicago? What if I'm stuck here?"

She smiles. "Then I guess you're one of us now. Welcome to the Resistance."

"But I have no experience being a fighter. It's my brother who was the fighter—"

"Is he a soldier?"

"Was—he was killed a year ago. In my world we're still too busy fighting each other."

"Yeah, Uncle Toll told me about all the wars. I guess it's one good thing about having aliens attack you—it gives everyone a common enemy."

"I never looked at it that way. I'm sure once they leave you'll all go back to hating each other again."

"Maybe. Who knows? We don't even know what the rest of the world looks like. Paris? London? Are they like us? Are they worse?

Like I said, it's the not knowing that's so damn frustrating. If only we could contact them. Organize a worldwide Resistance. But that's where the Zoktari has us beaten. The isolation has us cowering in fear."

"You're not beaten yet," I tell her.

"No, we're not." The smile returns along with a look of defiance.

Chapter Nine
Library

We wait in the train car another hour. Violet says once she's sure it's clear we'll move out. So we wait and watch for signs of Bruzers. There have been no more sounds of explosions. I hope the others, including that psychopath Brody, made it out alive. I'd hate to think I caused anyone's death.

"Okay," she says. "It looks clear. We should move out now."

"Where will we go—your home?"

"No, that would be too dangerous. Without a collar people would notice you too much. The Red Coats would be alerted and then it would all be over for you. I'll take you to one of my favorite places to hide."

"The War Memorial?"

"No. That's out in the open. They'd get us for sure. We'll hide out in the library."

"The library?"

"Yeah, there's a really huge one not far away—"

"I know it," I tell her. "I go there all the time."

"You do? That's weird. Maybe we've been there at the same time in the same place but just in different worlds."

"Creepy isn't it?"

"Not really," she says. "It's—I don't know. Kind of cool I guess."

"I wish I knew how to cross back over. I would love to show you my Chicago."

"Like a date? Do people still do that in your world?"

I'm glad of the darkness because she can't see my face getting red. I didn't think of it like that, but now that I do, I wish it were true. I wish I could take her out on a date and show her around. Take her away from all this suffering and death and fighting.

"No—not a date," I stammer, "just a—"

"Relax, I was only kidding."

"Does no one date anymore then in this world?" It sounds depressing, but I guess they have better things to do, like staying alive.

"Not like you think it is, but sure, people still meet and fall in love and get married. Father Wu did a wedding ceremony last week. Some people say they're not as legal as they used to be but legal's not high on anyone's agenda right now. It's legal in their hearts and that's all that matters."

"And you? Are you . . . seeing anyone?"

She hesitates a moment. A hand brushes away hair that wasn't in her face, while her voice almost falls to a hush. "No. There's no one. Boys aren't interested in me. They want to see a softer side. I'm rough as tree bark, Aunt Alice says. Too focused on fighting. I don't know if that's it. Maybe they just don't like my face. I'm not exactly glamorous."

"They're blind then. I like your face. I think it's perfect."

An awkward silence hangs over us. She finally breaks it and says: "What about you? You probably have lots of girlfriends in your world."

I stifle a laugh. "Oh sure, one for every day of the week and twice on Sunday."

"Really?" Her face is serious—almost as if she's disappointed.

"No, I'm only kidding." Does her face brighten? It's hard to tell in the dark. "There's no one I'm seeing right now. My friend Speckler keeps trying to get me to go out with this girl—Nancy Caldwell. She's the best friend of a girl he's madly in love with."

"So what's wrong with her? This girl Nancy?"

"Nothing. She's great. She's just not—the right one for me." This conversation has definitely taken a direction I didn't think it would ever take. First, I never thought I'd see this girl again. Then I find her and we end up hiding in a train car having the most intimate conversation while aliens are hunting us. Weird.

We move out of the train and into the shadows of the el. "Where did the rest go?" I ask. "Will we meet up with them?"

"Probably not. They all have their own hiding places—routes they know to take that will give them a chance. Father Wu will probably help most of them. He knows the area. It's best to travel in small groups."

"Father Wu's a priest?"

"Was—before the Zs arrived. I guess he still is, even though all religions have been outlawed."

I watch Violet. She looks calm. Maybe she's used to outrunning alien monsters and dodging laser beams and rockets. I feel a little embarrassed, as though I should be protecting her, providing her with a picture of peace and safety. Instead it's the other way around. She doesn't look worried at all and I feel much better just looking at her. In a way I almost feel like Speckler mooning after Amy Dierdorf. He must have come up looking for me. What did he think when I wasn't there? What's he going to tell Mr. Carnofsky if he asks where I am? What about my parents? I can only imagine what he might tell them. Would it be the truth or just let them believe I ran away or got kidnapped by some cult and taken to Mexico to be brainwashed. Who knows what story Speckler will come up with? He might even spill the truth. He may have to if I never return, if I'm stuck here for good. Will anyone believe him? Will it get to the government?

The moon has gone down. It's darker out than before which gives us better camouflage. We keep low and move silently. I'm glad Violet knows the way or else I'd be stumbling and breaking my leg over all the debris. We continue to follow the train line. It's more of the same—broken sections lying in piles of concrete and track. Another train—this one only a couple of cars—has been torched and is nothing but a blackened empty shell. It also looks like a fire has swept through the houses along the street.

"Does anyone live in these houses?"

"Maybe a few Scavengers holding up, but they move around, rarely staying in one place. Plus the Forbidden Zone is not a place you want to hide out in for too long."

We keep to the shadows as we head north. I recognize the street names but this part of the city is almost unrecognizable. Mostly it has to do with the fact that time has stood still for over ten years. Things that were just beginning to be built have stopped. The things that were built lay in ruins or are burnt to the ground. It is like a war zone, which of course it is—or was. I guess the war is over now. To the victor go the spoils and in this case the spoils is a whole planet and its people.

There are huge craters in the street from whatever alien missiles landed there. And more burnt-out cars. I'm beginning to think every car in the city has been destroyed, which really sucks since I just got my license. I'm about to ask Violet if anyone still drives when she says urgently: "We've got to take cover. Ravens!"

Two small ships come into view and circle above us, their lights flooding the ground. I follow Violet into one of the houses that are not totally burnt to the ground. There's barely anything left, only a half wall of the first floor, but enough for us to hide behind. We scrunch in tight into the darkest corner. Violet presses her body next to mine. I can feel her warmth, her heart beating, her shallow breathing just as she must feel the thundering of my own heart, the heavy breathing, the coolness of my body in my damp clothes.

We watch the ships. The lights get closer. Closer. We flatten ourselves as best we can but it's not good enough. The light hits us. I'm paralyzed, thinking any second will be my last, expecting the laser missile to come down. But then the light leaves us as the ship flies off.

"Why are they leaving?" I ask.

Violet is on her feet, moving out to the street. "They're not, they're landing. We really have to move now—there's going to be Bruzers on the ground sweeping for us."

We run.

It seems all I've been doing since crossing over is run. I need to get in better shape. If I ever make it back to my world I make a promise to start a running regimen. Maybe learn hand-to-hand combat to keep from getting thrown to the ground by hundred pound girls.

We come through the neighborhood and reach the south end of the Loop. I can see the skyscrapers ahead—or what's left of them. Most are only half-buildings, steel frames and concrete structures, famous buildings that started the age of skyscrapers that my History teacher, Mrs. Hederson, taught us about on a walking tour the year before. All gone now. I can only pray that the aliens will leave just as Violet says and the people of this Chicago can rebuild this once great city.

We reach a tall barrier—a chain fence—blocking our way into the Loop. This must be the barrier that begins the Forbidden Zone. I follow Violet as she leads me to a spot where there's a wide hole in the fence.

"Don't touch the wires—they're electrified," she says. She's skinny enough to make it through fine but I'm not. I find that being well fed has its disadvantages in this world. But I somehow make it through without getting myself electrocuted.

"That wasn't too bad," I say and smile. Her return smile disappears as she sees something over my shoulder. She starts to speak, to warn me, when she doubles over as if she's been punched. I reach for her and catch her just before she hits the ground. She's unconscious but breathing. I look back. There are two Bruzers approaching the fence, firing their rifles, which must be set to stun since no bullets or lasers shoot out of the muzzle, just a high-pitch pulsing noise. They have no effect on me since I don't wear a collar. I pick her up and put her over my shoulder. She doesn't weigh anything. I make a run down an alley and then another. I run to the library. My energy is renewed. I can't let us get caught.

I make it to Congress Avenue without a Bruzer or Raven catching us. The library is across the street. In my Chicago it's a distinguished-looking red-brick building with a green roof and large ornate owls decorating the top corners. Gargoyles of learning. But here it's missing half its roof; large sections of the brick facade litter the street while one owl has been knocked from its perch and lies in the middle of Congress. I dodge the owl to get to the front door. It's boarded up. I run around to the other side of the building and find a pile of debris stacked in front hiding the side door. If no one knew the building they wouldn't even know this side door existed. Luckily I've been here so many times I know all the entrances and exits. I squeeze around the debris and try the door. It opens.

I make my way inside to the circular lobby and gently lay Violet down then collapse next to her. I breathe easy for the first time.

The lobby is not completely destroyed. Though it's nothing like it is in my world—clean, safe, with marble floors and ornate paintings. The escalators to the upper floors obviously aren't working but it's not a total wreck.

I check on Violet. Her breathing is shallow but she seems fine. I wish I had some way of waking her. There's no telling how long she'll be out.

Almost out of nowhere a voice startles me. "What have we here, some competing Scavs?" Three figures appear. Boys. The place is quiet but I didn't hear them at all. They move like cats, or cockroaches.

I scramble to my feet, putting myself between them and Violet. I can see they're young, teenagers like myself. They look haggard, rough, and smell god-awful, as if they haven't had a bath in years. They spread out in a half-circle, blocking my escape on all sides.

"What's with your friend?" one of them, a tall mean-looking kid with scabs on his face, asks. It's not a friendly question. He points a stick at her and I can see it's some kind of walking stick like an English gentleman would have. It has a silver head in the shape of a lion with some dark stain on it. Blood?

"Bruzers," the one blocking my escape on the left says before I can respond. The other boy in the middle makes the pulsing noise the rifles make and the other two laugh, though I don't see anything funny about it.

"She's fine," I say. "Leave her alone."

"Leave her alone," the tall one with the stick says in a mocking voice. "We haven't even touched her."

"Not yet," the boy who made the rifle sound says. This brings another round of laughter and I tense up. I thought I only had aliens to worry about in this world. Now I know there can be things just as bad as aliens. This could get ugly. I have no weapon to defend us with. I wish Violet would wake up. She's a fighter. She would know what to do. I begin to tremble, not sure how to protect her. But I'll fight for her and do whatever I can to save her from these walking hyenas.

"They're not Scavs," the middle boy says. He's short, mangy-looking, with clumps of hair missing and one eye that looks closed. "I ain't never seen 'em before. Your mommy know you're out after curfew?"

"Maybe he don't have a mommy," the boy on the left says.

"Yeah—big bad Bruzers took his mommy away. Is that what happened Bruzerfood?"

"We're not looking for any trouble," I say. "Can you leave us alone please?"

"Oh sure, since you said please." More hideous laughter.

My palms begin to sweat.

The tall one points the deadly stick at me. "You're real polite, Bruzerfood. We're polite too. So why don't you please step outside and leave your friend with us. We'll be polite to her, too."

I tense up even more. My throat is suddenly dry and it's hard to swallow. I scan the room for something to fight them with, wondering if I can get to a brick or piece of wood before they all jump me. I put my hand instinctively in my pocket and feel something cold and smooth. My smartphone! I forgot I had it. I pull it out and point it at the boys as if it were a weapon. "You three better leave. I don't want to have to use this on you."

Their eyes go to the strange black object in my hand. I can sense their wariness. It's obviously something they're not familiar with. If all technology stopped twelve years ago, then none of them would know about smartphones like this.

"What is that thing? Some kid's toy you picked up?"

"Yeah, he's still playing with toys."

"It's not a toy," I tell them. "I got it off a dead Bruzer. It's a new weapon. Kills you instantly."

"You want us to believe you killed a Bruzer? You and what army?"

"I didn't say I killed a Bruzer, I just said I got it off a dead one. I'm working with them."

"You're working with them? You're a Red Coat? What are you— stupid, or just crazy? We kill Red Coats."

"Not before we cut all their fingers off first."

"Then all their toes," the short one adds. "Then their privates." Again the laughter, but not as loud as before. They're still eyeing my smartphone—wary of its potential.

"I told you, make a move and I'll kill you with this. Don't believe I'm working for them? Then how did I get my collar off?" I show them my neck, hoping that will convince them.

"It's true, he ain't got one," the middle boy says to the other two as if they can't see it for themselves.

"I don't know how you got it off but it won't stop us from killing you," walking stick says. He grits his teeth as if he just had a tooth pulled without any painkiller.

All three are tensed up and I sense they're ready to jump me so I switch the phone on with my thumb and pray there's still some battery life or that the plunge in the Chicago River didn't ruin it for good. It powers up instantly. The three instantly take a step back as it glows to life. I hold it up and aim it at them as if it were a gun or a phaser from *Star Trek*.

"I told you I don't want to have to kill you but I will if you don't leave."

They continue to back up but they don't leave. Maybe they're thinking of a way to attack, possibly thinking that I can't kill all three of them. I need to scare them some more. I open one of the game apps with a tap of my thumb. The sound effects start up and this makes them even more nervous. "I gave you a chance," I say. I tap the screen and it begins making loud laser noises. At the first sound the three turn and run. They head down the hall to the side door and squeeze through. I check to make sure they're gone. I can't believe they bought that little stunt. I almost laugh out loud.

"What was that all about?"

Violet's eyes are open but she looks woozy. "Some Scavengers," I tell her. "Don't worry. I scared them away. How do you feel?"

"Wonderful—getting shocked is my favorite thing."

"What can I do to help?"

"Nothing. The feeling will go away soon. I just need to rest some more. But not down here."

I help her to her feet and put her arm over my shoulder. "Where do you want to go?"

"Upstairs," she says. "But you'll have to help me."

"Don't worry," I tell her. "I carried you here didn't I?"

"Is that how I got here?"

"Yeah."

"Thanks," she says and then kisses me softly on the cheek. I feel my face getting red again.

"I can carry you some more if you want." My voice sounds hoarse, barely above a whisper.

"Once was enough, I'm not a doll," she says. She doesn't want to appear weak. I don't blame her. Weakness is a trait that could probably mark you for death in this world.

We go up the broken escalator to the floor above. I don't see many books on the shelves. I ask her where they all went and she says people took them to burn. "Since there's no heat left in the city people have to make their own heat and burn whatever they can. Few kids my age can even read. I'm one of the lucky ones. Uncle Toll and Aunt Alice made sure that all of us could read and write. Me and my cousins. They said the aliens won't be here forever and soon we'll need to get back to the way things were before. People need to be educated. So I like coming here and finding books to read. I like reading about how the world was before the invasion."

We go into a corner between two rows of empty shelves that are still standing and I help her to the floor and sit next to her.

"What was that thing you scared them off with?"

I show her. "My phone. I told them it was a weapon. I'm glad they believed me. I was worried I might press my music and then Lady Gaga would start singing."

"Who?"

"Never mind. It would take too long to explain." How weird to live in a world so much like mine yet one with no radio, movies, or television. I check the status bar on the phone. "There's no signal. I wonder if my parent's telephone number is the same here. But it does other things other than make phone calls. It's got games and photos—would you like to see some pics?"

"Pics?"

"Sorry—pictures? Photos?"

She nods and I open my photos. "Here's my friend Speckler."

"Why is he dressed like a Bruzer? Is he completely insane?"

"It's for Halloween. And yes, he is completely mental. But he's a good friend, even if he moves to the beat of his own drum and wants me to march along with him." I scroll through pictures of me and Speckler putting the Haunted Hotel together.

"You all look so . . . happy." She says the word "happy" like it's some kind of foreign word. I don't press her on it. I know she's seen nothing but misery since she was a little girl.

"How many pictures does it have?"

"Hundreds," I say. "But it doesn't just store photos, it also takes them." I hold up the phone and point it at both of us. "None of them will believe that I'm here. This is proof. Smile." I shoot a picture of us. I flip the phone around to show her. She's not smiling. She's looking nervous, confused.

"You're not smiling."

"I haven't had my picture taken since I was a little girl," she says. "It's weird." She stares at it for several minutes. "I look terrible." Her hand comes up to her face.

"No you don't."

"Everyone in your world is so perfect," she says as we look at other photos. "Like her. Who is she?" I tell her. "Nancy—the one who likes you? Yes, you can see it in the way she looks at you."

It's a group photo of me, Speckler, Nancy and Amy. Speckler's trying to put his arm around Amy and she's forcibly removing it. Nancy is looking at me. I never noticed the look in her face before, as if she wants to kiss me.

"We're just goofing around," I say. I quickly scroll to a new photo.

"You don't have to be embarrassed. There's nothing wrong with someone liking you."

"I'm not embarrassed," I say, which couldn't be more wrong. I don't want to talk about Nancy Caldwell or Amy Dierdorf or any other girl. I show her pictures of Mungo and talk about his comic book store.

"If this is a parallel universe then there must be doubles of everyone. I wonder what Mungo and Speckler are like here. I wonder if Speckler and I are friends here. Probably not since there are no more schools and that's where we met."

"I wonder what my double is like in your world," Violet says. I never thought about that, the idea of an exact duplicate of her in my world. But it wouldn't be exact at all. "Does she live with her parents?" she continues. "She must. Does she have any brothers or sisters?"

"Maybe. I'm sure she's not going around kicking alien butt," I say.

"Will you try to meet her? If you get back to your world?"

"No, I don't think so. There's only one Violet I'm interested in."

"You're interested in me?" she says.

"You know what I mean," I say quickly. "I'm sure she's nothing like you. We probably wouldn't even get along. She might even have a boyfriend."

"Her life is probably quite normal," she says, her voice turning wistful. "But if you do get back to your world and you change your mind and feel like looking her up, her name's Violet Ames. Her, mine, ours I guess, it's confusing what to call her . . . mother was—is—called Mary. Our father is George Ames."

"And you have no idea what happened to them? Your parents I mean?"

"They were taken like so many others. What's worse is that we don't even know where they were taken or for what reason. That's what's so terrible—the not knowing. Are they alive? Are they dead? Will I ever see them again? At least my double doesn't have these worries. I hope she never does."

"Would you want to meet my double in this world? This Ryan?"

"Maybe, even though it would be totally weird. That's of course if he's still alive. I told you that in the first few years they killed thousands here and took hundreds more as prisoners. Besides, no one lives in the houses they lived in before. Most are destroyed. It might be impossible to find out if he's alive and if so which part of the camp he's living in."

"But you could try to find out, ask around. His father is Walter—Walt Whitaker and his mother is Miriam Whitaker. They have another son named Jack."

"Jack Whitaker?" she says, as if she's heard the name before.

"Yes. He's probably still alive in this world."

She sits up straight. "There's a Jack Whitaker who's in the Resistance. He's one of the ones who went on the scouting mission out east."

"It can't be possible it's the same one." I scroll through my photo album until I find a picture of my brother. He's in his uniform from training camp in Fort Benning, Georgia. His head is shaved and he's smiling. It's a sunny day.

"That's him!" she says. "He has long hair but I'm sure of it."

I show her another photo of Jack before going off to boot camp. There's a photo of the two of us from the summer before when we went whitewater rafting on the Wolf River in Wisconsin. "I was scared to death of the rapids," I tell her. "But Jack kept laughing, wanting to go through them again and again. I was praying just to make it to the end without dying and here he was praying to go again. That was the last family trip we took." I stare at the photo. It's been a long time since I looked at it. Not since his death have I looked at any of the photos. To think that in this world he's still alive. I can't believe it. And he's a fighter, a member of the Resistance. Just like in my world. Maybe the two aren't so unlike after all.

"But you don't know anything about his brother—about my double?"

"No. There are a lot of us in the Resistance from different camps in the city. We don't all meet together. I've never spoken to him so I don't know. Maybe your double is in the Resistance and I haven't seen him, or maybe I've seen him but I just don't remember."

Great, I'm unforgettable in this world.

"What's wrong?"

"Nothing, just thinking of something."

"I'll try to find out about your double," she says.

"I don't want to meet him, even if I am stuck here. It's better that way. Besides, I'm sure if the aliens saw us together they'd think something is wrong."

"Ryan, I just thought of something. What if it's the aliens who brought you over? Their technology is so much more advanced than ours—I mean, they traveled all across the universe. Maybe they know how to travel from one universe to the next? Or bring people from one universe to the next. They might not even be from this universe."

"That makes sense, but why would they bring me here? For what purpose? How do they even know I exist?"

"I don't know. But it's better not trying to find out. Whatever they have planned for you can't be good."

"Maybe it has something to do with all the people they have rounded up. Maybe they're sending them back across to my world."

"Have you heard about it in your world? People coming from this universe?"

"No, and I think that'd be something we'd all hear about unless the government found out and are keeping them hidden away."

We talk some more, going over this idea, but we can't come up with any reasons why the Zoktari would want to bring people from another universe into theirs. I don't think we have any technology in our world that would benefit them, if they are so advanced. Cell phones and laptops wouldn't be anything to them.

We make a decision not to tell anyone other than her Uncle Tolliver that I come from a parallel universe.

"If people find out that there might be a way to escape this world for a better world, I don't think you'd be safe. I said I wouldn't want to cross over, that there's still too much work to be done here, but I can't speak for everyone. Most would probably jump at the chance to escape this world, escape the Zs and the Bruzers."

"Maybe I won't be here much longer. Maybe I'll cross back on my own or find another door or window. If we go back to the hotel—"

"I think it'd be crawling with Bruzers by now. Why were they there in the first place? That area's been a Forbidden Zone for years—no one's lived there. It seems they might have been expecting you."

"I never thought about that. But if I can't return then what will I do?"

"You can stay with us until we decide what to do."

"But I don't have a collar? Everyone will notice me you said. I'd stick out like a rodeo clown at the opera. Maybe I should just hide out here, or somewhere else."

"Okay, we can decide that later. I'm really tired. I need sleep."

I'm exhausted as well. I close my eyes but it seems neither of us can fall asleep. We don't talk anymore though, each of us lost in our own thoughts. An hour goes by and eventually I hear Violet breathing steadily. She's asleep. She's curled up next to me, our bodies close together. I watch her until my own eyes start to get heavy. I close them for a second and before I know it there's someone shaking my shoulder telling me to wake up.

I open my eyes and there's a bright light above me. I bring a hand up to shield my eyes. "Violet?" She's no longer next to me. Who took her?

"You can't lay there, young man. I'll have to call security if you don't get up."

There's an elderly woman bending over me. I'm still in the library but I can see people walking about. Books fill the shelves and the place is clean and orderly.

"Where's Violet?" I jump to my feet. "Violet!" I shout, but she's nowhere around. People stop and look at me as if I'm crazy.

"Are you okay? How did you get in here? You didn't spend the night here did you?" She backs away from me thinking I must be homeless or crazy or both.

"This is impossible," I say. I can't be back in my world! I can't. But I am. I wander out, down the escalator, which is working. I walk outside and it is my Chicago. No ships in the sky. City busses and cars drive by. I've crossed back over to my world and now I know one thing—it wasn't the building at all. It's me. It has to be. And is it something the aliens are doing? Controlling me? So if it is me and not a specific place, then how do I get back? Because I have to get back there. I know there's no sane reason for me to feel this way—that being in that world increases the chances of my death—a very painful death—enormously. Yet, I can't shake the idea that I belong there somehow. That it's my purpose to be there. To be with Violet.

Chapter Ten
Super Friends

The first thing I have to do is call Speckler and find out what happened after I disappeared. It's morning time. About ten o'clock. I hope my parents aren't home. On Saturday they often head to Costco and stock up on five hundred rolls of toilet paper and giant boxes of Cheerios. I don't want to have to explain my whereabouts. If Speckler didn't freak out and blow everything I should be okay. But knowing Speckler, maybe he thought I was gone for good and told them everything. What will I say when I show up? *Oh yes, I was in a parallel universe running from killer aliens but I'm back now—what's for lunch?*

I take my phone out but before calling Speckler I look at the photo I captured the night before. I stare into her green eyes. I never knew they were green. What is she doing now? What will she think when she wakes up and I'm not there? Has she already woken up? Did she think I abandoned her or that I crossed back over to my world? I hope she doesn't think I left her there. I hope she knows I can't control this thing that is happening to me, because if I could I would go back to her world in an instant and be there when she wakes up so that I'm the first thing she sees.

I call Speckler.

He answers on the first ring. He probably slept with the phone next to his pillow. "Dude, what happened to you?"

"I crossed over," I say. "It happened for real this time. Not just seeing a face in a reflection but I was in their world."

"I thought so. I freaked out when I couldn't find you. I waited all night, me and Charlie. We looked all along the river. We thought you might have drowned or something."

"I did end up in the river but I didn't drown. I thought it would bring me back here but it didn't. But I know one thing for sure—it wasn't the building at all, it was me."

"What do you mean it's you?"

"I can't explain right now. I'll tell you when I see you."

"Where are you? Do you need me to come get you?"

"No, I'm good. I'm downtown. I'll take the train home, change my clothes and then go straight to your house. But I need to know what you told my parents. Please don't tell me you told them anything about this."

"What kind of an idiot do you take me for?"

"You really don't want me to answer that do you?"

"I told them you were spending the night with me and that your phone's battery was dead."

"Did they buy it?"

"Please, I could tell your mother that you really did become a zombie and she'd believe it."

"Probably, but my dad would want proof."

I hang up and get on the train. It's surreal going through a city that isn't destroyed and doesn't have giant spaceships up in the sky. But for how long? If this is a parallel universe and both universes are identical then there are Zoktari and Bruzers out there somewhere. Maybe they're on their way here right now, or they've been here waiting on the dark side of the moon. Maybe we're on our last few days before it all ends just like in Violet's world. What then? Should I contact the government? The president? I'm sure they'll think I'm a nutjob. Once more I wish I could cross back over. I need to learn more about these aliens, and more about the Resistance. How do they fight them? Kill them? I don't even know what the Zoktari look like. Maybe they look just like us and are already here. I look around the train and see several suspicious characters that look like they could be aliens.

I almost miss my stop I'm so absorbed with thinking about this. A couple of blocks and I reach my house and open the door slowly. I don't hear the TV, which is a good sign. I carefully close the door behind me and then head to the stairs. The hardwood floors creak like an old coffin even though I try to tiptoe.

"Is that you, Ryan?" My mother pokes her head out at the top of the stairs. She's got a full laundry basket in her arms.

"Yeah, it's me Mom." I try to sound as casual as I can, as if I wasn't running for my life a few hours ago.

"How was it last night? Pretty scary?"

For a second I think she knows everything and she's referring to the Bruzers and the Zoktari, but then I realize she's asking about the

Haunted Hotel. "Yeah, it was pretty scary. We had a lot of people. Made a ton of money."

"So it looks like the New York trip is back on?"

"It's back on."

"Good. I know your father will be happy to hear that."

"Dad? Why would he be happy? He hates all this art stuff."

She comes down with the laundry basket. I take it out of her hands and we go down to the laundry room down in the basement.

"No he doesn't," she says while sorting whites from the colors. "He's just very practical. It's hard for him to see the career benefits. You know he never went to college. You'd be the first one in the family."

"I know. Did he ever try to talk Jack into going to college instead of joining the Army?"

Talking about Jack with my dad is a taboo subject, but it's different with my mom. Since she's been active in the family support group she's learned to deal with Jack's death in positive ways whereas my father has yet to get over it. I can talk freely with her about Jack.

"No. I think he envisioned Jack rising up to be a four-star general one day."

"Four star general? Don't you have to be an officer first? Jack was just a private."

"Your father knew Jack wouldn't stay a private very long. He knew he had leadership skills and ambition. He wouldn't be happy taking orders. He figured it would only be a matter of time."

I tread carefully with my next question. "Mom, do you ever think about what would happen if Jack were still alive?" *Because he is alive—just not in our world.*

She gives me a sad smile. "All the time. Sometimes I imagine getting letters from him asking about the family, asking for advice. Sometimes I even write back to him."

"You do?" That sounds kind of crazy—but not too crazy. I sometimes have imaginary conversations with him like the real ones we used to have. We shared a bedroom when we were younger and lived in a smaller house. I could talk to him about girls and school and stuff. Unlike Dad, he never thought being an artist was dumb.

"Sure I do. I tell him how you're doing. How you're planning a big trip to New York. I get him caught up on his cousins and aunts and uncles and about your father and work. Then I think what we would do as a family when he comes home to visit. The dinners I'd fix. The places we'd go. You know your father always wanted to visit famous Civil War battlefields? He used to talk about taking you and Jack some summer—just the three of you."

I never knew that. I mean, I knew he was a bit of a Civil War buff, always watching the History channel and that Ken Burns documentary whenever it came on. But a road trip with the three of us? "Just because Jack's not here, doesn't mean we can't still go. Life doesn't have to stop. Maybe we can do it in Jack's honor. It might even give Dad some closure."

"I know your father. For him, it wouldn't be the same without Jack. He always thought Jack would have liked it more than you. You were always more of a pacifist."

"Yeah, I'm sure Jack would have loved it. He shared dad's love of war history. But there might have been some cool stuff I could have drawn. Cannons and things. I'm not totally against war." *Especially if it's a war against aliens.* "Is Dad here?"

"He went to Home Depot to get a new snow shovel and some bags of salt. We're supposed to get an early winter this year. He should be back soon. I know he wants you to help rake up the leaves and clean out the rain gutters."

"Okay, but I have to go see Speckler first."

"Didn't you just come from Ralph's?"

"Yeah, but I forgot to ask him some things. Now that we know we're going to New York we have to start planning."

"But that's not until Spring Break. You got months to plan."

"There's no time like the present. I just need to change first."

"Yes, you do. I know you were just pretending to be a zombie, but do you have to smell like one to?" She laughs. I'm glad she can still find moments like this to laugh about things. It reminds me of her old self before Jack died. Since then there hasn't been a lot of laughter in the house.

I shower and finally examine the cut on my leg from crawling through the broken window in Chinatown Square. It's not deep and I patch it up with a good wide bandage. I dress quickly and hop on my bike and race over to Speckler's house before my dad gets back. I don't want to get stuck doing a day's worth of weekend chores. There's too much I need to tell Speckler.

"Wow, this is so amazingly weird," Speckler says for the millionth time. "She looks so . . . real."

"That's because she is real, dummy." I snatch my phone out of his hands and wipe his tortilla-chip-stained fingerprints off the glass.

"Yeah, but seeing a drawing of her is one thing. Seeing a photo of the two of you together is just mind-blowingly weird. I'm talking major *Twilight Zone* weird."

"I know how weird it is, you don't have to keep saying it."

"Okay, but you have to tell me every single detail. Do not leave anything out." He's excited and looks like he hasn't slept all night. Who has? We're alone in his room. I can hear his mom running the vacuum cleaner downstairs. He has a younger sister but his dad took her to soccer practice. His room looks like a hurricane hit it. He's crashed out on a large blue beanbag chair with the new *Halo* game on his X-Box.

"I can see you were real worried about me."

"Hey, it's how I deal with stress," he argues.

"Stress? You want to know about real stress? Try having *real* killer aliens hunting you down and then see how you deal with stress." I begin to tell him what happened and he only stops me to ask a dozen questions.

"Can you please let me finish my story?"

"Wait," he says. He goes hunting in one of his desk drawers and pulls out a small video camera. "We should record all this while it's still fresh in your mind."

That's actually not a bad idea. "Okay, but don't interrupt me while I'm telling it."

"But you leave out a lot of important details."

"I'll be thorough."

He sets up the camera on a tripod. I sit down and begin the story all over again. I start with cleaning up all the body parts after the Haunted Hotel and then turning to see—what I thought was Speckler in his alien costume—a Bruzer. I continue to tell my story, taking my time and trying to fill in all the details. Speckler stops me a few times to make clarifications. A more detailed description of the alien ships—and no I didn't see any Zoktari so I don't know what they look like—and more details about the Resistance. I don't know much. I describe Violet's uncle—Tolliver Ames, as best I can even though it was pretty dark in the church. No, I don't know which church it is. I was running for my life so I didn't even know which street I was on. Somewhere in Chinatown. Speckler gets very interested when I tell him I recognized Sam from the diner.

"What? Wait! You saw Sam?" He can barely control himself.

"Yes. At first I thought it was the Sam you and I know but it wasn't. It was a different Sam."

"What do you mean it was a different Sam?"

"Mungo was right, it's a parallel universe, an exact duplicate to this world—with the same exact people."

"You got to be kidding? A parallel universe? I just thought it was another world—not a parallel universe!" He starts pacing around the room. Maybe he's thinking of an alternate Amy Dierdorf—one where she would be madly in love with him.

"Can I continue my story now?"

"Of course."

I talk about Violet. It's strange telling him about her. And telling it makes me feel like it was so long ago, that all it is is a story I'm telling. That somehow she isn't real and that we didn't share an adventure together. I explain about the attack from the Bruzers and our escape. How Violet and I hid out in the ruined el train and then in the library.

"The library? You went to the library? What, you went looking for books? With aliens after you?"

"No. We went there to hide. There's few books left anyway, most of them have been burned for heat. So it was a good place to hide, until we ran into some Scavengers—"

"Some what?"

I explain how so many people lost family members to the Zoktari and how some kids who have no one to look after them decided to live on the street. I also explain how I chased them away with my smartphone and how I was lucky it still worked.

He looks puzzled. "They've never seen a smartphone before?"

"Dude, their world pretty much ended twelve years ago when these aliens attacked. They don't even have electricity."

"No iPods? No Xboxes? No movies or TV? That has got to majorly suck."

"I don't think they're missing any of those things—they do have other things on their mind other than watching *Jersey Shore*. They are trying to fight for their lives you know?"

"Right. Fight for their lives—like a real life *Halo*."

"Yes, like real life *Halo*." If Speckler can only imagine their world in connection to a video game then more power to him.

"So keep going," he says. "What happened after you chased off the Scavengers?"

"Nothing. We lay down to get some sleep—"

"Sleep? You were sleeping together—on a first date? Leave it to you, Ryan, to have to travel all the way to a parallel universe to get some action."

"Okay, can you turn that off? First thing, I wasn't getting any 'action' as you call it. We were not on a date—"

"Kind of sounds like a date, if you ask me."

"No one's asking you. This wasn't a date and we were not 'sleeping together.' I mean, we were sleeping together—sleeping next to each other—I don't know why I'm explaining this to you. We were not on a date, moron! Now, can I finish the story—because I haven't even gotten to the best part yet?"

"There's a better part? Does it involve the super-duper-double-nasty? Wait, let me get this turned back on."

I give him a look that says *I will rip your head off if you say another word*. He gets the look, gives me a zip lip sign and I continue. "I show her the pictures I have on my phone. She recognizes my brother Jack. She knows him. She says he's a member of the Resistance and that he left with a group to try to make contact with others outside of Chicago. Can you believe that, Jack's alive!"

"Wait a minute, your brother also crossed over?"

"What? No. Not my brother here, my brother there."

"Oh, parallel brother. This can get confusing. You didn't meet your parallel self did you? Did you meet parallel Speckler?"

"I didn't meet anybody besides the parallel Sam. There was no time. We got to the library and then went to sleep and when I woke up I was back in this world."

"And you don't know what triggered crossing back over?"

"I don't know what triggered it in the first place. Why me?"

"I don't know. I think we better call a special meeting of the Super Friends."

"What Super Friends?"

"You know—you, me, Mungo, and Charlie. We have to discuss this and get some answers. Who knows, you could cross back over at any time."

"I never thought about that. At first, I just thought it was because of the building."

"It still might be. We don't know yet. Maybe your body just had a longer reaction time than Charlie's did. Maybe once you cross over your body's on an immediate countdown. Tick. Tick. Tick. And then zhoop! You're back here."

It didn't sound any crazier than any other theory—which there were none at this point. "All right. Let's get to Mungo's. I'll call Charlie and see if he can meet us there."

Mungo closed the Pages of Peril early. He'd never done that before, but of course he's never known anyone who crossed over into a parallel universe before either. This is definitely a special occasion.

Charlie left Sam in charge of the diner and joins us about an hour later. We go into the back room and sit in a circle among boxes of comic books and an odd collection of memorabilia he hasn't unpacked yet.

I tell them the same story I told Speckler. They don't interrupt as much and so I'm able to keep it brief. There isn't that much to tell anyway. I'd only been in the other world for less than eight hours. Of course I had no way of knowing at what time I made the leap back to our world. Was it the moment I fell asleep? Later? If time works exactly in both worlds then I slept for at least three or four hours before I crossed back over.

"The real question," Mungo says when I finish, "is what prompts it. Is it a window opening up and somehow you slip through or is it specifically aimed at you? If we were all standing at that same spot would it have taken all of us?"

"If it's aimed specifically at Ryan then it had to be aimed at me too," Charlie says. "I don't think that's it. I still believe it has to do with the building. It's where we both crossed over."

"But Ryan crossed back at a different location," Speckler chimes in. "The Harold Washington Library. Does that place have a doorway as well? And what about the Bean?"

"We can't rule it out at this point," Mungo says. "Maybe there's something happening where multiple locations are popping up. Until we know for sure that it only takes Ryan—or Charlie—and no one else who may be standing right beside them, then we won't know if it's the place or if it's the person."

Speckler throws an arm around my shoulder. "I guess I have to stick to you like glue, buddy. Wherever you go, I go."

I untangle myself from his arm. "Even if where I go is a parallel universe?"

"Especially that. I wonder what my doppelganger is like? Is he as cool as me or is he some weirdo? No, don't answer that. I'll just assume he's as cool as me. I wonder how many aliens he's killed? Maybe he even keeps their heads as trophies in his room. You know, mounts them on the wall like they were lions or tigers. Hey, I just thought of something. What if when Ryan crossed over to their world—the Ryan duplicate crossed over to ours. Maybe, your Ryan and my Speckler and your Mungo and your Charlie are sitting around right now discussing the very same thing?"

Mungo shakes his head. "What you're talking about is not just a parallel world but a mirror world—where everything is exactly the same, happening the same way and at the same moment. But we know it's not. They were invaded by aliens but we weren't. That's a major difference. Because of this alien invasion, the world as we know it is quite a bit different from theirs. Technology stopped being invented. The pop culture we know of in the past twelve years doesn't exist there. People who are dead here may be alive there and people who are alive there may be dead here."

"My brother Jack is alive," I say.

"That's because there's no war in Afghanistan. Who even knows if Afghanistan even exists anymore as a country?"

"But it's interesting that he still turned out to be a soldier. He's in the Resistance. He's fighting the aliens."

"I don't think we'd be too surprised at our counterparts. At least in many ways they'd be much like we are."

"Maybe our world is heading for an alien invasion as well," Charlie says. "Maybe we should warn the government."

"Why haven't we been invaded?" Speckler asks. I'd been wondering the same thing.

"Who knows?" Mungo says. "Maybe it's a small thing. Obviously these aliens exist. Maybe they just haven't detected our planet yet. If they do, I'm sure we'll suffer the same fate though."

"So we should contact the government?" Speckler asks. "Do you think they'll believe us?"

"I don't even believe it and it happened to me," I tell them honestly.

"Me too," Charlie says. "For years I almost convinced myself that what had happened could not have been real. I'd experimented with some heavy drugs at times in my life and I just figured maybe I was having a delayed reaction."

I nod my head in agreement. "My father thought I was on drugs after the incident at the Bean—and I didn't even tell him about what I'd seen. If I can't convince my family there's no way I could convince the government."

"Not without proof," Speckler says.

"How can I get proof?"

He pulls out his smartphone and smiles. "Apple may not be around anymore in their world but thank God we still have it. Next time you cross over make like Spielberg and take lots of video and photos. The ships, the creatures—the Bruzers right? The city. Everything."

"That's if there is a next time. It's been ten years since Charlie crossed over and he still hasn't crossed again. What if I never cross back? Or, what if those aliens attack us tomorrow?"

"Speckler's right," Mungo says.

Speck looks at him. "I am?"

"Yes. The government will never believe us without good solid proof. But Ryan's right, too. He may never cross back over again. It might have been his one time."

I don't like that idea. I was counting on seeing Violet again. "So what do we do? Tell them or wait, risking an invasion and countless deaths?"

"I say we wait for now," Mungo says. "Telling them without any proof will only make us look like a bunch of raving lunatics one donut short of a dozen. Like it or not, we have to wait until Ryan crosses back over again."

"We could take to the internet," Charlie says. "Get a grassroots movement going."

"The only grassroots movement we'd get is all the crazies hiding in the weeds," Mungo says.

It's settled then. We wait until I make the next crossing. I'm determined to make this happen. I don't know if just willing it can make it happen, but I put all my determination into crossing back over and seeing Violet and getting proof.

Later, crashed out in my room, after raking and bagging several huge piles of leaves to appease my dad, Speckler and I have a moment to discuss what's happened. He brings up the idea of searching for the Violet in this world. I hesitate. I know that my Violet is curious about knowing what her parallel family is like— mother, father, brothers or sisters—but I'm only interested in one Violet and she's a world away. A universe away.

"Who knows? Maybe this is God's way of putting the two of you together," Speck argues.

But I don't want God putting me and this Violet together. I want to be with the other Violet. But I can't tell Speckler this. He'd only mock me and tell me how we could never double date if I'm dating a girl from a parallel universe. Besides, it wouldn't fit into his plan to get Amy.

The other Super Friends are not much help either. Charlie's begun to act weird when I come over and ask to walk the hotel. There's a resentment I sense in him, as if he hates the fact that I crossed over and he didn't. Knowing that this other world exists doesn't seem to satisfy him if he can't be the one to see it and experience it. And lately he's been talking about selling everything, the diner, the hotel and moving to Montana to wait out the alien invasion.

"I was afraid of this," Mungo says when I explain Charlie's behavior to him.

"Afraid of what?" Speckler asks. He looks up from the latest issue of *Green Lantern*.

"He's going into survival mode. Feeling the world will end soon so he thinks it best to start planning for it. Almost like a self-fulfilling prophecy. A part of him actually wants the world to end so he can be proven right."

"Mungo," Speckler says, "sometimes you are so far above us it's like living in Einstein's shadow."

In return of this compliment, Mungo throws a waded up piece of paper at him.

"But it's not the end of the world," I say. "People have survived. And Violet says the aliens have begun leaving. There's only one mothership up in the sky above Chicago—maybe it's the last one left on earth.. She says there were dozens. But in the last few years they've begun to leave. So there's hope that they'll be rid of the aliens for good and begin to rebuild their lives."

"Sure. Stands to reason," Mungo says. "Rape the earth for as much as you can get and then take off for another planet to do the same thing. I just hope they don't do any more destruction before they leave."

"Like what?" Speck asks. "The place is already decimated."

"Sure it is, but there are people left, and you said not all the buildings have been destroyed. There's more they can do, is all I'm saying. And don't get me wrong, I'm not saying they will. But it happens. Before a conquering force leaves they put the place to the torch and kill the remaining inhabitants."

"Why would they do that?" I ask, though I'm not sure I want to know the answer.

"Who knows? Send a message. Make sure earthlings don't rise up and go after them. Maybe there are other aliens competing for the same resources. They make sure they won't get their hands on any of it. That way they have an edge on them." He sees the reaction his statement has on me. He reaches up and lays his hand on my shoulder. "But maybe not."

"The people have to get out of there," I say.

"You said they were like prisoners though," Speckler reminds me. "The collars keep them from leaving or rising up."

"If they can get the collars off they might have a chance."

"Have they done it yet?" he asks, his nose still buried deep in the exploits of Hal Jordan.

"No, they haven't."

I feel totally depressed at the thought of this. The feeling gets worse once November ends. Thanksgiving weekend was a particularly depressing time. I barely touched any of the food. My mother made a big deal thinking I was sick, but how can I stuff my face when I know that Violet and her people are practically starving to death? I can only imagine that winter will be much worse. The weather outside is cold and there has already been a light snowfall. Winter will be here soon and with it only more suffering for them. I remember they all looked thin, gaunt, as if they hadn't had a full meal in years. The weight of Violet in my arms as I carried her to safety. Like a kid's rag doll. So the sound of football games and people laughing and cheering only remind me how much we have compared to them. It also reminds me how quickly it can all come to an end. One day we're celebrating Thanksgiving and the next we're being massacred by killer aliens for no good reason. Maybe Charlie has it right. Maybe the best plan is to high tail it to the mountains and build a survival fortress. But that's the selfish way out. It just ignores the problem, and makes others deal with it while you try to save yourself. I know now that I need to cross over more than anything. If I don't get proof to our government then we're all doomed.

Chapter Eleven
Winter Wonderparty

I'm in no mood to party.

It's already been over a month since I left Violet sleeping in the library. It's December already. Several inches of snow are on the ground. Nothing has happened since then. No visions. Nothing. Not even a flicker of a headache.

I'm a wreck. I think about Violet constantly. I stare at her picture, now downloaded on my desktop, every day. She's the first thing I see when I get up in the morning and the last thing I see before going to bed. I fight the urge to track down her double. Speckler thinks I should do it, which only confirms it's a bad idea. He thinks maybe this whole thing is some cosmic way to get us together, that we're meant to be together. But I don't want to be with this Violet—whoever she may be. I want to be with *my* Violet. My Violet. It sounds weird to say this, as if somehow she belongs to me.

The Super Friends have yet to come to any decision about what to do. Mungo still believes it's best to wait until I cross back over again and then I can take pictures and videos to bring back as evidence to convince the government. But as the days and weeks go by it seems more and more likely I may never cross over again. Then what? No one thinks we can convince the government without proof, which I agree. Speckler thinks I'll cross over at any minute and sticks to me like a bug on a windshield. He's even stopped stalking Amy just to be by my side. And Charlie? Charlie grows more and more paranoid each day. Now that everything he saw has been confirmed—and in the worse way. He's been talking more and more about his plan to move out west, buy a cabin up in the mountains and stock up on supplies. He feels the invasion could come any day now and so it's best to be prepared. A part of me thinks he might be right. After what I saw, a cabin in the woods and playing Davy Crocket might not be the worse idea. Not for myself, but for my parents and Speckler's parents and little sister. The more people we can save the better. We should be prepared. That's what Violet and her world were not. The invasion happened in an instant and they were caught completely off guard. What if we could plan? Be prepared—not just to survive in some crazy shack in the mountains, but be prepared to fight? But in order to do that the government has to be on our side and that still can't happen until I cross back over and get the evidence.

So I wait. And I hope. It's a weird thing to hope for. Like putting yourself purposedly into the jaws of death.

I don't tell the Super Friends how badly I want to cross back over, not even Speckler, the original Super Friend. I can't talk to him about Violet. My feelings for her. Because I don't even know what those feelings are. I only knew her for a short time, but in that short time I felt as close to her as I've been to people I've known for years.

So I continue to wait. And while I do Speckler plans a big winter party he's calling his "Winter Wonderparty." To some extent it's to celebrate the success of the Art Club and our Haunted Hotel fundraiser. Partly it's just to have an excuse to get Amy in his house, possibly drunk. With beer goggles on he thinks she might see him in a better light. I tell him she'd have to be in complete darkness in order to see him in a better light.

"Wait and watch," he tells me while he empties a bag of tortilla chips in a big plastic bowl.

"Okay, but don't say I didn't warn you. I don't want to pick up the pieces after she completely annihilates you."

"It's a waiting game, Ryan. And she doesn't know how long I'm willing to wait."

"Till hell freezes over?"

"Precisely."

"And what if the Zoktari come before that? What happens then?"

"That's where you come in my friend."

"Me? What are you talking about?"

"Once we get proof and we warn the government we'll be heroes." He smiles triumphantly as if it's already been decided. Simple. We cross over, shoot some videos, then we pop back. Except it's not so simple. He still believes there's a good chance that he'll cross over with me if he stays by my side.

We finish setting up the party. His parents are out of town with his younger sister enjoying the indoor water parks at the Wisconsin Dells with another family, so he has the house to himself for the weekend. I had to talk him out of doing an extreme theme party. He wanted Zombie Christmas, but I told him I was through with dressing up as zombies and aliens. I want to focus on real aliens, not pretend ones. So he decided on doing "Winter Wonderparty."

There's not a bad turnout. With these things you never know, and it's not like Speckler is the most popular kid in school. We never did hang out with the elite, but we were never the social outcasts either. So most of the Art Club has shown up—including Amy and Nancy, who gives me a big smile when she arrives. I make an excuse to go talk to Wally to avoid having a forced conversation with her.

The party is down in the basement. Speckler borrowed a projector from Mr. Carnofsky and has the sci fi classic *Forbidden Planet* projected up on the wall. The sounds off, which is probably a better way to view most of these old movies. Besides, with the music playing you wouldn't be able to hear it anyway.

Speckler is running around like the perfect host checking on everybody. Linda and Marty are in a corner by themselves and Speckler makes sure they're keeping it at least PG 13. Wally has a drinking game going on, so that whenever Robbie the Robot appears in the movie everyone has to drink. There's a cooler full of beer and someone brought a bottle of rum and some fruit punch. Everyone's having a good time. Of course, Speckler doesn't lose sight of Amy either. Every chance he gets he goes over to talk with her and to see if she needs anything. She's in a good mood and doesn't give him too much of a hard time. Or maybe it's the booze. I notice she's on her third cup of rum punch. At this rate maybe she will be seeing Speck in a good light.

I try to have a good time, but I can't get Violet out of my mind, nor the fact that I'll either cross over at any moment or I'll never cross over again. Speckler tries to cheer me up and I think a part of the reason for throwing this party is to do just that.

"You should have invited her," he tells me when we have a chance to talk. We're back upstairs in the kitchen. I came up to refill the salsa bowl for the chips and to give myself a break from Nancy. My attempts at avoiding her don't work. She keeps cornering me and wanting to have these deep conversations about art, telling me how talented I am and that I could be the next David Hockney or Jasper Johns, two artists I've never been that crazy about.

"Who?" I say playing dumb. I know full well who he means.

"Alterviolet," he says. This is his clever name for the Violet that lives in this world.

"And say what? Hi, you don't know me but I know your double in a parallel universe. Do you want to go to a party?"

"Yes," he says a little too loud, he's also been hitting the rum punch a little hard. Me, I've been sipping the same lite beer for the past two hours. I need to stay sober just in case I cross over. "That's exactly what you could say. I mean, it would be the best. Pickup. Line. Ever." He punctuates each word with a head bob as if he were rocking out at some concert.

"Here." I thrust the salsa bowl in his hands. "Why don't you take this down stairs?"

"Okay," he says, still a little too loud. "But promise me that before the night is over you'll call her. Promise me."

"All right, I promise." I say it just to get him off my back. I don't have her number but there are enough computer geeks downstairs who can find it for me in a flash. Wally, for instance, besides being in the Art Club is also president of the Computer Club. He could find it with his eyes closed, except he's probably too drunk to even find the "shift" key on the keyboard.

Speck pauses at the top of the stairs. "Are you coming down?"

"In a minute," I say. "I'm going up to your room to find another movie to put on. We can't keep watching *Forbidden Planet* over and over."

"Good idea. Just don't get any of those damn romantic vampire movies." He makes a vomiting noise.

"You know you secretly love them," I say.

He smiles and makes a shushing noise with his finger over his lips.

Going up to get a movie is just an excuse to get away form the party. Once I'm in his room I plop down on his beanbag chair and close my eyes. Outside the window I can see snow flurries dancing around in the wind. The window rattles softly. Where is Violet right now I wonder? I hope she's warm, wherever she is.

I hear a soft noise, light footsteps outside the room. "Can you give me a few minutes alone Speck?" I say before he comes in. I open my eyes and look up but it's not Speckler. It's Amy.

She gives me a Cheshire grin. "Speckler says you came up to look for a movie. I thought you might need some help."

She comes in and stands over me, slightly toddering from side to side. "Not having a good time are you?" she asks. "Nancy can be a bit of a bore."

"It's not Nancy," I say. "I'm just not feeling great."

"I noticed. Anything I can do to help?" There's no mistaking what she means, which is weird since I never had any indication that she even liked me.

"No, thanks. Maybe we should go down and join the party." I start to get up from the beanbag chair, which is never an easy thing to do. Amy steps forward and pushes me back down, then lands on top of me.

"Hello there," she says, her face inches from mine, casual, as if she were meeting me by accident at the mall.

"I don't think this is a good idea," I say. "You know my best friend is madly in love with you?"

"And I'm madly in love with you," she says and then kisses me hard on the mouth, her tongue trying to find out what flavor of gum I'm chewing. I can't say it's not enjoyable, but it's really the last thing I want. So I push her away.

"Come on, Ryan," she says. "Who knows, maybe we're meant to be together."

I laugh at this. I can't help it, it's too damn funny.

This visibly bothers her. A girl like Amy doesn't get laughed at too often. "What are you laughing at? I don't see what's so funny about it."

"If only you knew," I say.

"Knew what?"

"That the girl he thinks he's meant to be with lives in a parallel universe."

Amy and I look up. Speckler is standing in the doorway, a dark look in his eyes.

"What are you talking about?" Amy says. She doesn't feel the animosity coming from him—probably too drunk—but I can feel it.

"Nothing," I say quickly, giving him a hard look to shut him up. I push Amy aside and finally get to my feet. As the only sober person in the room I figure it best to make a quick exit.

"You two look like you're having fun," he says sarcastically.

"You know it's not like that," I tell him.

"Like what? Like my best friend is trying to steal my girl?"

"I am not your girl, Speckler," Amy says from down on the floor. She's rolled off the beanbag chair and looks like a turtle on its back.

"No, I can see that."

I put my hand on his arm to calm him down. "Come on, she doesn't mean it. She's been drinking a lot."

He knocks my hand off. "And what's your excuse? You haven't been drinking a lot. We're you hoping for this?"

"You know I wasn't."

"Do I? I don't know. I told you to call up Alterviolet, but now I know why you don't want to. I see who you really care about."

"Who's this Alter-what's-her-name?" Amy says. "What is she—some kind of performance artist?"

"She's supposedly his dream girl—"

"Shut up, Speck!"

"Why shouldn't she know?" He looks at Amy who's still struggling to get to her feet. "Her name's Violet—"

I push him against the wall. "I told you to shut up about that!"

"What are you going to do?"

"What's he talking about?" Amy says, now fully on her feet but for how much longer? She's weaving like she's standing on the deck of a ship trying to sail through rough seas. "Who's this girl Violet? I don't know any Violet at school."

"She doesn't go to our school," Speckler says. "She doesn't go to school at all."

"Why not?"

"Because she—"

I hit him in the mouth. I don't want to hurt him—he's still my best friend—but I have to shut him up. "I'm sorry . . ." I manage to say, before he hits me back. He doesn't pull his punch. I fall back against the door, my head reeling. He's angry and curses at me.

"Stop fighting!" Amy yells stepping between us.

"I trusted you!" Speckler says. He goes out and down the stairs.

I start to go after him but Amy grabs hold of my arm. "Let him go. It's better he found out now."

"Let go of my arm, Amy."

She lets go, looking like she's about to cry. "I just wanted to be with you. Is that so bad?"

"No, it's not bad at all. I'm sorry. It's just . . . not meant to be. I don't know what you have against Speckler. He's really a great guy and you shouldn't treat him like shit."

"I don't care for Speckler," she says.

"That's obvious," I say. I leave her standing there.

I don't go back down to the party. I knew this was a bad idea, and now it's turned into a disaster. I don't think I could make Speck listen to reason, so I grab my coat and leave. It's cold out and the snow flurries have increased into a light snowfall. I feel numb as I walk back home.

Chapter Twelve
Aquarium

I text Speckler as soon as I get home. I apologize again and tell him we'll talk on Monday after we've both had a day to cool off. He doesn't respond to my text and on Monday he refuses to talk to me. At least he doesn't punch me. Good. He's no Nuke Fist, but I was surprised how hard he hit me. I guess jealousy and rage can give a person extra strength. Or maybe Speckler's a lot stronger than I thought he was. Could be the beanpole physique and straw arms are just a front for untold power.

Amy is also giving me the silent treatment except for a quick text she sent the next day that read: PLS SAY NTHNG! She didn't need to text me. I wish I could forget the whole thing ever happened. During the week though Nancy keeps asking me what's going on. She obviously doesn't know what happened up in Speckler's room. I guess Amy didn't say anything. I evade her questions as best I can and say that Speckler and I just had a disagreement and leave it at that.

My parents are a different story. It's obvious that something is wrong. I can tell them some of the truth, that the girl my best friend's in love with says she's in love with me.

"What are you going to do about it?" my mother asks over dinner. My father of course is silent on this matter. He sits at the head of the table in his favorite Bears throwback jersey, a number fifty-one Dick Butkus. He used to tell me and Jack about seeing Butkus play in his last game at Soldier Field. It became just another thing he shared with Jack, the football star, that we can't talk about.

"Nothing," I say. "I don't love this girl. She's okay, but she treats Speckler rotten and I told her so. Plus, I don't want to lose his friendship."

"Does he know this?"

"I've texted him a dozen times and tried to talk to him at school but he's ignoring me. He'll come around though. It's like that time in the seventh grade, when he found out that Kevin Shaughnessy invited me to his birthday party but didn't invite Speck. He didn't talk to me for two weeks after that, thinking that I was dumping him to hang out with Jimmy instead. But soon as he found out the truth we were good as gold. He just needs to realize I wouldn't give up our friendship over a girl."

"It happens sometimes," my father says. The comment surprises me.

"Your father stole me way from his best friend," my mother confides with a smile. She gives him a wink as she passes him the meatloaf.

I look at my father like he's a complete stranger. He doesn't look the type to steal anyone's girl from anyone. He's not a bad looking guy at all, but he's no Clooney. "You did? I never knew that."

"He wasn't my best friend," he says. "There was a group of us and Dominic was in love with your mother, but I knew she didn't care for him, so I asked her out."

"And then what?" I ask. Getting information out of my dad is like trying to pull a tooth out of a crocodile.

"Nothing. He got mad and stopped hanging out with us. He eventually found someone else. I think he married her after high school—"

"Claudia her name was," my mother adds. "They divorced a year later. I guess it wasn't meant to be."

This doesn't make me feel any better. "I just hope Speckler gets over it quickly."

My mother gives me a concerned look. "Why? What's going on with you two? You've been having all these secret meetings lately. And I happened to see that photo you left on your computer."

I drop my fork on the plate. "Mom, that's my private computer."

"Hey, don't talk to your mother like that," my father chimes in. "Nothing you have is private in this house unless you bought it with your own money. Last time I checked it was us who bought you that computer and your phone. So what's this picture? Is it porn?"

"God no!" I say. "It's just . . . some girl I met."

"Not Amy?" my mom asks.

"No. I told you I don't care about her."

"So this is a girl you do care about?"

"Yes, I mean I think so. I just met her. Besides, I may not see her again."

"Why not?" she asks. "Did you have a fight as well?"

"No. I told you I just met her. She doesn't live here." I dig into my meatloaf to avoid their probing looks.

"Where does she live?" Now I know I've blown it. I should have just kept my mouth shut, or kept her photo off my computer.

I think for a moment before saying, "She lives in Canada. She was just visiting some family here. I met her when we did the Haunted Hotel." *Canada?*

"That was over a month ago."

"I know how long it's been."

"Is that why you've been so depressed? You can still talk to each other with video calls and texting. It's not like when we were young. Our parents would have killed us if we made a long distance phone call. Right, Walt?"

"Hunnhh," he grunts in agreement.

I tell them sure we can still talk, just to end the conversation. I wish I owned a special computer—one that can make video calls from one parallel universe to another, but I don't tell them this. I wonder when I will tell them about the other universe. How will they take this little bit of news?

The week goes by and Speckler continues to ignore me. I text him for the umpteenth time asking that we put this behind us or he'll never be able to cross over with me. We'll never be heroes. I'm hoping this will convince him. He finally texts back and says: CROSS OVER URSELF—AND STAY THERE!!!!!!

Friday is our last day of school before Christmas vacation. On Monday Speck and his family leave for Rivera Beach, Florida to spend Christmas with his aunt and uncle and their family. So if I have any hope of repairing our friendship it'll have to be soon. Friday is also the second of the "Artists Field Trips" that Carnofsky has planned for us. Since it's too cold to be outdoors, Mr. C decided that we should study the beauty of a different kind of nature—the underwater kind. So the plan is to spend the day at the Shedd Aquarium studying color, design, movement, and texture in fish and other amphibious animals. We're to take a series of sketches and put it all together in a final piece that represents what we discovered. I thought the idea was kind of stupid when he first told us, but any chance to get out of school is always a good one. I never thought about the beauty of fish before, but since looking up some of their exhibits on line I'm actually pretty excited to be here. It's not just fish, but they have snakes and monkeys and lizards and penguins. Even dolphins and beluga whales. Too bad Speckler still isn't talking to me. This could have been so much fun.

The bus ride to the Shedd Aquarium is a strange one. Usually Speckler and I sit together and he keeps things pretty lively. He can be very funny when he's not being totally obnoxious and that's only when he's bugging Amy. Now he's not bugging anybody. We're not sitting together. He immediately sat down next to Wally when he got on the bus. I was hoping this might be a chance for us to talk and patch things up. Wally was surprised when he sat down next to him but now is going on and on about the New York trip in the spring. I can see that Speckler is barely listening.

Amy has avoided me since the party. I'm glad. It would just make things more complicated. The rest of the kids give me some space and don't pester me about my "breakup," as some people call it, with Speckler. They know something's up, most of them were at the party, but it's clear that no one knows what happened. Mr. C even pulls me aside once I'm off the bus to ask if everything is okay between me and Speckler. I tell him we had a bit of a fight but we'll work it out. Then, to change the subject, I tell him that this is an awesome idea. He smiles and says that you can't beat the art of nature.

As we line up and go inside I notice our class is not the only one visiting this day. There are at least two other high schools doing field trips to the aquarium. Not art classes like ours—I don't think—but for some other reason—biology or zoology. So it's quite crowded with teenagers doing various studies and projects—and quite noisy. Just like the trip to Millennium Park, Carnofsky tells us to spread out and find something interesting. We're to have at least three ours of our own time looking at various exhibits, drawing what we find interesting, before we have to meet back at the bus. Hopefully, in that time, I can convince Speckler to talk to me again, or else it'll be another long awkward bus ride back to school.

I follow close behind Speckler when he heads off to the Caribbean Reef. This exhibit is in the middle of the aquarium and is the first thing you see when you enter. It's a huge circular tank that holds a miniature coral reef. There are sharks and rays and moray eels and dozens of colorful fish. There's even a diver in the tank feeding some of the fish. Wally, who's still with Speckler, says it would be so cool if one of those sharks suddenly went berserk and attacked him.

"Those sharks aren't dangerous," I say. "Those are bonnetheads and aren't known to be man-eaters." I'm standing a few feet behind them. I have my sketchbook out but there's nothing on it. I figure I'll have plenty of time to plenty of time to draw. Patching up my relationship with my best friend is priority number one.

"You're probably right," Wally says. Speckler doesn't even turn around.

"Hey, Wally," Speckler says. "Let's go check out the anaconda."

"Sure," Wally says, giving me a quizzical look before he follows Speckler over to the Amazon section. I watch them go and then follow after them. I wonder how long Speckler can keep avoiding me. Maybe I can corner him down by the penguins and finally work things out with him.

The snake is huge. Even though it's coiled up it must be at least thirty feet long.

"How would you like that wrapped around your body?" I ask them. "I bet it could swallow you whole."

"I wish it would swallow you whole," Speckler says. "Stop following us will you?"

"Who says I'm following you? I want to get some sketches of a new super hero I'm drawing. He's called . . . Anacomet." It's dumb but it's the first thing that comes to mind. "He gets his powers from both an anaconda and a comet."

"How is that possible?" Speckler asks without thinking. When he realizes he's talking to me he frowns angrily.

"Oh, it's possible," I answer. "You see, the snake bites the man while the snake was infected with alien comet dust making the man part anaconda and part super alien comet. Hence—Anacomet." I have to smile at my own quick thinking. Who knows, there may be something to this Anacomet. Maybe turn the dynamic duo of Nuke Fist and Kid Fantstic into a triumphant trio.

"Well, you would know about aliens wouldn't you?" he says. "Come on Wally, let's go see the giant iguanas." Wally and Speckler walk off a few feet before Speckler spins around and says, "Don't you know I don't want you around?" He says it low so no one else can hear.

I give him a smile and say, "You'll have to talk to me eventually."

"No I don't," he says.

"Yes you do."

"No I—look, I'm not going to argue, so stop following me. It's not going to happen."

"Oh, it's going to happen," I say.

He shakes his head and hurries on to the iguanas. I wait a minute before following. Maybe he's right. Maybe I should just let it go for now. If it took two weeks when we were thirteen maybe it'll take three weeks this time. I know he'll eventually simmer down, but I don't know if I can wait three weeks. So I eventually go after him.

There are more students here. They're all bunched up in front of the glass looking at the iguanas, tapping the glass to get their attention and making noises. I can't get next to Speckler so I hang back. Maybe if I move ahead to the next exhibit he'll catch up to me, then he won't think I'm following him. Plus, it has to be less crowded than this.

I turn around, a little too quickly, and collide right into a girl. "I'm sor—" I start to say then realize the face I'm looking at. "Violet!"

I drop my sketchbook and wrap my arms around her in a tight hug. I can't believe it's her, but then there's a violent push and she shoves me back.

A hand grabs hold of my shoulder and spins me around. "What the hell are you doing?" A tall, beefy blond kid glares at me. "Who is this guy, Violet?"

"I never saw him before in my life," she says. She looks different. Her hair is longer and styled. She has makeup on and is wearing a schoolgirl uniform for one of the Catholic schools. She's not wearing her trademark black combat gear. And she doesn't have a scar! This isn't Violet. I mean, it is Violet, but it's not my Violet. It's Alterviolet!

The Viking steps between the two of us. "You better have a good reason for sexually assaulting my girlfriend."

"I'm sorry, I thought she was someone else," I say. I can't believe I did it again. First with Sam in the church, and now this. But this is much worse. Still, I can't help but stare at her. It's her but it's not her. The eyes. That's what's different. They're the same color and shape, but they don't have the same look in them. They haven't seen

118

what Violet has seen. Death. Misery. Suffering. It's true then that the eyes are the windows to the soul. Her soul, Alterviolet's soul, is one of comfort—shopping, dating, hanging out with friends—not fighting for one's life, scarred by brutality and pain.

She looks at me. "What do you mean, you thought I was someone else? You called me Violet. How do you know my name?"

"Yeah, how do you know her name? Are you stalking her?" They're both angry and loud. People are taking notice, ignoring the snakes and frogs and snapping turtles. A crowd starts to form around us. I take a step back. Maybe I can still get out of this without causing more of a scene.

"Look, I said I was sorry. Let's just forget it."

The Viking's not having this. I guess his blood is up and he wants satisfaction. Two thousand years of Nordic barbarism is hard to suppress. "Uh-uh. No way." He grabs me by the front of my shirt. "You're not going anywhere until you explain yourself."

I break the grip on my shirt and push him back. But he throws a punch at me. I haven't been punched since I was eight and now I get punched twice in one week. But unlike Speckler this guy has obviously been hitting the gym. His punch knocks me back several feet before I lose my balance and fall to the ground. I don't know if he pulled his punch and I don't want to know.

Blood drips from my nose and I wonder if it's broken. It hurts like hell. If it is maybe it'll give me some character. I struggle to get to my feet. The guy's ready for round two. The crowd is now all around us and I'm sure the familiar yell of "Fight! Fight!" went out, though my head is still ringing from his first punch and I'm a little dizzy. I'm not eager to feel the second one, but maybe I can get one in before a teacher shows up. Where the hell are the teachers anyway?

But just as I set myself to launch my futile attack someone brushes by me and stands between me and my assailant. I can't believe it, it's Speckler.

"Calm down, Darth Maul," he says to the Viking. "I'm sure whatever the problem is we can work it out without resorting to violence."

It's already resorted to violence, but I don't say that. I'm just grateful he showed up. Does this mean we're friends again?

The Viking doesn't want to back down. Some of his fellow classmates are behind him, looking ready to join the fracas if called upon. If it came down to it, who else would stand with me and Speckler? Wally? Not a chance. Marty Kekner? And risk possibly getting his lips busted putting future makeout sessions with Linda on hold? Not even. I think it's just me and Speckler, the dynamic duo once gain.

"The guy attacks my girlfriend," the Viking, I'm sure his name is Wolfgang or Blitzkrieg, tells Speckler. "What do you expect me to do?"

"Attack is a pretty strong word," Speckler says. He points at Alterviolet. "Did my friend attack you?" The word "friend" perks me up. If it takes getting punched by a maniacal Viking to end this feud and make us friends again then it worked.

"No," Violet says. "But he hugged me."

"See, a hug is not an attack. If it were my grandmother would think I'm attacking her every time I visit, which I'm glad she doesn't because she always carries industrial strength pepper spray with her."

Several kids start laughing. Speckler does a good job defusing the situation. Wolfgang starts to unclench his fists and relax a bit. Alterviolet still stares at me like I'm a deranged pervert. I see Carnofsky finally coming through the crowd along with some other teachers.

"What's going on here?" he asks us.

"Just a misunderstanding," Speckler says. "I saw the whole thing Mr. C."

"Then explain why Ryan's nose is bleeding."

"Certainly . . . you see . . . he was walking and tripped and fell into this young lady and of course reached out to catch himself so he wouldn't fall. She thought he was trying to cop a feel and screamed like Elsa Lanchester in *Bride of Frankenstein*—and of course this is the Frankenstein monster who thought his woman was being attacked."

"Hey!" the Frankenstein monster, visibly insulted, exclaims. He's not much for wit, this one.

"Is this true, Max?" the other teacher asks the boy. So I guess his name isn't Wolfgang.

"I didn't see him trip. I saw him grab her."

"Violet?"

"I don't know, maybe he tripped. But he acted like he knew me and I've never seen this kid in my life."

"Do you know her, Ryan?" Mr. C asks me.

"He doesn't know her," Speckler interrupts. "When he tripped he wasn't saying 'Violet,' he was saying . . . buy a lot."

"Buy a lot?" Everyone repeats it with a skeptical look on their faces—mine included. I'm wondering how he'll explain this one.

"I told Ryan I was going to the snack bar to buy some . . ." He pauses as his mind obviously goes blank.

"Snacks," I say quickly.

"Yes—snacks, thank you. And I said should I buy a little or buy a lot? And Ryan says . . ." He turns to me.

"Buy a lot," I say. Well, that's our story, and I guess we have to stick to it.

Carnofsky definitely isn't buying it. "Speckler, take Ryan to the bathroom and help him get cleaned up. We'll sort this out afterwards. Boy, you have the worse luck with our field trips."

The crowd, upset it's ended so quickly, reluctantly parts to let us go. We head downstairs to the bathroom. I yank a handful of paper towels from the container, wet them under the faucet and begin wiping the blood off my face. It looks worse than it actually is. At least I don't think my nose is broken.

"Buy a lot?" I say to Speck.

He smiles his old smile. "Pure genius," he says. We both laugh. It feels good to laugh again.

"They'll never believe it. Did you see their faces?" Then I think of the one face I saw. "I can't believe it's her. It's Alterviolet. What are the odds of this happening?"

"A long shot. She's pretty cute but she has terrible taste in boyfriends. I hope your Violet has better taste."

"She doesn't have a boyfriend," I say.

"Yet," he says giving me a sly look.

I ignore the look. "What would you have done if the guy had attacked me again? Or you?" I say.

"Simple. I would've kicked him in his big Neanderthal balls. His neanderballs!"

"You probably would've missed and gotten more taint than balls," I tell him. We both crack up. "It's Nuke *Fist*, not Nuke *Foot*." We laugh even harder.

"Come on," I say, still laughing from the joke. "Let's go see if Carnofsky was able to talk them out of pressing charges. I'd hate to have sex offender on my record."

"What? For a little hug? How was it—nice? Did you feel some boobage?"

I open my mouth but he stops me. "Let me pee first and then you can tell me." He goes into one of the stalls.

I check my face in the mirror to make sure all the blood is off. My head is still ringing like the bells of Notre Dame, but I'm glad to have the old Speckler back, even though we have some difficult things to talk about. Or at least one difficult thing to work out— Amy. I don't know if she witnessed the exchange upstairs. I didn't see her face in the crowd. I think I heard her earlier asking Nancy to go with her to see the penguins. Maybe she expects to see them all dancing like in *Happy Feet*.

I'm anxious to get back upstairs. A part of me wants another look at Violet's double, even though I know I shouldn't. She may want a good explanation how I knew her name. I start think of an excuse when suddenly all the lights go off. "What the hell. Hey, Speck . . . you still in there or did you fall in?"

He doesn't answer. It's very quiet all of a sudden. "Hello? Speckler? Do you think they didn't pay their bills? Or is it a city wide blackout?"

There's still no answer.

"Hey, come on. You're still not giving me the silent treatment are you? I thought we made up."

I open the stall door. It's not completely dark. There's no one there though. I push open all the doors. They're all empty. He couldn't have left. I would have heard him.

I know why he's not there. "No way," I say to myself. "Not here, not now." But it is here and it is now. I crossed back over. My head wasn't ringing from the punch—it was ringing from the sensation of crossing over, though not as severe as before. Maybe the more I cross over the more my brain gets used to it. Maybe I'll soon be crossing over with no headaches at all.

Outside, the whole place is dark and silent. I head up the stairs to the main floor. Something cracks beneath my feet. There's ice on the floor, which crackles and crunches as I walk. There's light coming in from above and sections of the roof are nothing but large gaping holes. It's cold. My breath comes out in steaming puffs of air and I can see small drifts of snow on the floor where it came in through the opening in the roof.

In the center, the large circular Caribbean Reef is empty. The glass has been shattered and there's no water in the tank. The floor is littered with fish skeletons of various sizes. Then I see a dark shape on the floor. The diver! He's lying on his front. I rush to his side and turn him over and recoil in horror. There's nothing but a decaying skull behind the diver's mask. Who knows how long he's been dead? I hear movement above me. I look up and see a monkey jumping around the metal beams. It stops and stares at me. So not everything is dead. He eventually moves on to wherever he was going. I look at the exhibits. Most of them are destroyed, empty except for the skeletal remains of fish or turtles or iguanas. There are a few that are not destroyed. They still have water in them, but they've turned practically black. There's no power to keep them clean so they stagnated and are as dead as everything else. There's the dank smell of rot and mildew and death in the air.

I stand there in disbelief. Then I remember what I have to do, so I take out my smartphone and turn on the camera and begin recording. I make sure to get the exhibits and the dead diver, the monkey overhead and the destroyed Caribbean Reef. I compliment it with commentary of each thing I'm seeing.

I slowly make my way to the main lobby. The ceiling here has also been partly destroyed. There's more snow and cold. The gift shop is practically empty. I make sure to get the name of the Shedd Aquarium from the few remaining souvenirs—some stuffed animals, key chains, and refrigerator magnets. They also carry the date from twelve years ago. This should help explain things.

I leave the gift shop and push open the front doors. I step out into the noonday of a Chicago that's as alien to me as Mars. My view of the city before was at night—in the dark. A city blacked out. But now, in the light of day, I can really see the total destruction. All the familiar buildings are either gone or half-destroyed. The ones that are gone leave nothing but wide gaps in the landscape. The mothership is still in the sky, looming oppressive and deadly. Scary as hell. Like a giant bird of prey watching you, waiting to feast on your corpse. That would be after they make you a corpse. I make sure to get the few Ravens flying about, before zooming in on the mothership as best as possible. This is my most important evidence. There's no way the government can deny this is real.

I pan across the city over to the lake and then back. There's no one around. The street in front leading down to the Field Museum is empty. It would help if I could get a shot of some people and their collars, maybe even a Bruzer or two. But I'm glad there's no one around. What would they say if they saw me filming—especially with a device no one has ever seen before? They would probably think I am a collaborator.

I look back over to the lake. No ships or boats, even if it is wintertime. I wonder what to do—where to go. How can I reach Violet? She mentioned that Lincoln Park is a refugee city. Maybe that's where I should go. Maybe I can find someone who knows her—or her Uncle Tolliver. My jacket and scarf will hide the fact that I don't have a collar on. I zip it up tight then start to head down to the street when I see one of the Ravens heading in my direction. What do they have—some kind of radar that detects anyone who crosses over? There's only one place to go, and that's back inside.

There are no hiding places on the main floor, so I head downstairs to the large pool where they kept the dolphins and beluga whales for the shows. The pool is empty, except for the skeletal remains of one of the beluga whales at the bottom of the tank. There's a wide glass window facing the lake, and normally presents a cool backdrop to the aquarium, but most of it is destroyed along with that side of the pool. I guess the water drained right out and into Lake Michigan. I wonder what happened to the other animals. I'm sure dolphins and whales can't survive in a fresh water lake.

I'm glad for the opening, it allows me a chance to escape the Bruzers. I get ready to jump down into the empty tank and make a run for it out the open back to the lakefront. Maybe I can make it to the planetarium a little further along the lakefront. I'm thinking about my options when a hand grabs me from behind.

I turn around and stare into the faces of a group of ragged teenagers who look familiar, though the last time I saw them was in the dark.

"You again," one of the boys says. It's the Scavengers from the library—the ones I frightened off with my smartphone. Obviously they remember me. "What are you doing here? No one comes here. This place belongs to us."

"There's Bruzers coming," I tell them. "We got to get out of here."

"Why would Bruzers come here? They never come here."

"I don't know—ask them when they get here."

"I thought you were working for them. Where's your fancy gun? Grab him Slim!"

The one called Slim—which is funny since they're all skinny as a mop handle—grabs a hold of me locking my arms behind me. The one doing the talking, the leader of the three, still has the walking stick the silver lion's head with the bloodstains on it. He goes through my pockets and pulls out my smartphone.

"Here it is," he says in triumph. "How does it work?"

"Give it to me and I'll show you," I say.

He stares at me for a second before shoving the lion's head into my gut. He doesn't have much strength and it doesn't hurt too badly, but it does knock the wind out of me. I double over. When they pull me back up he breathes into my face. His breath smells as pleasant as road kill on a hot summer day. "Now tell me or we'll kill you."

Before I can offer some kind of snappy comeback ala Peter Parker, a loud crashing sound erupts from upstairs. The Bruzers have arrived. "I told you. We got to get out of here!"

The heavy footsteps of the Bruzers are loud and frightening. Slim releases his hold on me and tells the others he's not sticking around. He scrambles down the side of the empty pool and makes a run for it to the other side where it's open to the lakefront. The other two follow right behind. All three make a hasty escape to the outside. I'm about to follow, but just then a Raven drops silently down from the sky blocking their escape. The Scavengers freeze instantly, and then turn to run back but it's too late. The ship fires three quick blasts. I watch in horror as their bodies flame up and evaporate. Black smoke and the smell of burnt flesh fill the air.

I stare in disbelief and then realize my dumb luck. The Scavenger was holding on to my smartphone when he got vaporized. Damn! There goes my evidence. But it won't matter if I'm killed as well.

Even though my own fear grips me I turn and again make a run for it all the while expecting a burning ray to engulf my entire body. But it doesn't happen. I head into the penguin section—empty of all penguins of course. There's another set of stairs that lead up to the main floor. I glance up to the top and don't see any Bruzers at the top coming down to get me. I fear the place is swarming with them as I make my way up cautiously. It's brighter down in the pool area where the half-destroyed glass window lets in all the daylight, but upstairs it's darker. I don't know if it will be any advantage but it makes me feel better.

I make it to the main floor without seeing any Bruzers. Maybe they went down another set of stairs and are looking for me down below. I hope so. I consider my options. It's only a short sprint to the front doors. But they must have Bruzers outside standing guard—plus a small ship or two waiting to blast me and turn me into a pile of ashes like they did the three Scavengers. But I can't stay here. There are few places to hide and besides, it'll only be delaying the inevitable. Pretty soon they'd find me.

I hear a loud screeching noise. The monkey! It's still in the beams above and now is making all kinds of noise. *The damn dirty ape*! I'm sure the Bruzers are on their way to my location. This leaves me with no other choice than to make a run for it. I start to sprint to the main door, but just as soon as I start my run a Bruzer steps out and levels his gun at me. It doesn't look like the ones they use to zap the people with collars—this looks like it'll zap a hole right through me. I stop and put up my hands to show him I surrender. I just hope he recognizes the gesture. Maybe in his culture it's an insult like giving someone the middle finger.

He doesn't shoot me though so I guess he understands my intent. He walks cautiously forward till he's right in front of me. The monkey is still overhead making all kinds of monkey noises. I wish he would shut up. He's already done his duty—why keep screaming?

The Bruzer calls out in his strange language—but he doesn't finish. Out of nowhere, I guess it was hiding in one of the tanks, comes the anaconda. It's survived this whole time! Probably by eating half the animals. I guess this is what that monkey was shouting about. Maybe he was trying to warn me.

The giant snake wraps itself around the Bruzer, coiling and coiling until it has him choked to death. The Bruzer, a giant himself at nearly eight feet tall, struggles to get the gun in place and blow the snake apart. His finger on the trigger, he begins to fire at random. I drop to the ground to avoid being hit. Shots go wild as alien and snake wrestle together. It's a startling sight, one I can barely tear my eyes from, but I have to get away. Other Bruzers must have heard all the noise.

I make it to the front door and hope for the best. Just as I step outside there's a Bruzer standing there. He doesn't give me a chance to surrender. He slams the butt of his rifle against the side of my head and everything goes black.

Chapter Thirteen
Mothership

I see Violet.

She's standing on the jogging path by the lake. It's cold and windy and giant waves are splashing over the side up to her feet. She's just standing there. Not making a move. I shout at her to get away, but instead she turns her back to me and begins walking towards the water. I scream louder. She doesn't listen. I want to run to her but my feet won't move. I look down and see the anaconda coiling itself around my feet. It moves up my body, around my legs, and up to my waist, but I don't care that it squeezes the life out of me. I only care about saving Violet. The waves are still splashing over the side and soon she'll be swallowed up by them and carried out into the lake. I continue to shout as a Raven drops down and fires at her.

I open my eyes.

The dream feels real and I try to look around but I can't move my head. There's something holding it in place along with the rest of my body. My arms, legs, torso are held in place by something. Not straps or anything like that, just a force pressing me down onto the bed or table, whatever it is they have me on. I can only look straight up at the ceiling. It's a pale gray. Metallic-looking. There are lights from somewhere though I can't see where. Not from above. They're not bright, just a soft glow enveloping the room. Along with the soft lights, everywhere, as if coming from the walls and floor and ceiling itself, is a low metallic thrumming noise. A steady hum like a religious chant from a chorus of robots. Do robots have religion?

I'm not alone. There's movement in the room. A face comes into view. It's not human or a Bruzer's gask-mask covered mustardhead. It must be a Zoktari. The face is bone-white and smooth. The eyes are dark, the nose small, mouth thin. It wears a robe of some dark material that kind of shimmers as if it were made of water absorbed by moonlight. It speaks in a language I don't understand. A voice answers. There are others in the room. I try to move my eyes to get a peripheral look but I can only see the one standing over me.

He has some kind of instrument in his hand and he passes it over my face. A blue light shines in my eyes. It's warm and lingers there so long I want to shut my eyes but I find that I can't. They seem locked open. It's only when he turns off the blue light that I can finally shut them.

He speaks to the others. They answer. Another steps forward into view. He looks older than the first. Though his face is as white and smooth there is also a more seasoned look in the eyes. A look of experience. Of old age. He seems more in control. When he speaks the words are louder, rougher, more controlling. Is he a doctor? A scientist? A general? Will they cut me open? Remove my brain? Kill me?

Neither of these happens. At least not now. They continue looking at their instruments and studying whatever it is they need to study. Do they know I come from a parallel universe? They must. It has to be why they have me here. But where is here? Their ship? Maybe we're still at the Shedd Aquarium or some other place. The Field Museum? Are they preparing me to be one of their exhibits? I notice that my jacket has been removed. I'm still wearing my T-shirt and jeans though. At least I'm not stark naked. I take this as a good sign. If they meant to cut me open wouldn't I be prepped for surgery?

They seem to ignore me as they go about their business. It feels like I'm not that important to them. Maybe I'm just a lab rat to them. Maybe that's how they see all the humans. Insignificant. Lab rats or pesky flies to be swatted. Once more I'm left thinking about those I left on the other side. What is Speckler doing? What did he think when he came out of the bathroom stall and found me gone? He has to know I crossed over again. His idea of sticking close to me didn't work, or maybe he just wasn't close enough. I'm glad he didn't cross over with me. Not that I don't want him here—I'd love to have someone here to help me. But I also need someone over there, on the other side, to help me as well. Someone to cover my tracks, or notify next of kin.

I don't know how long I've been here. Hours? Days? I wonder what story Speckler came up with to tell Mr. Carnofsky. What did he tell my parents, if he's told them anything? I think about what will happen if I never return. Whatever story Speckler comes up with won't matter. He can probably cover for me for a day, but after that?

Will he tell the truth? Or just let them think I ran away or was abducted? Well, in a sense I am abducted. Except, I'm sure they don't call this an alien abduction on this side since the aliens are everywhere. It's only when you don't know aliens are there that they call it an abduction. When you know they are there, they probably just call it getting snatched or picked up or grabbed or whatever term they use here.

I think about Violet as the dream comes back to me. She was in danger and I wanted to save her but it's me who's in danger. I'm the one who needs saving, just as I did in the church in Chinatown. But who will save me here, wherever here is? She doesn't even know I've crossed back over. She'll never know. That's the worse thought. No one, here or back in my own world, will ever know what's happened to me. Because I am sure of one thing—the Zoktari will not let me go, or send me back to my world. If they have the technology to do that, which I think they do, they won't use it to send me back. Why would they? The reason I'm here has to be because of them. Because of their technology. It can't be my side. We haven't even traveled out of our own solar system yet, and haven't even been further than our own moon. We must seem like savages to them.

I close my eyes trying to drive this thought from my head. But it's no good. At least my parents had the knowledge of knowing how Jack died. They had a body to bury and mourn over. A grave to visit and lay flowers on and know that underneath the dirt are the bones belonging to their first-born son. Where will my bones end up?

What seems like an hour passes. The aliens remain intent on studying everything but me. Maybe they don't need me any more. Maybe they have all the data they need. And for what? Will they bring more of us from the other side? I think about Charlie. He crossed over once but then never again. I've crossed over twice, three times if you count seeing Violet's reflection in the Bean. Why did he never cross over again? Why am I so special?

They finally stop ignoring me and come back. It's the first one again. The younger one. But the older one is behind him, directing him. He has a different instrument this time, a kind of syringe with a greenish liquid in it. He presses it to my arm. There's a warm feeling for a second and then the warmth turns to fire. It feels like my blood is on fire! I scream. The one ministering the injection looks worried.

He glances over to his leader who only nods and says nothing. Was he expecting this? Is this how they'll kill me—death by liquid fire?

"Stop!" I beg them. "You're killing me!" I continue to scream but they do nothing but study their instruments.

It feels like I'm going to die, and I think that this must be it. This is the moment of my death. My whole body sweats as the fire continues to rage through me. But I don't die. The fire soon burns itself out and eventually the pain subsides. My body relaxes. I breathe normally again.

Then something happens.

A loud piercing noise like a warning alarm goes off somewhere. Not here in this room but outside. The Zs are surprised by this. The leader screams at them and one of them leaves to find out what's going on. He returns shortly and is obviously agitated by something. He jabbers at them and they all exit leaving me alone. I wish I knew what was happening. Are we under attack? Have the Resistance come for me? But that can't be possible. They don't even know I'm here, wherever here is. And why would they come? Most of them think I'm working with the Zs. They would think I deserved this.

Someone comes in. He goes over to some of the machines and does something. The weight that was pressing down on me vanishes. I can move my body. Are they moving me to another room? To a cell? An execution chamber?

"We do not have much time." The voice startles me. English! He—the voice is definitely male—is speaking English. But he's not human. He's Zoktari. He's young, dressed in the same shimmering black uniform.

"Time for what?" I croak. My voice is raw from screaming.

"They will be back soon. You will have to come with me."

He opens the door and peers out. "Come now—quickly."

I don't make a move. "Go where? Who are you? How do you speak my language?"

"Your language is not difficult." What seems like a smile appears on his face. "Mon'Wa'Zee—that is a difficult language. There are over two hundred words for hello—depending on—never mind. Like I said, we do not have much time."

"I'm not going anywhere with you until you tell me where we're going. Why would they be looking for me? Who're they? You're them aren't you? A Zoktari?"

"Yes, I am Zoktari, but I am not one of them just as you are human but not one of the humans on this planet."

"You know I crossed over from a parallel world? And what do you mean you're not one of them? You sure as shit look like one of them."

What he tells me takes me completely by surprise. He says, "We are from the same world—you and I. I am not from this world either."

"My world? You crossed over?"

"Yes. Now, please. If you want to have some hope of returning home you must come with me."

He turns and goes out the door. I have no other choice but to follow him. My head is still woozy with a dull ache but at least the liquid fire has burnt itself out.

The corridor is dark but not pitch-black. A similar glow is everywhere and I still don't know its source. Maybe it comes from the ship itself. Is this a ship? I ask my new companion, walking quickly ahead of me, peering around corners and anxious.

"Yes, we are aboard one of the Klokans." He sees my confusion. "The large ship above the city."

"The mothership?"

"If that is what you call it, yes."

We don't go far. He stops at a door and taps on a small screen beside it. I notice the similar V markings appear on the screen. It must be their written language. When he's finished punching in whatever code it was, the door silently slides open. We go inside.

The Z goes quickly about the room with his hands sliding down the wall checking for something. "It should be here," he says.

I look around. We're in another lab. There are large tanks filled with the same greenish liquid I was injected with. Something is inside one of them, floating in the green liquid. I go up to the glass and look inside. It's a human, naked, suspended in the liquid with long black tubes protruding from his body like tentacles. I can only see the back of his head but there's something about the figure that is eerily compelling. I move around the tank to see his face.

It feels like a steamroller just flattened me. The face I'm looking at is my own. My double on this side.

"Is this how . . ." I begin to say.

The Zoktari looks at the other Ryan floating in the tank.

"Yes. They have discovered how to take your counterpart and use it like a magnet to pull you from your world to this world."

"Is he dead?"

"No. He is being kept alive. He must be alive for it to work. If the link is severed you would immediately cross back to your own world."

"Then do it!" I tell him. "Sever the link. I have to get back to my world."

His face softens. "I cannot do that. If I did you would not survive for very long."

"Why not?"

"We are far above the city. If I sever the link you will cross over at this spot and drop down to your own city and perish."

"Is this how you crossed over? Using your counterpart in this world?"

"No. We have perfected another technique, one that allows us to cross back and forth without having to rely on using counterparts. We are afraid that these Zoktari may soon discover how to do this as well. We cannot let that happen. Now, I cannot explain more. We really must get moving."

"Why do you want to help me? Why don't you want them to be able to cross over? They're your people."

He finds what he was looking for. His fingers press a hidden panel, which pops out. Once removed it reveals a small opening. "In here," he says.

"Hey! I'm not going anywhere if you don't answer my questions."

He thinks for a moment. "All right, but we cannot wait here long. We have very little time and they will soon discover that you are missing. My name is Tarak Par. I am a scientist. I was on the team that discovered____" The word he uses is totally foreign and unpronounceable.

"What is that?"

"In your language, it might be translated as *transuniversal travelling*. The ability to travel from one parallel universe to another. As I said, we invented a device that allows us to cross over from one universe to another. But once over we discovered that our Zoktari counterparts are very different from us. We are a peaceful race. We are scientists, not warriors. But a thousand years ago the ones in this world diverged. A leader took power that had not taken power in our history. In fact, he was nothing but a minor figure, unimportant in every way, but somehow, because things were slightly different, he had managed to get a large following together and take control. He had very different ideas, and engulfed his world on a path bent on conquest. That is what led them here, and to so many other worlds.

"We studied them for many years, fascinated as to how they could be so different from us. But then we realized that if we discovered transuniversal travelling then surely they might have discovered it as well. So we sent a team that includes myself and several others to find out just how much they know."

"Why was this so important?"

"Because, if they have discovered the means to cross over into our world they would not like what they see. They would think we are nothing but a race of weaklings. Cowards, hiding on our planet when we could be out conquering other planets. We knew then that our world was in danger if they could cross over."

"But they haven't discovered it yet. My double—they use our doubles to bring us here. I knew someone else who crossed over. Did they also use his double?"

"That is likely since you are not the first, though I believe you are the most successful so far. They made many attempts, and always the double died severing the link before the person could complete the journey. But you are the most successful so far. Your double has not died and you remain here the longest."

"The first time I didn't cross over, but I got a glimpse of this world. I saw a girl and a Bruzer in the reflection of a sculpture. But I wasn't in this world—I was still in mine."

"They probably started the process to send you over and then stopped it. For that brief moment you were still in your world but there were images of this world reflected in the exact same spot. It is possible for you to glimpse these images and to project your own."

The War Memorial. Even though they don't have the Bean in this world, Violet said there's a downed Black Hawk helicopter they call the War Memorial. We each saw each other's reflection because they were probably in the same spot.

"And the last time I crossed? I was only here for several hours."

"Yes. They tried to capture you but you eluded them. You had some help I believe. That is when they decided to send you back to your own world and try again later."

"How did they know when to do it again? How did they know I was at the Shedd Aquarium?"

"They have people watching you—their people. They managed to send them over to your world but they cannot retrieve them. That is another reason you are important, so they can bring their people back."

"But that's impossible! How can they be on my world and not be detected?"

"These Zoktari have spent their scientific pursuits in other areas—mainly in the area of warfare. These ships, like this one, are far more advanced than anything we have. They also have the capability of transforming their bodies into similar species in order to infiltrate them and gain knowledge before they attack. They have assumed the appearance of humans. That is how they have gone undetected. But they can still communicate with this side. So in essence, they have been sending vital information already about you and your world."

The idea that I've been spied on by aliens is unsettling. Who are they? Is it someone that I know? Could it be Mungo or Mr. Carnofsky? Could it be Speckler? Impossible.

"And if they can cross over then they will attack my world as well—just like they've done here?"

"Yes, exactly like they have done here. It is their—as you say—*motis operandi*. Your ancient Latin has a style and grace to it that reminds me much of our language. But they will not stop at your world. If they make the breakthrough and can cross over themselves then none of us will be safe."

"Can you send me back? You have the technology?"

"We intend to do more than that, but we cannot stay here any longer to discuss it. We must get moving."

We move into the crawlspace. It eventually leads to a deep shaft that has a ladder leading deep down into the ship. There is hot air and a strong draft that comes up this shaft, strong enough that it feels like it will blow me off the ladder.

"Hold on tight," Tarak tells me, as if he had to. I follow him down. It's a long way but we stop before we reach the bottom.

There's another small opening and we enter another passageway where eventually he stops and taps the opening in a kind of code. Someone on the other side removes it and we exit. I expect to see another Zoktari but it's not. It's a Bruzer standing there.

"Do not worry," Tarak tells me, seeing my reaction. "He is a friend." He says something in another language, not the language of the Zoktari. This must be the Bruzer's language. He nods, says something and moves out into the corridor. We follow behind him.

"Is he from our universe as well?"

"M'Raug is from this universe. We have managed to forge an alliance with a few and convince them to support us. It wasn't easy. Most of them hate the Zoktari, and only do their bidding because of what they are threatened with."

"What do they threaten them with?"

"Total annihilation of their planet. I've told them that in our universe we live in peace with other species. And if we work together we can at least save our worlds in our universe, and maybe even one day work together to free them from these Zoktari. Maybe one day we will even make contact with your leaders and forge an alliance. The Bruzers—as you call them, but their real name is not all that difficult." He says something that sounds like "Bruzer" if it had ten other vowels and consonants in it. I think I'll stick with Bruzer. Besides, it's a lot more fitting. "The Bruzers," he continues, "crave independence as much as anyone. They themselves are by nature, despite the rather threatening appearance, as gentle and peace-loving a species as you will find."

We move quickly through the corridor of the ship and into an elevator that drops us down what seems like a thousand feet.

"What did you mean back there that you intend much more for me?"

"You will see, but we have to get you off the ship first."

The elevator finally stops and the doors open. We step out into a long circular room, with a row of small chambers all along the wall. "What are these?" I ask.

"Escape pods. We will drop you down onto the city, just outside one of the Forbidden Zones. I am afraid that you are on your own from there. You must find a place to hide, and then I will get word to you when we can meet. We need to put this on you." He holds up a collar, similar to the ones Violet and her people wear. I step away from the thing, not eager to have this around my neck.

"Do not worry, it does not work. It is just so that you can blend in. We have a tracking device implanted so we will know where you are at all times. Do you think there is somewhere you can go where you will be safe for a few days? It may take that long before we can meet again. Once they discover your disappearance it may be difficult to leave the ship."

"I think so. I've met some people here who might help me. They're in the Resistance."

Tarak smiles. "The Resistance? Even better. We may need their help if we are to succeed."

"But you haven't told me anything yet. How will I get back? If I wait too long my family and friends back home will be worried about where I've been. My friend Speckler is smart but he's not smart enough to give everyone an excuse that covers me for several days. They may even have the police and FBI looking for me right now. And if you say there are aliens already infiltrating us then I have to tell my government. I need proof. Can you help me prove to them that this is real? If we identify the aliens then that's all the proof they need. Can you do this?"

"You ask a lot. We do not know who these Zoktari look like or what names they are using. We know they have at least two, but there could be more. We may never know for sure. There are not many of us, and once your disappearance is discovered it will make it very difficult for us. They will suspect you had help in escaping. If they discover who we are we will have to cross over in order to escape. We cannot allow ourselves to be taken. If we do they will certainly discover our ways of crossing over. And if we cannot get to an escape pod we will have no other choice but to cross over wherever we are. If it is on this ship then we will drop from the sky and fall on your city. I guess that will be the proof your government needs. Unfortunately, if that happens, it may then be too late for our worlds. By then these Zoktari may have discovered a way to cross over and back."

"How do you plan to stop them?" I ask.

"We figured it has to be the same scientist who discovered it in our world. That scientist is stationed here on this ship." I think of the older Zoktari scientist who wasn't afraid of killing me with his liquid fire. He must be the one Tarak is talking about. "That is why we came aboard," Tarak continues. "To monitor his progress. All his work is here. If we blow up this ship then all his work will be destroyed as well. Good luck, Ryan." He reaches out his hand and instinctively I take it. It's a strong hand. Confident. Reassuring. But I don't feel any reassurance. Blow up a mothership? I don't think this is like *Star Wars* where there's a tiny air duct you can drop a bomb down into and blow the whole thing up like the Death Star.

They lock the deactivated collar around my neck and I step into the pod. There are straps that fit over my body to keep me secure.

"Once you land get as far away from the escape pod as possible. They will be sending ships to look for you. Get to the people that will help you. As soon as I can get away I will meet up with you."

I nod in agreement. It sounds simple, but it's anything but simple. They shut the door. I take a deep breath and wait. Then it feels like the bottom has dropped out and I'm falling. Fast. Faster. The pod doesn't appear to be slowing down. I think that it's falling out of the sky and will explode on impact. I grip the edges of the seat and shut my eyes to prepare for the worst. Then it begins to slow down and actually starts flying. I zoom down and soon jolt to a stop as it makes a landing. The hatch door opens immediately. I guess it's programmed to do that. I'm glad, because I have no idea how the thing opens. I undo the straps and step out. It's nighttime. The area I'm in is completely destroyed. There's not a house or building standing. It's all rubble. Once more I feel like a sitting duck, just waiting to get vaporized. I move quickly and see a battered street sign left standing. North Avenue. Good. I know where I'm at and which direction to go. I start running east towards the lake and the park. Violet said that she and the other survivors live in tents in the park. If I can make it without getting myself toasted, then hopefully I can find them.

Chapter Fourteen
Lincoln Park

Tarak Par was right. It doesn't take long before the ships come after me. I see several Ravens with their searchlights on heading straight where the escape pod landed.

I'm a good distance from where they are and hopefully have enough of a head start that they won't find me. Unfortunately, it's freezing out. Not a good Chicago deep-freeze, a bone-chilling freeze, but cold. Very cold. They took my coat leaving me with just my T-shirt. There are patches of snow on the ground and I try to avoid these so as not to leave any footprints. I'm sure they have plenty of Bruzers on the ground looking for me. But as long as I keep moving I should be fine, and soon enough my body heats up and the cold becomes less of a factor. But when I stop and rest it begins to settle in on me and I start to shiver.

I force myself to keep moving. I can't rest long. I have to put as much distance between them and me as possible. A quick check tells me the ships haven't moved very far, they're still scoping the same area. Good.

I soon reach the north branch of the Chicago River. On the other side, probably a mile away, is the park. Unfortunately, the bridge here has been destroyed. Maybe the river is the boundary of the Forbidden Zone. I could swim across but I'm afraid of getting hypothermia. If the air is freezing the water must be frigid. I remember my suicidal jump from the roof of the Hotel Zamboni. The water was pretty cold then and that was late October. Now it's late December and must be ten times worse. I don't think I could make it this time.

I scour the banks for a boat or something that could float me across, but there's nothing. I curse my luck. I'm so close. I could run down to the next bridge to see if it's still standing but I have a strong feeling it will be the same. Besides, I don't have the time to keep running north or south looking for a way across the river. Eventually they would find me and recapture me. I have no other choice. I have to swim.

I strip all my clothes off and bundle them up tight. I remove my socks and shoes and use one of the shoelaces to tie them all together. I may survive the swim, but if my clothes get wet then I'm as good as dead.

I wade into the river. It's worse than I imagined. The freezing cold instantly seizes me, grips me in its icy clutches tight enough to choke the life out of me. I tread through the water as quickly as I can and hold my clothes above me with one hand while trying to dog paddle with the other. My movement is slow and painful. My teeth chatter. My blood freezes. It feels like my whole body will turn into a block of ice and sink down to the bottom of the river. But I make it across and pull myself up onto the bank. My whole body shivers. I dab at the cold with my jeans to try and dry off as best I can. I don't want to put my clothes on while I'm still wet. I rub my limbs and force myself to move to unfreeze my blood and get it pumping through my body.

My hands shake violently as I try to pull my socks on. Who knew putting on a pair of socks would turn out to be the most difficult thing in the world? But I manage it somehow. I put on the rest of my clothes and move once again towards the park. What will I find when I get there? Will the whole place be guarded by Bruzers and Zs? Maybe they'll be waiting for me.

I can't think about that now. I have to make it there first. My whole body continues to shake and shiver as I run. It's excruciating, this feeling of freezing numbness that takes hold of me. I don't know what's worse, this, or the fiery juice the Zoktari scientists pumped through my body? I'm reminded of a poem we studied recently in English class. The poet wonders how the world will end. In fire or in ice? He reasons both are just as bad. I know what he means after having suffered both extremes in a short period of time.

A quick glance back tells me the Ravens are now moving in my direction, hunting me. This gives me enough incentive to fight through the cold and keep running. At least it helps take the cold away.

I soon reach an area of the city that still has some partial buildings left standing. It's not all rubble and devastation. If I need to I can take shelter somewhere and hide. Maybe I should. I ponder the idea of waiting until morning when the curfew is lifted. If I stroll into camp now will everyone be sleeping? Banished to their tents with Bruzers patrolling? I'll stick out more if I'm the only one walking around. Besides, who would take me in? A stranger wandering around, searching for someone named Violet and Tolliver. Who would help me? They may turn me over to the Bruzers, or just ignore me, leaving me to fend for myself.

I begin searching for a place to hide out for the night. I find it in one of the small stores along North Avenue that's still standing. It used to be a dry cleaners, and if I were hoping some clothes would be left behind, they're not. I hide in the back with a view of the front entrance. There's a back door just behind me. I check to see if it opens, which it does, so in case I need to make a hasty escape and the front is blocked I can run out the back.

I settle in and wait till morning. I know I won't get any sleep. I'm soon shivering once again. I pull my arms inside my shirt and hug my body as tight as I can. My teeth chatter. I desire nothing more than to be home in my warm bed, covers up to my chin, the heat blasting through the furnace. I make a promise to never take warmth for granted again, never complain it's too hot out. I'll forever curse the cold.

I go out the back and relieve myself several times during the night. I know this is a good sign. My body still works. My brain works. My heart works. It's a long night but I eventually stop shivering, even though the cold still wraps itself around me like a death shroud. I know I'll be okay.

The sun begins to rise. How many days has this been? I should have asked Tarak. If they took me Friday afternoon and I woke up Friday night then this should be Saturday morning. Unless I was unconscious for more than a day, which is possible. Who knows how long they had me in that room doing their experiments? This makes me think of the other Ryan—my double in this universe. He's still alive in that tank, but what sort of life is it being hooked to those tubes? Can he still think and dream or is he brain dead? What did Tarak call him—a magnet? Is that all he is now? A human magnet used to pull me over from my universe? Empty of all thought and emotion? And what will happen when they don't need him anymore? Dispose of him like garbage? Is that what happened to Charlie's double and who knows how many others? Tarak said I was the first one to work successfully. How many others failed by dying? At least I know I'm valuable to them. They won't kill me right away.

I leave the dry cleaning store. The glow of morning gets brighter as I make my way towards the park. No Ravens fill the sky. No Bruzers on the ground. The mothership is plain to see, though. Is it watching me now? Maybe they were hoping I would do this. Take shelter for the night. Hide until morning then track me to the park. I can't let this stop me from reaching my goal.

As I get closer to the park I can see a strip of blue in the distance. The lake. Lincoln Park is along the lakefront. It stretches several miles north from here. I remember all the times Speckler and I played here. Nuke Fist and Kid Fantastic fighting evildoers. The park is immense. A kid's own Wonderland. There's a zoo and a pond where we would rent swan boats and paddle around pretending to be pirates in search of lost treasure. Does the zoo still have animals or is it like the Shedd Aquarium? If food is scarce then I can only think they've eaten most of the animals. I wonder how does barbecued polar bear taste?

I can see the area here is not totally destroyed. Several large condominiums are still standing, but all of the houses and businesses around the park are gone.

I reach the park and it's just as Violet said it is. A giant tent city. A refugee camp. I didn't think I would see something like this here. It's like a third world country. The tents are homemade with whatever they put up. Tarps mostly. Few real tents. They stretch as far as I can see. They cover a large field all the way east to Lake Shore Drive, stretching on over the Drive and maybe even onto North Avenue Beach.

People are stirring about. I see kids, some elderly. They all have the collars on, even the youngest kids. There are large pots in front of the tents with some kind of broth steaming in them. Everyone looks hungry and is as ragged looking as the Scavengers. Life doesn't seem to be much better for them.

I get plenty of stares from people as I enter their camp. There are no barriers keeping me out or keeping them in. No Bruzers around as I far as I can see. I'm instantly aware that I look different. Despite the fact that I have a collar around my neck to blend in, everything else about me screams Outsider. My clothes are clean and new. I look like I haven't skipped any meals or gone hungry in a long time. Even though I'm not fat, and always considered myself kind of skinny, at least compared to Jack who was always the muscled-up jock. Compared to everyone around me I look like Arnold Schwarzenegger. How can they not be suspicious? This is going to be much harder than I thought. And I have no idea where to go. There are hundreds of tents—maybe thousands.

I approach a young woman setting out a pot for cooking. "Can you help me? I'm looking for someone. A girl named Violet and her uncle Tolliver. Do you know them?"

The woman gives me a surprised look then glances around hastily. "Where's your red coat?"

My mind draws a blank. "My red coat? I don't understand. I don't have a coat."

"You must be a Red Coat," she hisses at me. "Asking questions like that. I wouldn't tell you if I knew. Get along with you!"

Red Coat! She thinks I'm a collaborator. A traitor. I move on quickly. I don't want to create a scene, but I don't want to be thought of as a traitor. I can't explain to her why I'm not, why I look different than everyone.

The whole camp begins waking up. People exit the tents. I see more kids around, more old men and women. It seems like it's mostly kids and the elderly. There seems to be few young men. Does everyone in the city live here, herded in like animals? I look again at the condos along the park. I don't see any signs of people, but that doesn't mean they're not occupied.

I continue to get stares from everyone. Mean, hateful, suspicious. They know I'm not one of them and must all think I'm a Red Coat. Do collaborators actually wear red coats or is it just a nickname? A little girl comes up to me and says, "Where did you come from?"

I kneel down and smile at her. "From far away," I tell her. "Do you know a girl named—"

"Melissa!" a man shouts. I look over to see a young man approaching me with a knife in one hand and a dead squirrel in the other. There's blood dripping from both.

"I have to go," the girl says. She runs to the man who pushes her behind him.

I stand up and tell the man I didn't mean any harm.

He points the bloody knife at me. "Get back to your kind and leave us be," he says. A woman comes out of the tent behind him and drags the girl by the arm back inside.

My kind? Could he know I'm from another universe?

"What are you doing here?" someone else demands. A crowd has started to form.

Something sails through the air and hits me in the chest. I look down. It's a chunk of ice from the last snowfall. It's hard as a rock and if it landed against my head I'd probably be out cold.

"Go back!" someone yells.

Back where? They can't know I'm from a parallel universe.

I retreat from the crowd. "I just need someone to help me," I say.

"You'll get no help from us, Red Coat," the man with the bloody knife says. "After all you've done."

"But I've done nothing," I tell them. I need to convince them I'm not a traitor. But how?

"Listen to the Red Coat," a woman says mockingly. "He's done nothing! Tell that to my two boys and my husband! Tell that to everyone who's lost someone."

Now everyone is shouting at me, heaping pent-up anger onto me. Another chunk of ice is hurled and catches me on the shoulder. The next one might find an eye. I cover up and think to run. What else can I do? Stay here and get pummeled to death by ice?

But then someone steps in front of them and orders them to quiet down. "This boy doesn't deserve our hatred," he tells the crowd. It's Father Wu, the Chinese priest from the church. "I don't believe he's a Red Coat, and he's asking for our help. Did the father turn away the prodigal son? Did Jesus refuse to help the sick and hungry?"

"He's a Judas, Father," someone says. "Like all the others. He may not have the Red Coat but look at him. When's the last time he went hungry? Look at his clothes! His shoes!"

"He's here to infiltrate us," one of the old men says. He's a scarecrow of a man with a dirty yellow beard. "It's another purge." There are many who shout in agreement.

Father Wu raises his hand and quiets them. "If he is a Red Coat then he'll be sent back. We don't want to bring them down on us do we?" He indicates the condos across the park. I turn my head. There are now several men standing on some of the balconies. So people do live there—and probably a lot better than the ones down here. They've obviously seen the commotion and are taking a look. I spot several bright red coats on some of them. So it's not just a nickname.

The people look with hatred towards the condos. Heads shake in agreement. Some of the people begin to disperse; they go back inside their tents. Others remain defiant. Not just at me, but it seems at the ones watching from above.

"Let me question him," Father Wu tells them. "I believe there's more here than any of us truly know about." The crowd relents, eased by his calming words, but their hatred remains.

"It's Ryan isn't it?"

"Yes it is."

He lowers his voice. "Come on. Let's get you quickly inside." He puts his arm around me and guides me over to a tent. He stops at a young boy and tells him, "Go fetch Tolliver. Tell him—the boy has returned. He'll know what it means."

"And Violet too, if she's here," I say quickly. The boy looks at Father Wu who nods. We go inside the tent.

"Thank you," I say. "I think you saved my life."

"They wouldn't have killed you—not in broad daylight. It's lucky they didn't find you at night. Your body wouldn't be the first one to go missing and end up floating in the lake." I'm glad then that I waited till morning.

He notices my shivering and goes over to some clothes and gives me an old sweater to wear. It's a hideous green Christmas sweater with a large brown reindeer on the front. I don't complain, take it eagerly in fact, and thank him, grateful for the sudden warmth and kindness he's shown.

"While we wait, can I offer you some food? Water?"

"No food, but water would be great." I can't bear the idea of taking food from them, and can still see the faces of the children, the little girl who spoke to me. The squirrel in the father's hand. Is that what they cook in those pots—squirrel meat?

He pours me a cup from an old thermos and I drink it down.

"While we wait for Tolliver, do you mind explaining who you are? Violet told us an incredible story that you're actually from another universe? What did she call it? A paradox . . ."

"Parallel universe."

"Yes, that's correct. A parallel universe. I can tell you I've never been big on science fiction. Even as a child, when my friends were all reading Ray Bradbury and Isaac Asimov. But the world seems more fantastic than even they could have imagined."

"Violet wasn't lying to you. It's all true. I do come from a world where there are no Zs or Bruzers or Red Coats. At least not yet."

145

He nods. "I'm beginning to think so. You certainly don't look like a Red Coat, and you don't look like us. But we'll wait till Tolliver gets here before I ask you to explain more."

I ask him about the camp and what they do for food. I'm afraid of the answer but I have to know.

"They allow us several farms to grow food and keep livestock. But it's not much, and there are many mouths to feed. Our stores are getting low. We've managed to scavenge what we could, bags of rice and flour, canned goods. Of course the Red Coats take a large part of the share, before leaving us to dole out the rest."

It's bad, what he says, but I guess it could be worse. At least they haven't resorted to going full Soylent Green yet. "And why do people stay? There's no guards, nothing to stop you from getting out of the city."

"In the beginning many left, and then we would wake up and find a fresh corpse in our camp and then less and less the people talked of leaving. Besides, we still have shelter and food and companionship. Out there, there's no telling what lies beyond the city."

"Violet says you sent a group out to explore."

"I'm afraid we haven't heard from them. But at least their corpses haven't shown up either."

"One of them is Jack Whitaker, did you know him?"

"Sure. I know Jack. A good boy. Very dependable. Very smart. If anyone can survive out there it's him. But why do you ask about him?"

"My name's Ryan . . . Ryan *Whitaker*. Jack's my brother—*was* my brother."

Before Father Wu can reply the tent flap opens. I turn and there she is. Violet. She comes in suddenly and stops just as quickly. We stare at each other for a moment without saying or doing anything. It's like neither of us is quite sure what to do. She's wearing the same black coat, mismatched gloves, and a thin scarf. She looks cold. Her breath comes out in quick pillowy puffs. They must have run here.

"I woke up and you were gone," she says finally, breaking the silence. "I thought you deserted me."

"I wouldn't do that. I would never do that. I crossed back over. I woke up and I was back in my world."

146

"I think we should be more private about this conversation," Tolliver says. They come in and he closes the tent behind him.

We speak in a whisper. They naturally have many questions and I answer them as best as I can with all that I know. Now that I have definite answers it's easier. I explain what happened when I crossed over at the Shedd Aquarium and was taken on board the mothership. I tell them about the experiments and finding my double floating in a tank of green liquid. But the part that has them most interested is the part about Tarak Par and his group. It's here that the questions fly at me.

"How many of them are there?" Tolliver asks.

"He didn't tell me. He said several."

"But you only met him?"

"Yes. And a Bruzer he said was working with them."

"From their world—your world?"

"No, from this one. He said they managed to convince some of them to help."

"And he said he would blow up the mothership to stop them from discovering the secret of –what did you call it?"

"Transuniversal travelling—which is the translation of their word. And yes, Tarak said if it came to that."

"When will they do this?"

"He didn't say. I think it depends on how close these Zoktari scientists are in discovering how to cross back and forth. They know how to cross over, but they can't cross back. Not yet at least. That's why they need me. They use my double—the Ryan Whitaker in this world—to act as a magnet to pull me over and I guess once they release the magnet I cross back. Once they discover how to do it without my double then they can bring their own people not only back here, but they can cross over and back themselves. They'll attack my world just as they attacked this one."

Tolliver looks worried. His face grows dark. "How will they blow up the mothership? Did he tell you?"

"No, but he was pleased when I said I made contact with the Resistance."

"Did you tell him who we were? Did you give him our names?"

"No. You can trust him. You're both on the same side."

"I'm not so sure about that," Tolliver says. "If he blows up a mothership they'll think it was us. What then? Other ships will come and destroy us. He'll be signing our death warrant if he does that. None of us will be safe."

"But he has to stop them. They can't cross over into our world."

"I think we all agree that would not be good," Father Wu says. "But to ask us to sacrifice our lives for people many of us would not believe even exist is asking a lot. You may convince the three of us. But you won't be able to convince everyone."

"Maybe Tarak can convince them. He said he would meet me again. He said he can send me back to my world—and something else."

"What else?" Violet asks. She has been silent the whole time. But she's been watching me, staring at me.

"I don't know. He wouldn't say."

"When is he going to meet you? And how?"

"As soon as he can get away without being noticed. It's dangerous for them, now that the Zoktari know that someone helped me escape."

"How will they find you?" Father Wu asks.

"They're tracking me."

"How?"

"The collar," I tell them. "It's not activated, but there's a tracking device planted inside."

"So they can track you now? Here?" Tolliver says, his voice quickening.

I nod.

Tolliver stands up. He's agitated. "I don't like this at all. They could be on their way right now." He goes to the front of the tent. "I need to get our people ready. This could all blow up on us at any moment. They need to be prepared."

"What are you going to tell them?" Father Wu asks.

"I don't know yet. Certainly not this story." He hurries out.

"It's not a story," I tell them. "It's all true."

"It will help if you can prove it," Wu says.

"I can. I will. I know you can trust Tarak. He helped me escape. If it weren't for him I'd still be on their ship. They might be carving me up, taking out my organs or whatever. And what they did to my double—"

"To this Ryan?" Violet says.

"Yes. They've got him hooked up to their machines right now. And they've done it to others. Tarak said they finally found one who wouldn't die, who would stay alive long enough for their experiments to work."

Father Wu looks concerned at this information. "Then you are valuable to them. They may be on their way to look for you right now. I have to tell Tolliver this. If the Zoktari come for you then none of us is safe. And you saw the people's reaction to you. They believe you to be a Red Coat. Any one of them will turn you over."

He goes out of the tent and leaves me alone with Violet. I breathe easier. "I wondered when I would see you again—if I would ever see you again. It seems like it's been forever."

"I know. Almost like a dream," she says. "You were there, and then you weren't."

"I'm so sorry. If I could control this I would never have left you."

"I know that. So how is it—back in your world?"

"The same I guess. Boring. I had a huge fight with my best friend, but we made up."

"His name is—Spackle?"

"Speckler."

"Speckler, right. What was the fight about?"

"It's stupid really. A girl he's been in love with kissed me at a party and he saw it."

"She kissed you? Why did she kiss you?"

"She said she likes me. But she was drunk. I don't know. It was weird. I didn't want her to kiss me—"

"So you didn't like it?"

"No, I mean yes—I don't know. Like I said, it was totally weird. It was the last thing I wanted."

"So you're not interested in her?"

"Not in the least."

"Why? She's not pretty?"

"She's a fox—"

"A what?"

"A fox. You don't say that here—for a really hot girl."

"Hot?"

"You don't say that either?"

She laughs. "I'm sorry, Ryan. Of course people still say that. We're not some other planet. But go on. You said you had a big fight—but it's over. You and Speckler are friends again?"

"Yeah, we made up. It was—yesterday I guess. Is today Saturday?"

"We don't keep track of the days of the week here anymore. Each day is the same."

"Right. Sorry. I should have known that. Yes, we made up. And you wouldn't believe what happened. I met your double—in my world."

"You what? How? What is she like?"

"I'm not sure what she's like. It was brief—and awkward."

"What do you mean awkward?"

"I hugged her. Stupid. I thought she was you. I thought somehow you crossed over to my world. It was at the Shedd Aquarium and both our schools were there for a field trip. I saw her and freaked. I couldn't believe it. Then her boyfriend almost broke my nose."

"Boyfriend? She has a boyfriend?"

"Yeah, this big dumb brute. If you cross over you have to have a talk with her about her taste in boys. Unless of course that's your type."

"My type? I don't think I have a type. I told you we don't really go out on dates here."

"Sorry. A joke. But soon after that is when I crossed over. Speckler came to my rescue like the cavalry and probably saved me from getting murdered. But when I was washing up I crossed, that's when they pulled me over here."

"You said they have Zs in your world—disguised as humans?"

"Tarak said they're watching me and that even though they can't cross back they can still communicate somehow with their people here. If I cross back I need to find them and stop them."

"How is he going to send you back?"

"I'm not sure. I know that one way is to shut off the machine the other Ryan is plugged into. That will automatically sever our connection and I'll automatically cross back over from wherever I am. But I think he has another plan he didn't have time to explain. When I see him again he'll show me."

We're both silent. We look at one another and smile.

"So you hugged her," she says. "I guess it could have been worse—you could have planted a big kiss on her."

My face gets red. "I wanted to. I probably would have if I wasn't busy getting punched in the face."

"Really, you would have kissed her?"

"No, not her. I would have kissed you. I thought it was you."

"But she's probably much prettier than me. She probably has real shampoo that she uses in her hair. Makeup. And she probably doesn't have this?" She indicates the scar.

"No she doesn't. That's because she's not a fighter like you are. That's what that is—a battle scar. It reminds me you're tough and you won't take shit from anybody. And I wouldn't trade it for anything."

"You wouldn't?"

"No."

We talk some more. I ask her about going out in search of Jack and the others. She tells me they decided a small group will finally go out. They'll keep to the back roads and the farms, travel at night on motorcycles they have hidden away along with extra cans of gasoline.

"And will you go with them? Will you be part of the search party?"

"Yes. I have to go. I have to find out what lies beyond here."

"When do you leave?"

"When winter begins to clear and spring arrives."

I'm glad they waited. I'd hate to think I crossed over and missed her. I wish her luck. "When you meet up with them, tell Jack his brother is still alive."

"I will. I'm sure he'll be glad to know that."

"I'm going to ask Tarak if he can free him somehow. Get him out of there . . ." Suddenly my head feels like it weighs a ton. My whole body sags. I can barely keep my eyes open.

"You must be exhausted," she says. "When did you last sleep?"

"I don't know. Not last night. I . . . never felt like this though. The . . . Zoktari. They pumped something through my body. Some kind of weird green liquid. They want to see if they can control me without using my double. Maybe, that's doing it."

"And eaten? Rest here, I'll bring you some soup—"

"No," I tell her. "I'm fine. But I'll rest a little. Lie down for a second."

There's an army cot and I lay down and Violet puts a blanket over me. It's warm. I thank her. She tells me to sleep well. She'll keep a watch out. I smile and tell her I'll sleep for sure knowing she's got my back.

"Got your back?" she says. This time she really doesn't know what I'm talking about.

I soon fall asleep. My dreams are as frightening as before. But no giant snakes or watching Violet get blasted by the Zoktari. This time I'm back on board the mothership. I'm running, but not fast and not far. I look down at my body and see black tubes coming out of me. Out of my abdomen and legs and arms. I'm running in place, or on some kind of treadmill. The Zoktari scientist who studied me before, the older one, stands in front of me with a clipboard checking off certain items. I keep running. Faster. He keeps checking. It seems to go on forever, never ending, until a door opens and Tarak comes inside. The next thing I'm back inside the escape pod and once more they're sending me down. But it's not night. It's day and I can see Lake Michigan outside the window stretching below me blue and wide and icy cold. I know I will land in the lake and sink to the bottom and no one will ever find me again. They won't even know what happened to me. I bang on the door of the escape pod. I don't want to drown in the icy waters. I bang and bang and bang and scream for help and eventually I open my eyes.

Violet is standing over me, shaking me by the shoulder. Father Wu is behind her looking concerned.

"They're coming, Ryan. Bruzers and Red Coats."

Chapter Fifteen
Red Coats

The tent flap is open slightly and I can see that it's darker than before. "How long have I been asleep?" I swing my legs out over the side of the cot and sit up and rub my face.

"About ten hours," Father Wu says. "We were quite concerned. We tried to wake you several times and you wouldn't budge."

Tolliver comes in. "I see you're finally alive," he says.

"What's going on?" I ask. My brain is still hazy from sleep and it feels like I could easily sleep another ten hours. But I force myself to stand.

"They want everyone out. Groups of Red Coats and Bruzers are moving through the camp checking tents. You can't stay here."

I shake off the last remnants of sleep. I'm ready to run again. "Where can I go?"

"I don't know if anywhere is safe. If they have you tracked they'll find you easy enough."

"If they were tracking him they would have come straight here," Violet says in my defense.

"Maybe," Tolliver says, still skeptical. "But he can't stay here and put us all in danger."

"I'll help get him out," Father Wu says. "If we can get past the Red Coats, maybe he can hide in the market. At least until night falls. We can get him easily away in the darkness."

"I'm coming too," Violet says. "You'll need help."

Tolliver looks at her and I know he wants to object but he nods and says, "Okay. Don't make a target out of yourselves though. And certainly don't be a martyr. I'm sorry, Ryan. I have to think of my people."

"I understand. I don't want anyone to get hurt because of me. Don't worry. Even if they capture me I think it'll be okay. At least I have some friends I can count on up there. Maybe they're even down here now."

"I hope so," he says. "For all of us."

Father Wu gives me his stocking cap. I pull it low over my head, knowing it doesn't really hide me at all, but even a little is better than nothing. At least I don't look like I did when I first entered the camp, and already I blend in with no one giving me a second look.

The sun is setting as we move out. Outside it's pandemonium. Several Ravens are hovering above the camp but they're not firing. Not yet at least. Men in Red Coats are everywhere shouting for everyone to come out. There's Bruzers with them. Lots of Bruzers.

I keep my head down, trying not to make eye contact with anyone. I can feel the Zoktari ships above me though. Watching me. I think of the three Scavengers in the Shedd Aquarium and the Raven that vaporized them in less than a second turning them instantly into smoke and ash. I want to tell Violet and Father Wu to leave me, but I can't bring myself to do it. Violet holds me by the hand and the warmth of her touch gives me strength. I don't ever want to let her go.

The Red Coats are telling everyone to quiet down. Then a loud voice is heard above everything. It stops us and I have to turn and look.

The voice is in English. It booms out: "ATTENTION EVERYONE. HAVE YOU SEEN THIS PERSON? HE IS A WANTED FUGITIVE AND SHOULD BE TURNED OVER IMMEDIATELY."

Everyone stops and listens with their eyes fixed to something up in the sky. At first I think it must be a Raven, but when I see it I'm stunned. There's a giant hologram of myself fifty feet tall projected up in the sky. Everyone can see it. Can see me. What chance do I have now with a giant wanted poster flying above everyone's head?

A little boy points at me. "There he is, Mommy." That didn't take long. But then the mother knocks his hand down and shushes him.

"Don't worry," Violet whispers to me. "No one will turn you in if they think you're one of us."

There are no more announcements, though my image remains in the sky. We continue on our way with Violet and Father Wu leading me through the crowd. I try to keep my head down, my eyes from making contact with anyone, but everyone around us sees me, recognizes me, but they say nothing. I'm grateful for their silence but I hope it doesn't get them killed.

We steer away from the nearest group of Red Coats but they seem to be all around us, closing in like a net cast into the sea.

"How far is the market?" I ask.

"Not far," Father Wu says as he guides us in a snake-like pattern away from Red Coats and Bruzers.

I see we're heading towards the pond where we used to rent the swan boats. There's a large brick building next to it where Speckler and I would go and have a hotdog and fries after the boat ride. Maybe this is the market.

Father Wu stops us. A gang of Red Coats is coming toward us shouting and pointing metal batons at people, ordering them to move aside, or stand up so they can check them. Any boy near my age is looked over closely. One of these boys yells something at one of the Red Coats who turns on him and points his baton in a threatening gesture. Violet tells me these are "shockers," similar to what the Bruzers use but less powerful. "They can give you a nasty jolt—or worse, if they turn them up, but they won't knock you out."

I watch as he gives the boy such a jolt. It knocks him to his hands and knees. The Red Coat then kicks him in the side for being defiant, before moving on to the next group of people.

Violet indicates the vicious Red Coat. "His name's Lee Doyle," she says. "He's a wild dog who loves hurting people."

"A wild dog who embraces the devil inside himself," Father Wu adds.

I study this wild dog barking orders and snarling gleefully at people. He's short, solid, with what is usually described as a bullhead in comic books. His nose looks like it's been broken several times, like a British rugby player.

"He's also Hanes's number one henchman," Father Wu says.

"Who's Hanes?" I ask.

"He's the leader of the Red Coats. He was one of the first ones who crossed over to the Zs and became a collaborator. They rewarded him by making him Commander Hanes. He commands a small army of his Red Coats. Doyle is Colonel Doyle. They make up their own ranks and titles and give them out to those who please them."

We manage to avoid Doyle and his group and eventually, through a roundabout way, make it to the pond.

"It's not good," Father Wu says. "Just what I was afraid of."

We stand across the pond huddled together with other refugees. On the other side, in front of the building, there's a large group of Red Coats forcing people out.

"The market is taken," Father Wu says. "That was our best chance. Our only chance."

"It should be completely dark in less than an hour," Violet says. "If we can hold out till then and stay hidden in the crowds, we have a good chance of slipping past them."

Father Wu thinks for a moment and then nods. "All right, what else can we do? It may take a miracle though."

Violet smiles. "You're in the miracle business, aren't you Father?"

"I'm afraid miracles are hard to come by these days. But we should get away from here as quickly as possible. There're too many Red Coats and I don't like the smell of Colonel Doyle so close to me."

We move once more through the crowd away from the pond and market. There are more shouts and yelling as Red Coats and Bruzers break into tents and persecute anyone who fits my description. Several teenage boys with dark hair are stunned and dragged away. I only hope that once they realize they have the wrong person they'll let them go.

More people around us take notice of me. Though they look at me questioningly, some with suspicion and curiosity, no one raises the alarm. But for how long will they remain silent? Surely someone will want to save the life of one of the boys and turn me in? I try to keep my head down and follow Father Wu and Violet.

We head back to Father Wu's tent. I feel as though the net is getting tighter and tighter. I can see gangs of Red Coats and Bruzers all around me blocking any escape. I feel that even the dark won't be any kinder to us. And the Ravens hovering just above me? Won't they light up the area until I'm found? I keep these questions to myself. I don't want to burden Violet, she seems so sure she can get me out.

Father Wu stops us once more. "Red Coat."

A single Red Coat, young, hostile, is screaming at people and brandishing his shocker, shoving it into one person's face, cracking someone else with it. He pushes people aside. I can see no other Red Coat or Bruzer nearby. All the ones I've seen so far have been in groups—at least two or more. This one must have branched off to become more assertive, demonstrate his power. He's doing a good job of it. The people are frightened of him.

Violet and Father Wu turn to make a new route for us. That's when he spots me. Our eyes lock on each other. For a moment he seems surprised that he's actually seeing me. I don't think he was even really looking for me, just using his position to persecute people. But now that he sees me he smiles crookedly. I expect him to yell but he doesn't. Maybe he figures he doesn't need to yell. No one's ever defied him, and if they have, I'm sure he's dealt with them. He doesn't notice I'm with two other people—it's only me he sees.

"You there," he commands. He points the shocker at me. "Hold it!"

I stop and face him, not willing to risk running or causing any commotion. Not now. The crowd makes room, shuffling off to get out of the way. They may not help the Red Coats capture me, but they certainly won't help stop them either. I guess that's for the best. In the end every man has to look out for himself and his family.

"Take off that cap," he orders. He still doesn't notice Father Wu and Violet, who have stepped aside and are inching their way behind him. I want to tell them to get away, to leave me, but this has happened so quickly I cannot even make eye contact with them. I don't want them to do anything reckless and get into trouble.

I take off the cap and the smile on his face suddenly gets wider, as if he's won the lottery. Maybe in a way he has. Maybe he'll get a promotion for finding me. General Douchebag! A four star asshole!

He turns around to yell now for his comrades to come and help or to gloat about making the arrest of the century. Tolliver steps up to him. I didn't even see Tolliver in the crowd. He's fast. The man doesn't even get a word out before Tolliver slams his fist into him. He goes down like a sack of beans. He's still conscious though. But not for long. After he's knocked out Tolliver looks up and says, "Get him away from here."

Violet grabs me by the hand while Tolliver and Father Wu drag off the unconscious Red Coat towards a tent.

But as soon as we try to make our escape another gang of Red Coats spots us. They raise the alarm. More are on their way. Too many.

I break my hold on Violet. "Get away," I tell her.

We look at each other. It's the only way, but she's hesitant to leave. When she finally turns to move away they've spotted her. "Get that one," a Red Coat shouts. "She's with him."

They grab her, stunning her first with the shocker. They drag her away. I run after them but the others intercept. They try using the shocker on me. It doesn't work and I think this might be my moment. I try to break through them to get to Violet but there's too many. They tackle me to the ground and tie my hands behind me. They jerk me to my feet and haul me in the same direction.

I think they're bringing us to the nearest Bruzer but for some reason we go through the crowd away from the Bruzers. We head back to the market where they take us inside.

They sit me down in a chair. We're the only ones inside. No Bruzers. No Zs. I wonder why they didn't take me to them. Several of the Red Coats are holding Violet who still looks heavily dazed, but her eyes are open, looking around. She reminds me of an animal that's been cornered looking to fight to the death. I pray it doesn't come to that. I curse myself for putting her in this situation.

A Red Coat comes forward. He's tall, with a lean hard face, short dark hair streaked with white like a skunk. He wears expensive black gloves and shiny black boots. He looks better fed and better groomed than any of them. I figure him to be Commander Hanes. Next to him is the bulldog I saw earlier—Colonel Doyle—grinning like a mental patient.

Hanes removes his gloves. "Are you sure it's him?" he asks Doyle.

"It's him," Doyle says. "Look at him. He looks different than the others. And his collar doesn't work with the shockers." To prove it he pulls out his shocker and demonstrates how it doesn't work on me. "See. Never seen that before." He puts the shocker away in his belt.

"Why do they want you?" Hanes asks me. He looks slightly bored, mildly curious as to why I'm so important to the Zoktari.

I glance over at Violet and then back to Hanes. "Don't you know?"

He drops his look of boredom and frowns. "I wouldn't have asked if I knew." He nods to Doyle. The bulldog steps forward and slaps me roughly across the face. He's still wearing his gloves. Leather ones. My lip splits and blood runs down my chin.

"Leave him alone you dirty son-of-a-bitch!" Violet screams. She's completely alert now and struggling against her captors.

"Shut her up," Hanes says to the Red Coats holding her. Someone shocks her and her body convulses and she goes limp in their arms.

"Stop it!" I tell them. "I'll explain everything but let her go. She has nothing to do with this."

"I won't let her go," Hanes says. "And you will tell me everything or else we'll use the shocker on her all night. Have you ever seen what happens to a body after being shocked a thousand times? Not really the body—it's the mind that gets destroyed."

He's a madman. He would do it and enjoy it and we both know it.

"Now, tell me why you're so important to them."

I hesitate, trying to think of my options, of a good lie. In my hesitation he nods again to the Red Coats holding Violet. "No!" I scream. "I'll tell you. But you probably won't believe it, but it's the truth."

He waves his hand at the Red Coat who lowers the shocker. "All right. Go on."

"There's a parallel universe—a world that's an exact duplicate to this one. The Zoktari have invented a way to cross over into this other world and to bring people from that world to this one."

He looks at me for a moment and then says, "You're right, I don't believe you." He nods to Doyle who slaps me once again, and then to the others who shock Violet. She does her best to muffle a scream, probably trying to deny them any satisfaction that the pain they're causing doesn't hurt. But I see tears in her eyes as she struggles to hold back the pain. My own eyes fill with tears at the sight of her.

"Damn you!" My hatred for them boils over. "I'm telling you the truth. This is too crazy for me to make up."

"How do you know about it?"

"Because I'm from the other world. They brought me here. It's why they want me."

"Prove it," he says.

"I can't," I say. He nods again to Doyle. "No, listen! Look at me, you said so yourself that I look different and that my collar doesn't work. I look different because I am different. In my world there are no Zoktari ruling us. We still rule ourselves. There's no war with aliens."

"And the collar?"

I don't want to tell them about Tarak and the Zoktari from my universe. "I found the collar and put it on to blend in. It was never activated so it doesn't work." I have no idea if these things need to be activated or not. I'm hoping Hanes doesn't know this.

He thinks for a moment and then says, "All right. Suppose all you say is true. What do they plan on doing with you? Why did they bring you here?"

"I think they're testing their system. They're using me as a guinea pig to see if it works. They'll probably kill me when they don't need me anymore."

"And if it works? What do they plan then?"

"I don't know. An invasion in my world is my guess."

"And the girl? What's her involvement? She's not from your world, she's obviously one of us."

"I told you she has no involvement. She doesn't even really know me. I asked her to help me is all. I needed to escape them." I think for a moment and then decide to go for it. "That's what I'm asking you to do as well. I know you must hate them—the Zoktari. Despite the fact that you may have a better life than most you're as expendable as any of them. And they'll kill all of you before they leave no matter if you helped them or not. Or, maybe they won't kill you, but when they leave you'll be at the mercy of the others."

"Don't worry about us, boy," Doyle says sharply. "I'd like to see this scum make a play for us."

Hanes looks at me and his eyes narrow to thin slits. "Are you saying if we help you escape the Zoktari it'll be good for us? How do you figure that? The Zs will kill us for letting you go, and one act of kindness won't be enough to save us from this lot."

"It may not save you, but you'll know you won't be giving the Zoktari the satisfaction of seeing if their experiment worked. Don't you want to at least defeat them—even in this one small way? You can't be friends with them."

"Friends?" His face turns hard. "No, we're not friends. Far from it. But we know what side our bread is buttered on. And right now the Zoktari hold both the bread and the butter. I don't live in the future. Around here there is no future. There's only here and now.

And for right now all I can see is that the Zs want you and I'm going to give you to them. I'll give her to them as well. They can decide what to do with her. And yes, I want to defeat them. But you can't defeat them. I learned that early on. We all did. And we chose the side that gives us life and another day to live and a better way to live it rather than scraping in the dirt for a crumb of food. And handing you over will do exactly that because I know one thing. Not handing you over won't give me one more day of life."

"Do you believe the kid's story?" Doyle asks. "I can work on him some more. Let's hear what his story is with a few less teeth in his head. Or the girl? He's obviously fond of her. Let's crack some of those fingers." He smiles brutally. They're both alike. Hanes and Doyle. Two wild dogs who found a good way to make their brutality pay off for them. People like them have existed for thousands of years. There's no talking to them or reasoning with them.

"No," Hanes says. "Strangely enough I believe him. It does sound too crazy to have been made up."

"So we just hand them over?"

"Yes, Doyle. It's what they want and we do what we're told."

"But they're valuable. To both sides it seems. Why not hold on to them a little while longer. Maybe we can barter for them. Get them to let us leave like we planned."

Hanes thinks about this. His eyes dart to me and to Violet.

"All right. I'll think on it tonight. Another day won't make a difference. I don't think they'll torch the camp just for one boy no matter how important he is to them. Not this soon at least. And I'm sure I can convince them that we can find him in a day or so. Lock them in one of the supply rooms. I'll have an answer in the morning."

Doyle hauls me to my feet and drags me off after Violet. They throw us in a small room and lock the door. It's pitch black, no windows, but at least we're together and we're safe. For now.

"Are you okay?" I whisper to Violet. I want to hold her, comfort her, but my hands are still tied behind my back.

"I will be," she says, her voice shaky. "Let me get your ropes." Her own hands are free and she quickly gets the rope undone. I flex my hands, getting the blood back into them.

I feel her hand on my face. "How's your lip?"

"It's fine. At least Doyle wasn't wearing brass knuckles."

I move around the room, bumping into things. "Is there any way out of here?" I ask.

"This is the only door. And there was what, at least a dozen of them guarding the place? The only thing is to wait until morning."

"Do you think Hanes might let us go?"

"Hanes wouldn't let his own mother go, if he thought it would benefit him in any way. He's a tyrant and a murderer. You were right, if the Zoktari leave without killing all of us, then Hanes and Doyle and the rest won't live another day to enjoy their new freedom."

"What did Doyle mean when he said they were planning on leaving?"

"Who knows? A lot of people plan on leaving. They think they can find a place where the Zoktari don't exist and they can live free and easy. They probably see themselves living in some small town, setting themselves up as lords of the kingdom. But it's all just a dream. The thought of striking out with no food and no idea what's out there is too intimidating for most people. We have very little here, but at least we know what it is. Out there? Who knows? But it doesn't stop people from dreaming."

"Like the old west," I say. "They had these cattle barons that would own all the land and run the towns. Everyone would do what they told them to. Until Clint Eastwood rides into town."

"Who's Clint Eastwood?"

"A movie actor."

"Oh. They're all gone. The actors and the singers. All the celebrities. They've been either killed, captured, or are sitting in refugee camps like us."

"I guess everyone's equal now."

"Not everyone. The Red Coats have power. I'm sure if there are other camps in other cities they all have their own Red Coats ruling over them, doing what the Zoktari tell them to do."

"And you have no way of knowing what's going on in any of the other cities?"

"No. That's why the others left. They wanted to see what was going on, if it was as bad as all the rumors say it is."

"Do you think you'll find them? When you go after them?" I think of Jack—out there somewhere doing his best to survive.

162

"I hope so. If there are others who are alive, then maybe we can work together. The Zoktari are getting fewer and fewer. Maybe a final fight will push them away."

"Tarak said they were a race bent on conquering. Maybe they have other wars on other planets they're fighting. If their forces are stretched all across the universe then they can't keep that up for too long."

"Ryan, did this Tarak tell you what they did to all the ones they captured during the purges?"

"No, I'm sorry I didn't think to ask."

"It's not your fault. You had other things to worry about."

"You're thinking of your parents? What happened to them?"

"Not just mine, but everyone who's lost someone. We know that when the war ended and we surrendered, that they began to take people. They would just come in and take a great many people. At first we thought the Red Coats had given them names of everyone who was ex-military, or even a potential threat to them. But they would take kids as young as five. It didn't make sense."

"And you never knew where they took them or what they did with them?"

"No. Nothing substantial. Rumors were everywhere of course, but nothing could be confirmed. Maybe, if we find others on the outside they'll know."

"Is that your real reason for wanting to leave and go after Jack and the others?"

"I need to find some answers, Ryan." I can't see her face but I know there's a look of determination on it. "I need some peace to all this. The nightmares I have are all about losing my parents. I run after them but I can never catch up to them. The closer I get farther away they appear. I want an end to these evil dreams, or at least some answers. That's why I need to go."

I reach my hand out in the dark and take hers. I squeeze hard. "The next time I see Tarak I'll ask him. Maybe you won't have to leave to get your answers. I hope these dreams of yours will end soon and you'll get the peace you deserve."

"It's strange," she says.

"What is?"

"You. Us. I only just met you but yet I seem to have known you all my life."

"I feel the same way."

We're silent for a while. Then she asks me to tell her about my family. What I was like as a child. I tell her about Jack—my Jack, and the trips we took as a family. I tell her about meeting Speckler and the comic books we plan on writing and drawing together. She listens quietly to a life that's so different from hers and might have been hers if some crazed alien race across the universe didn't go on a rampage. I tell her what Tarak told me how the Zoktari in this world elected a leader he said was a person of no consequence in the history of his world, and how this person led them on a path of war.

"Is it possible for one person to do this?" Violet wonders. "Convince a whole nation that war is the answer?"

"Our own history proves it, time and again."

We talk some more. She tells me about her earliest memories of her mother and father, her uncle and aunt, and her cousins. She shares a story about getting her head shaved by a cousin who found her dad's electric razor and wanted to give her a smiley face on the back of her head so people would see her smile when she was coming and going. This was all before the Zs came and turned her world upside down. Eventually we stop talking. Violet curls up next to me and begins to sleep. I'm not tired. I guess my ten-hour nap was enough to keep me awake. Besides, I have too much to think about. I think about what will happen in the morning. I wonder where Tarak is and what he's doing. Maybe he was caught and he crossed over to escape and dropped out of the sky onto a world that thinks they're the only life form in the universe. What a wake-up call that will be. I can see the headlines in the *Tribune*: ALIEN DROPS OUT OF SKY! Maybe right in the middle of Wrigley Field. That would really be something, except it's winter time and there are no games being played. So maybe not Wrigley Field. Maybe right in the middle of rush hour traffic.

Violet stirs next to me. I don't want to move unless I wake her. I don't want to fall asleep either. I dread the coming of the morning.

My eyes must have closed because a loud noise wakes us both. There's fighting going on outside.

"Someone's fighting the Red Coats," Violet says. We go to the door and listen.

"Bruzers?" I say.

"I don't think so. I don't hear guns going off."

There are sounds of shouting and scuffling. And then the fighting stops. We can hear voices on the other side of the door. We both pound on the door to let them know we're here. We hope it's someone friendly on the other side.

The door unlocks and opens. It's Tolliver.

Chapter Sixteen
Transuniversal Travelling

Tolliver quickly explains what happened. Someone in the Resistance noticed the Red Coats bringing us into the market. He recognized Violet and immediately told Tolliver who put a plan together to rescue us. It looks like it worked.

I ask about Doyle and Hanes. I don't see them anywhere. There are several Red Coats who have been captured. They're tied up with cloth bags over their heads, probably so they don't get a good look at anyone in the Resistance.

"Unfortunately, neither of them were here," he says. "Probably asleep in their comfortable beds."

"What should we do with the rest of these," someone asks, and I notice Brody, the red-haired Resistance fighter who wanted to cut my liver out. He gives me a look that says he still wants to decorate his tent with my liver.

"Lock them in the storage room. Killing them won't get us anything. Not killing them will probably get us something."

"It won't be mercy, not from Hanes and Doyle," Brody says. The Red Coats are all locked away.

"What happened while we were locked up?" Violet asks her uncle.

"The Red Coats and Bruzers completed their sweep of the camp. Obviously you weren't found. They're finished, for now. I'm sure they'll begin again in the morning. By then I want Ryan long gone from here."

Violet nods. She begins to lead me away but Tolliver stops her. "Vy, I want you to get him someplace safe, and then I want you to return."

She frowns and juts her jaw out stubbornly. "I'll return when I can," she almost snaps at him. "Ryan doesn't know how to survive out here. I do. I'll help him as long as I can. I can't promise you I'll be back soon."

"It may not be long anyway," I say. I know Tolliver hates the idea that they have to put their lives on the line for me, a stranger with a wild tale that most of them don't believe. "Tarak could be coming for me."

"I wouldn't put any money on that," Tolliver says. "If a Zoktari does decide to show himself, he'll more than likely get his throat cut."

"They bleed just like we do," Brody adds, a maniacal gleam in his eye.

Ignoring Brody's bloodlust, I appeal to Tolliver and Father Wu: "Can you get the word out not to harm him if he shows up? I'm telling you, he's on our side."

"Was he on our side when they were killing us like pigs at the slaughter?" Brody says. "Why weren't they helping us then? Why wait until you come along?"

"There's not many of them, what could they do?"

"That's right, kid. Make excuses for them."

"I'm telling you," I plead. "Tarak's not like the others."

"How do you know? Because he speaks English like the Queen of England and told you so? You're freaking dumber than you look."

Violet comes to my defense and squares off in front of Brody. "Why don't you give him a chance? Maybe he's telling the truth."

"He's really got you fooled, hasn't he little miss lollipop? What do you think—the heavens will open up and an army of friendly Zs will fly down to rescue all of us? Wake up—"

"All of you calm down!" Tolliver orders. "Listen, Ryan. Right now we don't know what to believe. But I do know that come morning this place is going to be a madhouse once Hanes discovers you've escaped."

"But he won't be able to say anything to the Zs," Violet says. "He'll have to tell them he had Ryan in his hands and didn't turn him over. They won't like that. It should keep Hanes in his place."

"For the moment," Tolliver says. "But believe me, he'll take his revenge out on us some way."

"Let him," Brody says. "I've told you it's time we stood up to them and take them out."

"With what? Kitchen knives and rocks? They've got shockers, or have you forgotten?"

He holds up one of the shockers taken from one of the captured Red Coats. "We have them now, too."

"We have ten of them at best. They have hundreds. I know you're not good at math, Brody, but even you can see the odds are against us."

"Not in a surprise attack. I say we do it now. Tonight. When they don't expect it. Ten shockers can become twenty in no time. Twenty can turn to fifty. Then it's a fair fight."

"You're forgetting the Bruzers and the Zs. Are they just going to stand back and let us defeat their comrades? It's nowhere near a fair fight and you know it. You're not thinking."

"Maybe I'm the only one who's thinking," he says sulkily.

"We've had this discussion before. When the time's right we'll make our move."

"By that time we'll all be laying in a ditch with flies buzzing around our bones."

"I promise you, the only ones who'll be in the ditch will be Red Coats, Bruzers and Zs."

Brody mutters something under his breath and stalks off. For a moment Tolliver seems like he's about to go after him but then decides not to. Maybe it's best just to let him sulk.

We're ready to leave. Father Wu gives us a bag of food and some water. It's not much but I'm grateful just the same. We shake hands. I tell them all thanks, even to Brody who only glares at me. I know we'll never be friends, but I wish I could convince him that there are some Zoktari who don't want to see them dead.

Once more I'm heading out into a strange city that I barely recognize with Violet leading my way. We get through the camp easy enough. There are a few Red Coat and Bruzer patrols but nto enough to patrol the entire park. We slip past them easy enough and head south toward the Loop. Violet tells me the Zs blew all the bridges since the meeting in Chinatown. Just another precaution. I tell her about swimming across the river and that it nearly killed me. She tells me I don't have to worry. She knows where a boat is to get across.

There are oddly no ships flying about. The mothership of course is still sitting ominously in the night sky, but none of the Ravens are anywhere to be seen. There were none above the camp when we left.

We get to the river on the edge of the Loop. Most of the buildings have been destroyed but some are still standing. Any of them would be perfect places to hide out. I ask Violet why not just hole up inside one of them.

"Too risky," she says. "The Zs left a lot of little toys around for us."

"Bombs?" I say.

"Uh-huh. Nasty little buggers that'll blow your head off if you sneeze in the wrong direction. Most are so small and so well hidden that you won't even know you triggered it until you're singing with the angels. Whenever we hear an explosion we know it was some poor Scavenger's unlucky day."

We go down a set of stairs to a platform along the river. Sure enough there's a small boat tied up. We get in and begin paddling across the river. The water is pitch black. It's eerily quiet. And just as we reach the other side a Bruzer suddenly steps out from the shadows to meet us.

"Back!" Violet yells. We reverse our strokes and begin frantically paddling to escape.

"Wait," a voice calls out. A Zoktari steps out of the shadows to stand alongside the Bruzer.

"It's okay," I tell Violet. "It's Tarak. We can trust them."

I could tell that just telling her we can trust them isn't enough. She's visibly shaking as we dock the boat. I have to steady her as we get out. Her fear's apparent and I instinctively grab hold of her hand. She squeezes it hard.

Tarak smiles, then another Zoktari steps out of the shadows behind him. "This is Tanis," he says. Her face is slightly longer and narrower than his, her eyes larger. She studies us warily.

I introduce them to Violet. She stares at them in both fascination and fear. It's probably the closest she's ever been to a Zoktari. And one that speaks English. Maybe not as good as the Queen of England, as Brody accused them of, but good enough.

"You're still alive," I say to Tarak. "I was afraid you got caught and you had to cross over."

"It is very dangerous right now. They do not believe you were able to escape by yourself, and so they think that one of their own has helped you. But it is a foreign idea to them, this idea that they could actually be betrayed by their own kind. They expect loyalty and they get it. Even from the Bruzers and the ones you call the Red Coats."

"So you're free to move about? You can come and go from the mothership?"

"To some extent, yes. But we have to be careful."

"Do you have the device that will send me back?"

He smiles. "I told you it would do much more than that. It can send you back and it can bring you here. You will have the power to travel back and forth just as we do."

"So if they pull me over I can instantly use it to travel back?"

"As long as you're wearing it and it is activated, they should not be able to pull you over."

"You don't sound so sure about that."

"It has not been tested," he says.

I look at Violet and smile. "Does it work with just one person or can it work with more than one?"

"It only works with the one who wears it. It has a small radius so besides your body your clothes can pass through along with any small item you may have with you. Another person is too large, unless it is a baby. But even then I would not chance it. If it does not make the cross over completely then it may die."

The female Zoktari, Tanis, produces a small metallic device. "It fits here." Her English is as good as Tarak's. She places it on my left wrist. The device is thin, weighs very little, and can easily hide under the sleeve of my sweater. It has a display window much like the face of a smartphone and she shows me how to activate it. Just like a smartphone it's touch activated. A green light comes on. Then, what feels like a hundred pin pricks stabbing me at once shoots through my arm. There's an instant feeling of warmth, as if my whole body temp just rose ten degrees. I could have used this after my polar bear swim across the Chicago River. I flex my fingers to make sure my hand still works. It does.

Violet stares at the device with unease. "How does it feel?"

"Hot," I say.

"It taps into your entire nervous system," Tanis tells me. She shows me the right way to activate it. It's not difficult. Only a few steps to enter the code.

"How long does it take?"

"Once you activate the code it only takes a few minutes to prepare your body for travelling, and then only a second or two to cross over. You will cross at the same spot at the same time so you have to be sure of what is on the other side."

"I'm sure this spot is safe." I remember this platform along the river, except there are restaurants and cafes in my world. At this time though they should be empty.

"Then the device is ready. You need only activate the code and the countdown will begin."

"One more thing." Tarak points at the collar. The Bruzers that's with him, I'm certain it's M'Raug, removes the collar from around my neck. It feels good to have it off.

"Can you do the same for Violet?" I ask.

Tarak speaks to M'Raug who nods. "But she should wear yours—the one that is not activated, so she will not be noticed."

M'Raug removes Violet's collar and before he puts the new one on, she stops him. "Wait. Let me enjoy this for a few minutes at least. I've been wearing that damn thing almost my entire life."

"Of course," Tarak says softly. "I can only imagine how terrible it must be for all of you."

"You live with it and get used to it," Violet says. "It'll be good knowing none of them can ever shock me again."

"It also might help convince Tolliver and Brody," I say.

"Tolliver, yes. Brody, I'm not so sure about. He'll just think it's a trick to get us to lower our defenses."

"We are on the same side," Tanis says. "If we cannot trust each other we may never defeat them."

"You'll have to meet with my uncle and the others. Help me convince them."

Tarak nods. "It seems the only way. We will coordinate with you a meeting time and place." He turns to me. "When you cross back to our universe, will you notify your government right away?"

"Yes. My friends and I said that I needed proof before going to them. I may not have any video to show, but I won't need it with this." I hold up my wrist with the device firmly attached. "They'll want to meet with you as well. I know our president will."

"I may not be able to at the moment. Of course, in time I will be very pleased to meet with your president to discuss our alliance in this matter. But we still need to find out how much the Zoktaris in this universe know. We know that the experiments with your double is not the only ones they've conducted."

"What about the Zs who crossed over into Ryan's world?" Violet asks. "Do you know who they are? How many there are? What they look like?"

"No. That information is too highly protected. We would risk everything just to get it."

"I understand," I tell him. "But it would be extremely helpful in knowing who they are and where they are. My government will want to know for sure. If you find out will you let us know as soon as possible?"

"Yes. We will probably have to work with your government in stopping them."

"You can count on the Resistance as well," Violet says.

"Good," Tarak says. "Together we may stop them before any more are killed."

"And the ones . . . the ones who were taken?" Violet asks. "Do you know what has happened to them? Are they still alive?" Her voice is filled with hope and longing to finally have answers that have haunted her dreams and nightmares for years. But there's also a slight hesitation in her voice. She needs to know but she's afraid of the answer.

Unfortunately Tarak doesn't have the answers for her. "I am sorry," he says. "We were not with them when they first arrived. I do not think they were killed and I do not think they were taken to our home planet or to another planet. I will try to find out more."

"Thank you," Violet says. I know how hard it must be to look kindly on a race that have done nothing but murder and destroy, but I hope she thinks of Tarak and the others as allies and not enemies.

There's nothing left to do and Tarak says they need to get back to the mothership. I ask for a moment alone with Violet.

"Will I see you again?" she asks. "Now that you have the power to come and go?"

"I have a lot of work to do convincing my government—and probably the whole world—that this is real. But maybe if we agree on a time and place. The library maybe."

"When?"

"If today is Sunday, count out seven days and I'll meet you there. It'll be in the morning. I'll be the first one in and I'll cross right away at the same spot where we slept."

"Okay. I'll wait there for you. But don't worry. If you're not there I'll understand you have more important things to do—"

"There's nothing more important than seeing you," I say.

"I think saving your world might be a little more important," she says and smiles.

"Okay, a little. But not much. Maybe, one day, when this is all over, you can visit my world."

"I'd like that."

We stare at each other for a moment and then I take her into my arms. Her body is thin and feels brittle, but I squeeze her hard letting her know how much she means to me and that separating from her is the most difficult thing I've ever done. More difficult than losing my brother. There are tears in her eyes and I kiss her. She kisses me back and it feels good and perfect. I press my thumb gently to her face and wipe the tears away. My own eyes well up. "I'll see you in a week," I whisper to her.

She nods. "Good luck."

I tell Tarak I'm ready. I tell him about the library and how if he needs to get word to me he can either meet there or leave word somehow. He agrees that this is a good idea. I wish him good luck and hope he finds information soon.

I step away from Violet and the others and activate the code. My whole body begins to warm up even more than before. The headache returns, intense, sudden. I look into Violet's face and for a moment I smile through the pain and hold my hand up in a wave. She smiles back. Then she begins to fade as a white light glows around me. There's a flash and then it's gone. So are Violet and Tarak and Tanis and M'Raug the Bruzer. I'm standing on the platform. Same spot. Different universe.

"How did you do that?" A voice startles me. A homeless man is resting on the platform, wrapped in a dirty blanket.

"Magic," I tell him.

The headache is gone. I hope it's not like that every time I cross over. Maybe my body only needs to get used to it. I run up the stairs to the street. There are cars—late night taxis. All the buildings are in one piece. I breathe easy, but I miss Violet already. A week is too long to wait. I want to see her now, make sure she gets safely back to camp. But I have a mission. An important mission. Probably the most important mission in the history of our planet. But I can't go to the government first. Who would I go to? The president? There's one person I need to see before I do anything. So once again, because I have no money and my cell phone was vaporized, I begin to run. This time though no alien ships are trying to hunt me down, but there's urgency just the same. I just hope Speckler is still home.

Chapter Seventeen
Agent Polley

I stop at a newsstand to look at a recently delivered stack of newspapers in order to check the date. It is Sunday. Good. Speckler's family was planning on leaving for Florida on Monday. Christmas! I completely forgot that Christmas is only a couple of days away. I don't know how I could forget; I'm still wearing the hideous reindeer sweater that Father Wu gave me.

I'm exhausted by the time I finally reach Speckler's house.

The lights are out. The whole street's dark and quiet. A few snow flurries are falling. I make my way around the house and look for a rock to throw up at his window. I find a small stone and just as I begin to heave it a light shines on me.

"Hold it right there," a voice commands. I shield my hand up in front of my eyes to block the glare of the light. I see two people in uniform. Cops.

"Are you Ryan Whittaker?" one of them asks.

"Yes," I say. "What's this all about?"

"I think you need to tell us that. There's been an APB out on you for two days—ever since you went missing at the Shedd Aquarium. Are you okay? Have you been injured in any way?"

Damn you Speckler! is all I can think at the moment. *What story did you give them*?

"I'm fine," I tell them. "I just need to talk to my friend."

"You can talk to him later, after you talk to the lieutenant and the feds."

They put me in the back of the police car and we drive away from Speckler's house. They take me inside the station. They don't treat me like a criminal, which is good. I'm glad they don't search me and discover the device on my wrist. The place is nearly empty. I see a clock and notice the time. Nearly two-thirty in the morning.

"Is this Sunday?" I ask the officer. I want to be sure.

"Yes, of course it is," he says. "Don't you know?" He studies my face to see if I'm high. I guess I pass the test. He takes me into one of the small interrogation rooms and sits me down at a dull chrome table that's bolted to the floor. He asks if there's anything I want. I'm suddenly hungry and thirsty.

"A Coke," I say. "A candy bar maybe. Snickers?" He nods and leaves. There's a video camera up in the corner of the room. I wonder if I'm being recorded. Eventually an older man, Hispanic with short black hair salted with gray, comes in. I notice the Lt. bars on his collar. The name on his uniform says Vega. He smiles and hands me the soda and candy bar. I thank him and tear into the food and drink. I'm ravished.

"Wow, slow down, Ryan," he tells me as he takes a seat across from me at the table. "It looks like you haven't eaten in days."

I nod and look at him cautiously. How much should I tell him? I don't want to tell him the whole story. He's just a local cop. I need someone with real authority and clout that can get me to the president. I don't think Vega's pay grade is enough to handle alien invasions. Whoever I tell has to be able to keep this top secret.

Vega opens up a manila folder, peruses its contents for a second or two, before he says: "Want to tell me about your magic trick, Houdini?"

Magic trick? "What do you mean?" I mumble, my mouth full of chocolate and peanuts.

"Your disappearing act from the Shedd Aquarium. After your parents reported you missing we checked the surveillance cameras. We see you going into the men's room with your friend." He looks back down at a document inside the folder. "Ralph Speckler. And then that's it. You never come out. You want to explain how that happens?"

"What did Speckler tell you?"

"He says he came out of the stall and you were gone. He started calling your name and that's when the teacher heard him." He checks the report again. "Carnofsky. Your art teacher?"

"Yes. We call him Mr. C. He's pretty cool." I don't want Carnofsky to get into any trouble.

"He says you were in a fight and went into the bathroom to clean up. He came down to check on you and that's when he hears your friend calling your name. He asks where you went and your friend didn't know. Later, Ralph says you weren't feeling well and you must have left. But you never returned home. The school called your parents to tell them that you left your field trip. A big no no. You can't just leave a field trip on your own without telling anyone."

He waits for me to say something. I can't think of anything so he continues. "Your parents immediately called your friend and talked to his parents. They hadn't seen you. Your parents then waited for you to return and when you didn't they of course called us. Unfortunately, we couldn't do anything until you were missing at least twenty-four hours. That's the law. With missing teenagers, especially boys, they turn up sooner than later. But when you didn't turn up that's when we started our investigation. Hence, the surveillance cameras at the Shedd. Now, do you want to tell me what happened? How did you leave that bathroom without being seen on camera?"

"I don't know, maybe you missed me. I'm sure a lot of people were going in and out."

"They were. Some even looked a little bit like you since there were several schools there on a field trip—"

"There you have it," I say.

"I said a little bit like you. They weren't you. We looked closely. Very closely. For the whole day. We thought, maybe you hid out in one of the stalls, afraid the kid you got in a fight with was coming for you. But the cameras run even after the place closes and you never came out. We had to consider then that maybe you were abducted. Maybe you didn't come out on your own but was grabbed by someone, forced to wear a disguise, and then kidnapped. It's a long shot, I know, but we had to consider everything, no matter how implausible it sounded."

Implausible? If he wants to hear implausible he should hear the truth. But I continue to keep my mouth shut and act dumb, like it's no big mystery how I got out of there.

Vega continues: "We had to notify the FBI that we had a possible abduction. In fact, they're sending an agent down right now to talk to you. So if you haven't figured out that this is serious then you might start thinking about that. A lot of people are worried about you."

FBI! Perfect. They work for the federal government. I'd seen plenty of *X-Files* episodes. Hopefully, the guy they send is another Fox Mulder. Spooky Mulder.

"Well, what do you have to say?"

"I'm sorry everybody worried about me, Lt. Vega. It wasn't my intention to make anyone worried. But I'm all right now. I wasn't abducted by some perv in a trench coat. Look, I'm fine. Really."

"Fine? You look like you've been dragged through hell and back, kid. You obviously haven't eaten in a while and it seems you've been roughed up by more than just that lunk at the aquarium." I forgot about the cut lip Doyle gave me. There must be bruises as well. "If it wasn't for the Houdini act," Vega continues, "I'd just chalk it up to another kid out getting his kicks. Drugs, girlfriend. But from what I hear you don't do drugs and you don't have a girlfriend. That doesn't leave much."

"How long do I have to stay here?" I ask. I need to get back to Speckler. Even though I know it wasn't his fault that all this happened. I guess if Mr. C didn't hear Speck call my name then he could have easily said I'd left and everyone would have believed him. No cops. No FBI. No need to check surveillance cameras.

Vega's face hardens. He jabs a finger into the metallic table. "You'll stay here long enough for us to get some answers. You say nothing happened but we both know that's a lie. You've cost this city both time and money looking for you. Now you're found. We're glad you're safe. There are way too many missing kids out there who never turn up—unless it's a body in an unmarked grave. So your parents are one of the lucky ones who get a good phone call rather than the one where we tell them your child's body has been found. But we need to clear up this mystery so we know for sure and until then you're going to remain here. Think about it. I'll give you ten minutes."

He slams the folder shut and leaves the room. I drain the rest of the soda. I'm nervous as hell but I can't tell him anything. I'm sure what he's telling me is all a bluff to scare me. They can't hold me here indefinitely. I'm pretty sure as a minor I've got some rights. But what do I tell him in case they do? That damn surveillance camera! If it wasn't for that I'd be fine. How do you explain disappearing from a men's room at a popular tourist attraction where there are cameras all over the place?

The ten minutes go by fast and the door opens before I come to any decision. But it's not Vega coming back for another round of interrogation. Another man walks in. He smiles at me. He's middle-aged with light hair that's a bit unkempt. His face is pink and his clothes are a bit rumpled. A beige suit with no tie. He has a badge clipped to the lapel of his coat that says VISITOR. He has a laptop case with him, which he sets on the table.

He reaches out his hand and says, "Hi Ryan. I'm Agent Mitch Polley with the FBI."

This is the FBI agent? He looks like the manager of a grocery store not a federal agent. He's definitely no Fox Mulder. We shake hands.

He sits down in the seat vacated by Vega. "So, the prodigal son returns," he says.

He's not smiling so I don't know if it's a joke or not. "You're really with the FBI?" I say. I still can't believe it and think maybe Vega is sending in another cop—maybe the night clerk—to get me to talk.

He takes out his wallet and shows me his ID. He's FBI all right. "We're not all James Bond and Tom Cruise," he says.

"James Bond is British and works for British Secret Service, and Tom Cruise, if you're referring to *Mission Impossible*, wasn't FBI either. He worked for IMF—Impossible Missions Force."

Polley nods. "Right, you're into movies. Your parents said something about that. Vega says you don't want to tell him where you've been or how you got out of that bathroom."

He waits for me to respond. These cops love to make statements and then wait for you to respond. "That's true," I say. I look over to the small surveillance camera they have up in the corner of the room. I do this to give him the hint that what I have to say can't be recorded. He doesn't get the hint and instead takes out his laptop and boots it up. I shake my head. This is the guy who's going to get me to the president?

He takes something out of the laptop case and slides it across to me. It's an 8 x 10 photograph. "Tell me about Violet," he says.

"What?" This completely startles me. I look at the photo. It's the one I took with my smartphone. Me and Violet at the library that first night.

I look at Agent Polley. What does he know? "How did you get this?"

"Off your desktop computer. I'm sure you've seen enough movies where the kid goes missing and the police investigate. They talk to the parents about where you might have gone and then they

179

give them access to your computer just to see if you made any emails to anyone saying you're coming over or making plans to run away together. There were no emails of interest but there was this photo. Your mother says she's a girl who lives in Canada. At least that's what you told her. I was never good at geography, but I do know that Chicago is not in Canada. So tell me about the girl. Violet Ames."

"There's nothing to tell." Once more I look deliberately at the camera up in the corner. Once more he doesn't notice.

"I think there is something to tell. And it's good. Real good. I've always loved mysteries—maybe that's why I got into law enforcement. And this is one doozy of a mystery bagel just waiting to be devoured. But for some reason no one wants to tell the truth about this. Certainly not you and not your friend and not this girl—"

"You talked to her? Why did you do that?"

"Because like it or not she's involved in this. Follow me on this, will you? A kid goes missing right after getting into a fight that involves a girl. Everyone's account is that it was all a misunderstanding. Then we find a photo of you and the girl on your computer—something you look at everyday. So she must be important to you. But when we talk to the girl she says she's never met you before. We show her the photo. It's her but it's not her. Maybe she has a twin running around and she never knew it. There are differences in the two—the scar for one. Who knows, maybe she does have a twin she doesn't know about who lives in Canada. Is that it?'

"No. But it's not her. I swear. Please don't talk to her again, she has nothing to do with this."

"It's kind of hard to ignore. Even her uncle's getting involved. He wants to talk to you as well."

"Her uncle? Tolliver?"

Polley studies me closely. "For someone who says this girl has nothing to do with this, you sure know a lot about her. Like the name of an uncle. Yes, his name is Tolliver. Sgt. Tolliver Ames. He's Chicago PD."

Boy, how dumb can I be? I just blurt out everything. And they have it on camera! I'm sure he really wants to talk to me now. I make a vow not to say anything more—at least not here with the camera recording everything.

Polley frowns at me. "Nothing? You're going to clam up now? After you've spilled some things. Okay, if that's the way you want to play it. Maybe you'll have something to say about this."

Once the computer is on he clicks on a video. "This is from one of the cameras at the Shedd Aquarium." I figure he wants to show me eight hours of footage of me not coming out of the bathroom. Is this how they plan to wear me down? Bore me to death? It might work.

It's the footage of the corridor outside the bathroom, the one that leads up to the main floor and down to the pool and penguin area. It's in black and white but still clear. You can see the stairs going up to the main floor so it's pointing away from the direction of the pool—the spot where the Scavengers got vaporized. People are coming and going. Speckler comes out of the bathroom looking frantic and calling my name. Then Carnofsky is seen coming down the stairs—obviously to check up on me. He talks to Speckler and then goes into the bathroom to make sure Speckler didn't miss me. Maybe I'm hiding in another stall or the trash can? There's no audio but I can guess what's being said. Speckler looks nervous. Scared. You can almost see the gears turning in his head as he realizes I've crossed over into the other universe and what he'll have to tell people. Mr. C comes out a minute later and they talk some more before they both head back up the stairs.

Polley stops the video. "And of course you never come out. At least that's what the video shows. But you did come out, right?"

"Yes," I say, surprised by the question.

"Of course you did. Or else we'd be having this conversation in the men's room of the Shedd Aquarium. Except it wouldn't be this conversation it'd be another conversation—one where I say, why don't you come out of the bathroom kid, you can't stay in there your whole life. You follow me so far?"

"I follow you."

"Good. Because I want us to be on the same page, and if at any time we're not on the same page you let me know. Because I just hate it when I'm not on the same page with someone. Okay, so it's established that you did come out of the bathroom. But what's not established, and this is where you're definitely on one page and the rest of us schmucks are on another page, is just how you came out of that bathroom. Am I right?"

181

Again I nod and say it's true and once again I look up at the camera and once again Agent Polley ignores this obvious sign I'm giving him. No wonder at his age he's working the late night shift.

"Okay, good. So I want you to help me get to that page you're on. And we're going to begin with this." He indicates the video, but I don't see what he means. Do we really have to watch the whole thing? "As I said, we poured over these images looking for you to come out. Everyone was certain you came out later, much later, and they scrutinized these last hours of the day and the hours into the night and the hours the following day. But I took a different approach. I thought, maybe we're focusing on the wrong time. Maybe we ought to be looking at the time when you enter the bathroom, before your friend comes running out shouting holy hell for you. And that's when I came across this. Take a look."

He shows me some more video. Once more it's the corridor outside the men's room, but the time frame is earlier. I watch myself coming down the stairs with Speckler. I'm wiping blood from my nose and Speck is laughing about something. I can't even remember what it was. We go into the bathroom. The video continues running. Then two men, who seem to be following right behind us, stop outside the bathroom. They look out of place. They both are wearing suits, are thin, and even in the black and white video you can tell their skin is also quite pale. Almost like albinos, and then, suddenly, something about them seems familiar. They confer with each other for a second and one of them goes into the bathroom. A second later he comes out and nods to his companion, who removes a device from his pocket, the size of a small handheld tablet, keys in something on the screen and then they leave. A minute goes by and then Speckler comes running out, but the two men have left. Agent Polley rewinds the video and freezes it on the two men. I stare at them. They have to be the Zoktari infiltrators. I don't even remember the one coming into the men's room. Of course I was busy cleaning blood off my face and talking to Speckler. But it has to be them. And then I remember. The Bean! Speckler made a comment about an albino punching a text into his Blackberry. That albino was a Z! Who knows how long they've been following me? The device was used to contact the other side. Was he telling them to send me over or to stop the process? Was that why I was in my world but seeing Violet in her world in the reflection of the Bean?

"Most of my fellow agents didn't think these two were of interest, but judging by the look on your face I'd say I'm getting to the page you're on. Am I right?"

I look Polley in the eye and then dart to the video camera and back to him.

"Okay, still want to give me the silent treatment."

Jesus! How dumb can this guy be? Just when I thought he was pretty smart about zeroing in on the Zs he completely ignores every signal I give him! I'm ready to just come right out and ask for his superior, when the door opens and Vega comes back in.

"Get anything out of Marcel Marceau here, Polley, or should I get the jumper cables?" He laughs at his own joke.

Polley shakes his head. "It's like trying to talk to a brick wall. The kid's got to go to the bathroom. Maybe after he relieves himself he'll feel more like talking."

Bathroom? I don't have to go to the bathroom. Where did that come from?

He takes me by the arm and lifts me to my feet. "Come on, kid."

"I'll get an officer to take him," Vega says.

"Don't bother," Polley tells him. "I need to use the john myself. Too much damn coffee."

He walks me to the bathroom and we both go in. I'm thinking maybe he wants me to explain how I can disappear from a bathroom. Or maybe he wants to get me alone so he can strong-arm me. I tense up, not sure what his plan is.

Polley stops and leans against the sink and crosses his arms. "All right. We're alone. No cameras, just like you've been itching for ever since I came in."

I breathe a sigh of relief. "Thank God," I say. "I thought you would never get the hint."

"Give me some credit, kid. I was born at night but I wasn't born last night. So start talking. We don't have much time."

"Okay, but what I'm about to tell you is going to change your life in ways you've never imagined."

"All right. You got me hooked, now reel me in."

"First, can I count on you to keep this top secret? For now? You'll probably have to tell your superior, and he'd have to go to his superior—how many superiors do you have?"

"You want my whole chain of command? How far up?"

"All the way."

"You mean—"

"Yes. The president."

"Don't worry about the chain of command. Just tell me what you know and let me worry about how far it needs to go. If it's serious enough it'll get to the people who need to know."

"I'm not worried it getting to the people who need to know, I'm just worried it getting to the people who don't need to know."

"What you have to say better be pretty damned important—"

"I told you it is."

"But you haven't told me what it is. What are we talking? Terrorists?"

"No. Aliens."

"Illegal aliens?"

"No. Alien aliens. Like . . . you know, outer space aliens."

His face suddenly drops and he swears under his breath. "Do I look like the schmuck of the century to you kid?"

"I'm not lying and I can prove it."

"How?"

I roll up my sleeve to reveal the device.

He looks at it. He's not impressed. "And this is what you used to disappear out of the bathroom? You had, what? Captain Kirk beam you up to the *Enterprise*?"

"No, I didn't use this. I just got this. Listen, this is going to get a lot weirder, but it's all true and I can prove it. But you have to listen."

"I've been doing nothing but listening to you. So far all I've gotten is your *Twilight Zone* story. I know you're a big movie fan and this may seem like a movie to you but I don't want to be an extra in your little make believe world. So cut the crap, and tell me how you got out of that bathroom."

"Okay." I take a deep breath. "Aliens in a parallel universe who have taken over the earth—the earth in this other universe—are experimenting with what's best called transuniversal travelling. This is the ability to cross from one universe to another. Through their experiments they sent two of their people here—the ones pointed out on the surveillance camera—the albinos—but they can't bring them back. Those two are stuck here. Then they started doing experiments with humans, knowing that each of us has a duplicate in

184

the parallel universe. So they used my duplicate in that universe to pull me over to their world. Like a magnet. But I escaped from them. First with the help of Resistance fighters—survivors of the invasion. Then later with the help of aliens from this world who had also discovered a way to cross over. A much simpler way. This device. They've been studying their counterparts for several years, seeing if and when they would discover this device themselves."

"Why study them? Why not help them, if they're the same?"

"That's just it, they're not the same. They're the same species and come from a duplicate planet in a duplicate solar system but that's where it ends. The Zoktari, that's what these aliens are called, are completely different from their counterparts in this universe. They are ruthless and cruel and have completely taken over the earth. The Zoktari in our universe are peaceful. They're scientists. They know if the other Zoktari discovers how to cross back and forth they will conquer them just as they conquered earth. That's why we have to work together to stop them. Starting with finding those two on the camera who were following me. Even though they can't cross back to the other universe they can still communicate with them, which is what you saw them doing. They contacted their people on the other side and that's when they activated their machine to pull me over."

I wait for Polley to react. All he says is, "Prove it."

"I can't do it here."

"Why not?"

"I can only cross where I know I'll be safe. This building may not be standing in that world. Or maybe the Zoktari or the Bruzers are standing right here. It's too risky."

"What are Bruzers?"

"The Bruzers are another alien race who have been conquered by the Zoktari. They've been turned into their soldiers, but it's the Zoktari that run things."

"And the girl? What does she have to do with this?"

"The girl in the photo lives in the parallel universe. We all have an exact double in this other world. Me, her, even you. That's why the Violet in the Shedd Aquarium didn't know about the photo. And it's how I know about her uncle Tolliver. But the one in the other world."

He thinks about this for a moment. His face is impassive, unreadable. I can't tell if he believes any of what I just told him or thinks I'm completely nuts.

"So where can you do it?" he asks. "Where is it safe to cross over?"

I don't get a chance to tell him. Vega walks in. "What's taking so long in here?"

"Nothing," Polley says. "We were just talking about the Cubs starting pitching. What gives?"

"The kid's parents are here. They want to take him home. Did you get anything out of him?"

Polley pauses for a few seconds and then says, "No. Nothing."

We walk out and Vega says, "Cubs fan huh? You should stick with the Sox. At least they won't break your heart every year."

Mom and Dad are standing in the waiting area. When I come out Mom rushes over and gives me a tight hug. It seems like forever since I've seen them but it's only been a couple of days. She releases me, steps back, then notices my face. "What happened to you?" She instinctively reaches out and touches the cuts and bruises. Her own face is worried. It looks like neither of them has slept since I mysteriously vanished.

"Nothing, Mom. I'm fine." I notice the look on Dad's face. It's a mix of anger and relief. I know he's relieved I'm okay but the anger will come out soon for not calling and making them both worried. I guess Vega told them I wasn't abducted or anything, but I also don't look like I've been having a party either.

"And what are you wearing?" She pulls at the sweater as if she wants to pull it off of me. "Where did you get this ugly thing?"

"A friend gave it to me," I tell her.

"Where's your coat? Why didn't you call us?"

"Where the hell have you been?" Dad says finally, unable to keep silent.

"I'll tell you about it when we get home." I turn to Vega. "Am I allowed to leave?"

"You're allowed, but we're not done yet. After you get some sleep and a good meal in you we'll talk again, Ryan. We need some answers."

I look over at Agent Polley who's been watching me the whole time. I can only imagine what he's thinking. I'm glad he covered for me in front of Vega. Maybe he is one to keep his mouth shut.

"I'll pay you a visit later, Ryan," Polley says. He introduces himself to my parents and gives them his card.

"FBI?" my father says when we're in the car. "Why is the FBI involved in this?"

"They had to call them," I say. "It was procedure. They thought I might have been kidnapped."

"Were you?" my father asks. He's watching me in the rear view mirror.

"Not now, Dad," I say. I slink down in the back seat. I'm exhausted. I close my eyes. The next thing I know my mom is shaking me and telling me we're home. I must have dozed off.

"Are you hungry?" she asks. "I can heat up some soup or make a sandwich?"

"Yeah, a sandwich would be great. Thanks, Mom. I really need a shower first. Can we talk when I come out?"

My father looks like he wants to shake the story out of me, but then he relaxes and tells me to make it quick.

I grab some clean clothes from my room and strip off my old ones. I punch in the code to release the device from my wrist. It unlocks and suddenly the warmth that was shooting through my body subsides. I check my wrist. There are tiny puncture holes from where the device clamped on to me. I hide the device in one of my dresser drawers under some T-shirts. I figure I'll be safe for a while without it on. The Zs must still think I'm in their world, probably still hiding in the camp.

I step into the hot water and at once feel guilty that while I'm here I'm safe and warm and fed but back in the other universe Violet is cold and hungry. The water they clean themselves with is frigid lake water they have to boil. I want to bring her here so she doesn't have to suffer another moment in her life. But the water feels good. I have no clue how to tell my parents the truth but since I already laid it out to Agent Polley I figure the best thing is to do likewise and just tell them everything from the beginning. But I also need Speckler, but I don't want to get his parents involved. The fewer people who know the better. I decide to tell them without Speck and hope for the best.

No one says anything for a long time. I've told them everything, from the beginning, starting with seeing Violet's reflection in the Bean. I even have the drawing I made. Anything to help convince them. But it's the device that draws their attention. They both stare at it like it's a dead cat someone threw on our front lawn. It's now locked securely back on my left wrist. I started getting paranoid standing in the shower, thinking what would happen if I cross over right then, completely naked.

"I don't understand any of this," my mother finally says. "It's all just too crazy. You crossed over into a . . . what did you call it?"

"A parallel universe, Mom. It's an exact duplicate of this world. Including the people. There're duplicates of all of us in this other world."

"A world overrun by aliens?" my father says with a total lack of belief. I don't think he'd believe it even if I crossed over right then and there. Maybe I'll have to just to convince him.

"That's right. I know it sounds crazy. It is crazy. But I was there. Twice. And now I can go there as many times as I want."

"Because of that . . . thing?" he says pointing to the device.

"Yes. Transuniversal travelling—crossing over from universe into the next. I have to keep it on just to be safe because they could try to bring me over at any time."

"The aliens?" my father says.

"Yes. Zoktari. They're called Zoktari, Dad. They can pull me over into their world by using my double. But if I wear this it should counteract their own device. At least that's what Tarak believes. It hasn't been tested yet, unless they've already tried to pull me over. So it's only a guess. But if I disappear when I'm wearing it then we'll know it doesn't work."

"And what do they want with you?" my mother asks.

"Please, Miriam. Don't encourage him. Listen, Ryan, save this bullshit story for the police or the school but in this house I want the truth!"

"I am telling you the truth. You have to believe me because it's going to get pretty weird pretty quick around here."

There's a knock at the door. I nearly jump out of my skin.

"Who the hell could that be at this time?" my father grumbles as he goes to the door. We follow him to the living room.

"I saw the light on," Polley says once the door is open. "I thought you might still be up."

They invite him in and he joins us at the dinner table. My mother asks if he wants something to eat and he thanks her but says no. "I see you've shown them the doohickey," he says indicating the device.

"Did he tell you his wild story as well?" my father says.

"He did."

"And?"

"And it's pretty wild. But there's a lot about this case that's pretty wild. The girl. The disappearance from the bathroom. That thing."

"I don't know what to believe," my mother says. She doesn't handle surprises very well. I'm sure she never thought she could get news that could easily outdo my brother's death.

I look at the three of them. "I'm telling you I can prove it. With this. I punch in a code and then I cross over. It's almost instantaneous. But I can't do it here—it has to be someplace I know I'll be safe. Can you get me into the library at this time?"

"Which library?"

"Harold Washington."

"It'll take making some calls to some people. They'll want to know why."

"Okay. Not there then. It'll have to be out in the open. Away from the city. A farm field. It should be safe there."

Polley thinks about this. "If it doesn't work, and I end up looking like a schmuck—"

"I know, you'll do something really, really terrible to me—"

"No. *I'll* do something really, really terrible to you," my father says.

My mother looks at him crossly. "No you won't, Walt. C'mon, let's get our coats. Ryan, you can use one of Jack's old ones."

"I thought you got rid of all his clothes?"

"Not all of them."

We drive outside the city till we get to farmland. Polley drives with my dad up front and my mom and me in the back. It's a quiet ride. The sun is just about to come up. Twenty-four hours ago I was running for my life, hiding out in a half-destroyed dry cleaners while aliens searched all over for me.

We reach the first farmlands outside the city.

"What if the farmer's up?" I ask Polley. "They might wonder what we're doing out in his field."

Polley shakes his head. "Farmers only get up early in the summer. I grew up on a farm. And it's still dark enough they won't be able to see much even if there is an early riser. You said it wouldn't take long."

"It won't."

We park along the road and march out to the center of the field. The ground is hard and covered with patches of snow. It's bitter cold, with a wind that cuts through you. I zip the coat up tighter. It's Jack's old letterman jacket from school. I wonder why Mom never threw this out. Sentimental I guess.

"Do we need to do anything?" my mother asks once we're out in the middle. "Hold hands or pray or anything?"

"It doesn't work like that, Mom. You should all stand back though and give me some room."

"Are you sure you know what you're doing?" she asks. "What if you do it wrong and your arm disappears or something?"

My father looks at her sternly, as if she were a child. "Miriam, please. Nothing is going to happen. We came all the way out here for nothing." But there's doubt in his voice, like he's trying to convince himself it won't work rather than firmly believing it. For a moment I think what if it doesn't work? What then? I'll never convince anyone. I have only one chance to get my parents and the FBI to believe me.

I hesitate a moment, take a deep breath, and then punch in the code. The warmth shoots through my body. I look at the three of them and smile. It's working, I think to myself as they fade away.

Everything refocuses. Another instant headache. I feel nauseous but it soon goes away. I look around. The farmhouse is nothing but a burnt-out wreck. Burned down long ago. No Zoktari or Bruzers or people about. No Ravens up in the sky. Good. I get ready to cross back. They must be totally freaking out. But then I see something out in the field. It looks like a scarecrow, but from this distance it's too big to be a scarecrow. And what would they scare? I'm sure there haven't been crops growing out here for several years. I head over to take a look. When I get closer I see it's not a scarecrow at all—or maybe it is, just not to scare crows.

It's the body of a Bruzer tied up on a cross. Dead. The gas mask is off and it's mostly skeleton. Its corpse is shrunken inside its tattered black uniform. Why is he here? Who put it up there? It can't be the Zoktari. It has to be the people. Maybe they left it as a kind of warning. A big screw you to their invaders. Was it before or after the house was burnt to the ground? And why didn't the Zoktari or Bruzers remove it? Maybe they don't honor the dead like we do with funerals and burials or cremations. The sight of it gives me the creeps and shivers run up and down my body. It brings the whole war home. In war, nobody wins. It just brings out the worst in people. I wonder if Jack ever saw anything like this? Or did anything like this? I like to think he didn't.

I punch the code back in and cross back.

The feeling is worse. I drop to the ground and heave up what's in my stomach. My head feels like its been whacked by the hammer of Thor. My parents and Polley rush over to me. My mother tells Polley to call for an ambulance.

"I told you to be careful. You shouldn't have done it," she says to me. "You'll get yourself killed."

"I'll be okay," I tell her. "It's just a side effect. It'll pass."

And it does.

I get to my feet. "Well?"

I look at my father. He looks shocked and for once is speechless.

I look at Polley. "I need a drink. A big one," he says. "Then I need to get you a meeting with the president."

Chapter Eighteen
Infiltrators

"I don't like this," Mungo says. "We should be in the Oval Office discussing strategy not in your parents basement. There're aliens on this planet and you guys are doing nothing to find them."

Polley has called all of us together. It's the day after Christmas. Speckler is here. He convinced his parents not to go along with them to Florida, telling them I was feeling depressed and needed his best friend. He gave them a story that I was missing my brother and was feeling like jumping in front of a moving train. They believed him, and let him stay with me.

It was a strange reunion between Speck and me. We had just made up as friends, and then I go and get whisked off to another universe leaving him to make up some excuse. He apologized for not having a good story to tell Carnofsky. I told him there was nothing he could have done, it happened so fast. But it was probably better this way, now that the FBI are involved.

I haven't left the house since my return. Polley thinks it's best to stay low. He wanted to meet the others involved in this—Mungo and Charlie. Especially Charlie, since it happened to him first. He did a video interview with Charlie and then one with me. We're waiting on information from his superior, a man named Richard Gost. Polley says he went to Quantico, the FBI Academy, with Gost. It didn't sound like he liked him. Maybe it's jealousy. Gost has obviously risen up in the ranks while Polley is still a low-level field agent. Well, at least he won't be low-level after this.

Later that Sunday morning, after my trip in the farm field, Polley went home and thought about all this for a long while. I asked him if he had his big drink and he smiled and said "several." Then he called and woke up his superior—Division Chief Gost—and said he had important information that couldn't wait. He drove to his house and explained everything. That night, along with a very skeptical Gost, we drove back out to the farm fields, this time with Speckler. I told them I wouldn't do it unless he was there. I also told Polley I wanted a different field with the excuse that it wouldn't look good if the farmer did see people two days in a row. I didn't say anything about the Bruzer scarecrow.

Once more I crossed over and this convinced Polley's boss. Things were moving now, but not moving fast enough to suit any of us.

"Why doesn't the president know yet?" asks Charlie. He's been hostile to Polley ever since he was brought in. Mungo told me he's gotten worse since finding out we've been spied on by the alien infiltrators. He thinks an invasion might be imminent.

"That will take time," Polley tells him. "Gost is busy getting to the director. Once he has the Director of the FBI on board then he'll get the president."

"I can't just keep popping in and out of one universe into the next for each person," I say. "I convinced you and Gost, isn't that enough? How come he doesn't have a team of agents on this? An army of agents should be all over the city looking for those two."

Polley smiles. "Look at me kid. I'm forty-seven years old and I live alone. I've been a special agent my entire life and I figured I'd retire as one. The reason I was called into your case was that it was Christmas time and everyone else has family and are off enjoying the holidays. So it landed on my desk. Most of the shit cases land on my desk. So when Gost's superiors hear the story I'm going to tell them they'll look at me and think I'm drunk and crazy. Poor drunken Polley, they'll say. Never got to advance and so now in the twilight of his career he's gone off the reservation. It'll take a lot of convincing, so if you have to pop over a dozen times then so be it."

"All right. Sorry. I know it's not easy, but I've never been good at waiting."

"So what's the plan, G-Man?" Speckler asks.

Polley's eyes narrow and he has a strained look on his face. Putting up with Charlie's paranoia is one thing, but Speckler's wackiness is something else. And Speck seems to have gone out of his way to clash with Polley. For one thing, Speck now sees our little group as not just the Super Friends, but as the Avengers. It's us against the aliens and he's ready to go toe-to-toe, mano y mano with them. Just what Polley doesn't want—a total loose cannon ready to misfire at any moment.

"The plan, *Ralph*,"—he refuses to call him Speckler—"is to observe. Keep an eye out and look for anything suspicious. You all have the photo of the two men."

We nod.

"And if we see them?" Speck asks.

"Do nothing—and I repeat, do nothing but call me."

"I think we should all be given guns," Speckler whispers to me. "Pretty little Glock, loaded and locked." He points his fingers in the shape of a gun and pretends to be taking it out of a shoulder holster.

"Put that away," I tell him.

"Gost should be moving faster on this," Charlie says. He's pacing about the room, slamming his fist into his palm. "Who knows what's happening on the other side?" He stops and points at me. "You should cross over, Ryan. Find out what's happening. You said there are aliens from this world who infiltrated them? You've made contact with them. Go back and find out what they know. They could be planning an attack at any minute."

I shake my head. "I don't think that's possible. They'd have to have the ability to cross over and back and Tarak assured me the Zs haven't discovered that yet. Besides, it's impossible to contact him. It's not like he has a phone where I can call or text."

"Maybe he doesn't know as much as he says he does. How do you even know he's on our side? Maybe it's all part of their plan."

"He gave me this didn't he?" I indicate the device. It's locked on tight and activated. I can't take the chance that I've been spotted by the aliens so I've decided to keep it always on, always activated.

"You think that means he's trustworthy? It could be nothing but a Trojan horse. This device he gave you might be the prototype and they've tricked you into testing it out for them."

"Calm down, Charlie," Mungo says. "You're acting paranoid."

"Christ! We should all be paranoid! Am I the only one who knows how serious this is?"

"I think we all know how serious this is," Polley says.

"Come on, Charlie. Let's go get some air." Mungo takes him by the arm and hustles him upstairs.

"Sorry about, Charlie," I tell Polley. "I shouldn't have told him that his double was killed while perfecting this technique. I think I might have pushed him over the edge."

"You're friend's been over the edge for a while. That's the last thing we need right now—for him—for any of you—to go off half-cocked and blow this thing."

"I for one am going full-cocked," Speckler says. Once more the finger-gun comes out.

Polley and I both shake our heads at him.

The rest of the week goes by with nothing new happening. There's been no news from Gost. In the meantime, I've been a prisoner in my own home, feeling locked up down in the basement like the village idiot. Polley says he can't risk me getting seen by the aliens who might be watching the house.

I don't know what I'm going to do come Sunday morning. I haven't told Polley about my planned rendezvous with Violet. I certainly don't plan on missing it, but I hate to risk the whole thing. What if the Zs are watching the house? Maybe they've moved in next door. The Henderson's haven't been seen in months. Sure, they said they were going to Phoenix for the winter, but is it true? Maybe they were under the influence of alien technology. Maybe they weren't the Hendersons. If these aliens can take our form maybe they can change forms to look like any of us. Sure, in the photos they looked nothing like the Hendersons, but who knows?

Mom and Dad are even worse. They've been treating *me* like an alien. It was bad enough when Dad looked at me like I was on drugs, now I'm the crazy parallel-universe crossing teenager. Maybe he's thinking I'm the double. I haven't even told them about Jack. I didn't want to. Mom hinted about it once and I really had to hold my tongue to keep from saying anything. If I told her that Jack's double is alive and well on the other side I'm afraid she'll want to steal the device and cross over herself. I can just picture her running around the other world asking for Jack Whitaker.

Sunday finally arrives. The library will be open in a couple of hours and I plan on being the first customer in. I've heard nothing from Polley in the last two days. During our last conversation he assured me that Gost had spoken with at least the Deputy Director of the FBI. I don't know what his reaction was, but no one has come knocking on my door and I haven't had to pop over into the other universe to prove my story to anyone else since Gost.

"I need to get out of here," I tell Speck. He's been sleeping over every night. His family is due back in another week. His parents have called him every day to check on him and to make sure I haven't offed myself.

"Going stir crazy? I can imagine. You want me to run over to my house and bring you back some more movies?"

"No. I'm sick of watching movies about alien invasions. If I have to watch *Independence Day* one more time I'm going to cross over and never come back. But this is different. I didn't tell you this."

I tell him about my appointment with Violet at the library. If nothing has happened then she should be there waiting for me. I don't want to think of the other scenarios—if she didn't make it back, or if the Red Coats grabbed her.

"But Polley said you can't leave. In fact, he personally told me my number one job in all this is to make sure you stay put."

"Really? He said that?"

"Yeah, really. And it would be kind of a dick move if I fail in the one thing I've been tasked to do."

"You know what else would be a dick move?"

"What's that?"

"Not helping your best friend when he needs you the most."

"I see your point. But what if it goes wrong? What if the president's on his way over right now?"

"Don't you think Polley would have called me if the president were on his way?"

"Good point. How long do you plan on crossing over for?"

"I don't know. I know I can't stay long, but once over there I'm sure it's going to be hard to leave her. She's all I've been able to think about this past week. Not even meeting the president is as important as seeing her again. In fact, I'd blow off all the presidents on earth just to see her again."

"She's that important to you?"

"Yeah, she really is that important to me."

"I guess I was pretty stupid to think you'd ever have a thing for Amy."

"Yeah, it was pretty stupid. I wish you could meet Violet. I wish I could bring her here where it's safe."

He nods and rests his hand on my shoulder. "Okay, so how do we do this crazy thang?"

"I can't tell Mom and Dad. Dad would go ape shit if he knew I was going to go to a public place and cross over. It's hard enough for him to agree to me crossing over in a farm field at night out in the middle of nowhere. So I need to sneak out and hope that they'll understand. I'll leave them a note telling them not to worry and that I'll be back soon. Like that'll do any good." And then I think of it. "Yeah. Go up and tell my mom that you're going back to your house to get some more movies, and then you'll go over to Mungo's to get some comic books. Check out where my dad is. If it's clear then as you leave just come around the back and give a knock on the window. I'll have it open so I can squeeze out."

It works better than I thought. My dad is off running errands. My mom was cleaning the kitchen. She offered to take Speck home but he said he could use the exercise. The only difficult part is squeezing out the tiny basement window. But I manage to do it and together we head off to the train.

We reach the library a few minutes before they open. There's already a group waiting. Mostly homeless people who need a warm place to stay all day and a clean bathroom to use.

I lead Speckler up to the second floor to the same spot where Violet and I spent the night together.

"It's not the most romantic spot in the world," he says when he sees it.

"It's even worse when it's completely destroyed."

"What did they do with all the books?" he asks.

"Used them as firewood I guess."

"Or toilet paper."

"Both are in short supply."

I check to make sure it's clear. "Okay, there's no one around now, but what about when I return? What if there's a whole class of kids doing research on—" I remove a book from a shelf and read the title: "*Mating Rituals of the South Sea Islands.*"

"Don't worry about that," Speck assures me. "If you return at a set time, I'll make sure there's no one around."

"How will you do that?"

He smiles. "I've got my ways."

I laugh. "Okay. What time though?"

"How much time do you need?"

A week. A month. A year. A lifetime. "Can you give me . . . two hours?"

"Take four," he says. "The place closes at five, so there shouldn't be many people in here. I'll just take this to pass the time." He takes the book from my hands. "So be sure to return at five o'clock. Does your watch work over there?"

"Yeah, it should." We synchronize our watches so that we're on the exact same time.

"Good luck," he says. "And give her a kiss for me."

"Go get your own kisses. Amy is still available."

"I'd rather kiss a wolverine," he says.

"You say that now. Maybe Nancy . . ."

"She only has eyes for you. Both of them do. It's not easy living in your shadow."

"Shut up. My shadow? That tiny little sliver? When I get back we're going to get you a girlfriend. I may even get Agent Polley involved."

"So I need the full resources of the FBI to get me a date? How pathetic."

We both laugh. It feels good. I'm anxious to go and I tell him I'll see him at exactly five o'clock. We shake hands awkwardly as if I'm about to go on a long journey. In a way I guess it is. I say a silent prayer, hoping she'll be there when I cross over. I'm nervous as hell as I punch in the code and disappear into another universe.

She's waiting for me.

Her face lights up when I materialize. Mine as well. She rushes forward and she's in my arms and I'm holding her once again. "Did you have any problem?" I ask once we finally unclench.

"None," she says.

"No Scavengers to worry about?"

"No. Strange they seem to be getting fewer and fewer. I wonder if the Zs are rounding them up?"

"Has there been any trouble in camp with Hanes and Doyle?"

"Not much, other than cutting our rations at the market. I don't know for how long but if they continue it much longer they'll have a riot on their hands. Even Uncle Tolliver is now siding with Brody on this one. He's talking about taking the Red Coats down."

"That'll have terrible consequences," I say. "The Zs?"

"Will probably destroy the entire camp. We're talking about having a mass exodus if it comes to that. If we take out the Red

Coats, we'll scatter. Take off in all parts of the city and keep going. Most will head south since its warmer there."

"What about your plans to go out east in search of Jack and the others?"

"I don't know. Things are changing quickly."

I don't like the sound of this, the doubt in her voice, the fear. Now, more than ever, I want to bring her back with me. But I can't. And then her face changes and she erases the fear and once more it's the strong beautiful face I remember. "What about you? How is it going on your side?"

I tell her about Polley and Gost and the madness of waiting to hear if they talked to the president. I tell her how I'm going crazy forced to be a prisoner in my own home.

She's worried that I might have made a mistake by coming here. "Ryan, promise me you won't do anything stupid just for me. If you don't show up I'll understand you had a good reason not to. I don't want you to put your life in danger for me."

"It's not dangerous," I assure her. "I'm sure the Zs still think I'm hiding out somewhere in this world. They don't know the power I have with this." I indicate the device. "Oh, I almost forgot. I brought you something." I take the present from my pocket, a small box wrapped in red and green Santa Claus wrapping with a pink bow on top.

She looks at it curiously. "What is it?"

"A Christmas present. I don't know if anyone still celebrates Christmas—"

"Not like they used to. But some of us still gather in secret to pray and sing the old songs. Father Wu leads us in remembrances of the old ways." She looks at the box, not sure what to do.

"You just rip open the wrapping. Don't worry. It's how everyone does it, especially if you're a kid. There's nothing better than Christmas morning when you're a kid. Seeing all those presents under the tree and going wild ripping them open. Go ahead, open it."

She rips off the paper and opens the box. "It's a necklace," she says. "What is it?" she asks, studying the talisman.

"It's called a dreamcatcher. It's a Native American symbol. It's supposed to protect you from bad dreams and only let the good dreams in. I remember you telling me about the nightmares of chasing after your parents. Do you like it?"

"Like it? I love it." She throws her arms around me and kisses me. It feels so right. Perfect. I never thought I could feel this way about someone. I always thought Speckler was a fool deluding himself that he was in love.

"Let me put it on you." I lock it around her neck underneath the collar. It's definitely a much better accessory than the collar. "I sent my friend Speckler to look all over the city for it. There. Let me see."

"How do I look?"

"Beautiful," I tell her.

She blushes. "Really?"

"Really."

She kisses me again.

"I also brought you this." I pull out a chocolate bar. "I hope you're not allergic to chocolate."

"I don't think I am. I haven't had it since I was a little girl." She tears into the chocolate like it's also a Christmas present.

"I can bring small things with me when I cross over. Ask Tolliver and Father Wu. I can bring medicine, other small things. I wish I could bring a thousand of these chocolate bars and a ton of other things. Unfortunately, it has to be small things I can fit in my pocket. But I can cross over and over. Maybe guns?"

"I'll ask him. Guns would work. I know that's what Brody would want. Medicine definitely."

"Okay. I'll talk to Agent Polley and hopefully they can start getting it together."

The rest of our time goes by quickly, and the next thing I know it's time to return. We make a promise to meet again in another week. Same time. I ask her if Tarak or Tanis has contacted her.

"No. Neither of them."

"I wish I had some way to make contact with him. I wonder what's been happening on the mothership. Hopefully, I'll have better news for you next time I see you. Maybe I'll have met with the president by then."

We kiss and cling to each other. I tell her to be safe and don't take any chances. She tells me the same thing. I check the time, dreading the moment when the second hand indicates exactly five o'clock.

"I have to go now." I step away and raise a hand to wave goodbye. She waves goodbye in return. I punch in the code and cross back over.

There's less of a headache this time but I still feel nauseous. I don't spew up anything though.

It takes several seconds to orient myself to my universe. It's not easy standing in the same place in two different worlds. Speckler is standing by the bookshelves. I guess he didn't have to do anything to clear the area out. I half expected him to be streaking buck-naked across the library with everyone in hot pursuit. I smile and begin to tell him everything that happened but the look on his face tells me something's wrong. Two men step out from behind him. One has a gun in his hand with a silencer on it. They're wearing suits but I know they're not FBI. I recognize them instantly. They're the two Zoktari infiltrators.

"I'm sorry, Ryan," Speckler says.

"Don't worry. It's not your fault, Speck."

"You both will come with us," one of the Zs says. They look human, but if you study them more closely you can tell they're not. Their skin is white—too white. They have no hair on their face—no eyebrows or lashes. They both have hats but I can only guess they have no hair upon their heads either.

"If we don't go with you?"

He waves the gun. "We will kill you both." I know he means to do it. Why not? His people killed millions. What are two more?

They have a car parked across the street. They put us in the back. The one with the gun sits up front but keeps the gun pointed at us. The other one drives south.

"Where are we going?" I ask.

"To our home. You will be our guests."

"Why? What do you want?"

"How did you cross back?"

They can't see the device, covered up by the sleeve of my jacket. I don't say anything.

"You will tell us," he says plainly. The simplicity of the statement and all it implies sends shivers down my spine.

I look at Speckler. The comment got to him as well. He looks nervous and afraid. I'm also afraid but at least I have a means to escape. All I need to do is punch in the code and I'm gone. But

Speckler is stuck, and if I disappear what will stop them from killing him? I have to make sure he's safe first before I try to escape.

We don't drive very far, heading out into an industrial section of the city. We pull in front of an old factory building standing alone. It looks abandoned. They take us inside. It is abandoned, except for some very sophisticated computer equipment that would make Bill Gates salivate with envy. What they have set up I'm sure is light years ahead of what we have.

They pull out a couple of chairs and sit us down.

"So I will ask you again—how did you cross over?"

I hesitate, my brain scrambling to find something to tell them. But it's too late. He fires the gun, shooting Speckler, who falls back. Without thinking I dive at the Z knocking him to the ground. He wasn't prepared for that, which gives me a slight advantage. I'm able to knock the gun out of his hand, which skids across the concrete floor of the warehouse. The other Z immediately goes for the gun. I'm glad they both aren't armed. I punch the Z in the face. It dazes him. I get to my feet and run for the door while punching in the code.

"Stop!" the other Z yells.

I turn around just as I begin to cross over. There's a look of astonishment on his face as he sees me fading out then fires several shots at me.

When I fade into the other world I immediately check myself for wounds. None of the bullets have hit me. I crossed over just in time; a second later and I would probably be dead. Just like Speckler. I can't believe those bastards shot him! All I think about now is getting revenge.

I look around. The warehouse is nearly destroyed. There's no roof and it tilts downward on one side. Luckily I'm in a safe area. I run outside to the back of the warehouse. I punch in the code and cross back. I look around for something I can use as a weapon and see an old two-by-four. Just as I bend down to pick it up someone grabs me from behind, clamping a hand over my mouth. I think it's the Zs as I'm dragged back behind a small shed. Polley is there in a flak vest. He's armed. The one holding me is an agent, outfitted in full combat gear. He lets me go.

"They killed Speck! They shot him just to get me to talk!"

Polley curses. "Why didn't you stay put?"

"I know. It's all my fault." Tears are in my eyes. My best friend is dead and I can't believe how stupid I was.

"Okay, forget it. How many are inside?"

"Just the two of them. How did you find us?"

"Your folks called me and said you pulled a Steve McQueen and made a great escape. We didn't know where you went but then I remembered you saying you wanted to cross over at the library. I wondered why there. I figured it was special in some way—maybe having to do with that girl. I pulled up just in time to see both of you being taken out."

"I just had to see her. I know it was stupid and I never should have done it." I'm practically sobbing, wracked with guilt over causing my best friend's death.

"All right. What's done is done. We need to go in and extract these two. What else did you see inside? Weapons?"

"Just the one gun I think." I tell him about the computer equipment.

"Okay, good. Let's do this quick." He gets on the radio and tells the agents they're going in. There are several glass windows and they shoot gas canisters inside. Several agents in gas masks rush the door and burst in. Gunfire is heard and then one agent comes running out carrying Speckler over his shoulder. They just make it before the other agents come out screaming to get down. There's an explosion and the whole warehouse erupts in a giant fireball.

Chapter Nineteen
Uprising

All the agents made it out alive, but just barely. The alien infiltrators never made it out. I guessed they planned it that way in case their cover was blown.

"They had the whole placed rigged," the agent tells Polley. I hear the scream of sirens. Ambulances and other emergency vehicles must be on their way. "Your friend," he tells me, "is still alive."

I rush over to Speckle who manages a smile despite the pain. He's shot in the side. It doesn't look serious but there's a lot of blood. "Hold on, Speck."

"I guess we got them," he says.

"We got them."

"Dynamic duo," he says weakly and raises his fist.

"Yeah," I respond, my voice choking. "Dynamic duo."

When the ambulance arrives, the paramedics give Speck a quick patch-up to stop the flow of blood, load him on a gurney, and pop him into the back of the ambulance as if they were closing him in a drawer at the morgue. I want to ride with them but Polley holds me back. He tells me I'll need to debrief the others.

"What others? Has Gost returned?"

Polley nods. "And he's not alone."

"The president?"

"No, not yet. But the Director of the FBI is here as well as the Secretary of Defense and several top NASA scientists. Expect them to have the most questions. Also be prepared for all of them to be skeptical. Remember, only Gost and myself have seen this so they'll want more proof than just the word of two agents—even if one of them is a Regional Director. It took some time to get them all to come out here. You can't imagine what it took to get them this far."

"I can imagine."

I don't want to go. To hell with all these big wigs! My best friend may die because of me, but Polley convinces me that I have to see the bigger picture. He tells me they're waiting for me at a highly secured location. The fact that all of them are here is top secret, no one in Washington except for the very top officials even knows about the trip. They all came separately and arrived in as much a low profile as possible.

After some reluctance I agree, but make him promise to take me right to the hospital once we finish.

"It's a deal," he says.

After paramedics check me out I'm given the okay. Polley calls my parents to tell them I'm fine and that he'll bring me home once I've had a chance to tell my story to the others and check on Speckler at the hospital. It's clear from the conversation that my dad doesn't like this but what can he do?

We drive almost an hour to a secluded suburb outside the city. A lot of thick woods and towering pine trees surround a very expensive-looking home with a tall black iron gate out front. I figure it to be some kind of safe house. Men in black suits with earpieces open up the gate to let us in.

Gost is inside with several other men and women sitting around the living room talking and drinking coffee and tea. They all stand up when we enter, a look of eagerness on some faces, serious skepticism on most of the others. I'm introduced to the Director of the FBI as well as to the Secretary of Defense and to the rest of the team. I can't remember anyone's name. All I can think about is my friend lying on an operating table. Polley told me the hospital would call as soon as he came out of surgery, so I try to put these thoughts aside until I know more. Polley tried to reassure me, telling me it was a low caliber pistol and that the wound didn't look life threatening.

They all want to hear from me so I give my story. All of it. From the beginning. They listen and take notes and ask many questions over and over. Polley was right, the NASA guys have the most questions. Most are technical, scientific gobbledygook that maybe if I went to MIT or took a load of advanced quantum physics classes I might make some sense out of, but my interests have all been artistic not scientific, so I just shake my head and tell them over and over I don't know, I don't know, I don't know.

I show them the device. They all crowd around to get a good look at it, to feel it, tap on it, and study its display window. The NASA guys want to immediately take it apart and I say no way. "It's the only thing that keeps me from being dragged into another universe." They look at each other and smile. Another universe? They'll want a demonstration of course. Proof.

"Is this even possible?" the Secretary of Defense asks. She's a tall woman with a gaze that could melt steel. She also has one of the strongest handshakes I ever felt. I had to make sure there weren't any broken bones afterward. As the first female Secretary of Defense, she has a reputation of being a hawk on defense in order that no one thinks she's soft. I figure this should work in my favor.

"Up until now, the idea of multiple universes has only been a theory," a tall white-haired NASA scientist explains.

"It still seems like a theory," she says. "Even if the boy does disappear how do we know he's going to another universe?"

"Where else could he go?"

"Who knows? His parents' garage? A science lab somewhere? All I'm saying is that we only have his word on this. There's no pictures or video of this other world. If he really does disappear, we have no proof that he goes to a parallel universe."

"The kid disappears all right," Division Chief Gost says. "Both Mitch and I seen it happen. Right Mitch?"

Polley nods. "I believe what Ryan says is a hundred percent correct. We're scraping up samples of alien DNA right now. And not from a parallel universe, but right here in this one."

"We'll get to that in time," she says. "The supposed aliens—"

"There's nothing supposed about it," I burst out. "They almost killed my best friend! And I told you I took some video but one of the Scavengers took my phone."

She turns her tense gaze on me. "Then was killed by one of the alien ships? Is that it?"

"Yes. I know it sounds unbelievable, but it's true." I hold up the device. "Isn't this proof enough? Nothing like this exists. It's alien technology."

"Calm down, Ryan," Polley says.

"I can't calm down. My friend gets shot by one of those aliens who infiltrated us. And those people over there are suffering far worse. We have to get them help. Food, medicine, weapons."

"What do you want? To declare war on a race that we aren't even sure exists for a people we also aren't sure exists?" So much for being a hawk.

"What if they do exist?" asks the FBI Director. "We can't turn our backs on—what would basically be ourselves. If this is true, then those people over there are us. We have to consider an attack on them an attack on us. It amounts to the same thing."

"You know what else amounts to the same thing?" I say. "When they finally perfect this technology—and Tarak says they're pretty close—then an attack on us will be almost certain. Helping them now will help us later before it's too late. You weren't there. You didn't see what they did to the city. How completely destroyed everything is. The millions who have died."

The Secretary of Defense looks at me, her gaze softening just a bit. "Okay, Ryan. But you're asking a lot. Not just of us but of yourself as well. Do you know what this means? Do you know how much your life will change?"

"It's already changed. And I'll do whatever it takes to help them. I don't care about myself."

"Why is it you care so much," she asks. "Is it the fear that what they did there will happen here?"

"That's part of it. But I've met these people over there. I've seen them suffering. And like you said," I turn to the FBI Director. "They are us. I've seen my own double being used like a damn lab rat. I've seen them blast people to bits. They don't care how much suffering and death they cause. We have to stop them. And I'll do whatever it takes. But you have to believe me. You have to trust me."

"We'll need to see if that works first."

"Of course."

"And if it does?" the FBI Director wonders. "We can't tell the American people about this. Imagine the uproar."

"How do we make a formal declaration of war without telling anyone? I'm sure you mean Congress as well?" someone asks.

"We can't keep this to ourselves then," the white-haired NASA guy says. "The whole world will be affected by this. The whole world *is* affected by it."

The Secretary of Defense shakes her head. "That's up to the president to decide if and when he lets other leaders know. Right now we have to play this one step at a time. This is a whole new territory we're stepping in and right now we don't have all the facts."

"So not even Congress will know right now?"

"God, especially them. The whole story would be leaked in ten minutes. But we don't make any formal declaration. It's been done before. Too many times, but this is different. Right now it's a humanitarian effort. We'll have to wait and see if it stays that way."

The NASA guy turns to Polley. "What about the two aliens? What do we do about them?"

"As I said, whatever remains are left from the blast site are being scraped together right now. We'll analyze what we get, but it won't be much. I don't know what it will tell us. I wished we'd gotten them whole, so we could find out how they take on our appearance. For all we know they could have hundreds here. Thousands."

The meeting eventually ends. I answered all the questions I could answer. They'll need a couple of days to set up the demonstration. It has to be done so that no one observes it.

Polley takes me to the hospital. Speckler is out of surgery. The doctor says he's lucky that the bullet passed right through him without hitting any major organs. There are two agents standing guard out front of his room. He'll like that he's being treated with such high security.

"Did we get them?" he asks weakly.

I tell him what happened right after he was shot.

"You idiot," he says. "You always have to play the hero don't you?"

"Hero? I was running for my life scared shitless. A second later and I'd be dead—it was that close."

"I guess Violet would never know how close she came to being a widow."

"A widow? We're not married, Speck."

He gives me a grin. "Not yet," he says.

"I don't think it's ethical to marry someone from another universe."

"At best it's a gray area. What was it like meeting with the honchos?"

"Frustrating. I had to answer every question a million times."

"Are you crossing over again for them?"

"Yeah. They'll need to secure a spot and make sure the area is blocked off. It's all very top secret. But at least it should convince some of them."

"Why not all of them?"

I tell him what the Secretary of Defense said.

"Your garage? What do they think, that you invented a teleporter as a school science project? What have they been smoking?"

We laugh and he winces in pain.

"No more jokes until you get better," I tell him.

"That shouldn't be long. Doc says I should be out of here in a week. At least I'll have as cool a scar as your girlfriend."

"Yeah, too bad you can't tell anyone how you got it."

His face drops. "What are you talking about?"

"Polley says you can't tell anyone that an alien shot you. Not even your parents when they get here."

"What's the story then?"

"Polley says he'll come up with one and brief you on it. Something simple like getting mugged."

"How are they going to explain the explosion in broad daylight?"

"A gas leak. Polley says the government's pretty good at inventing stories and covering up the truth. Leave it to the experts he says. He even said they'll give the school a story what happened with my disappearance so they don't suspend me for going AWOL during the field trip."

"Well, that's convenient. Do you think they can get me out of Mrs. Lardmuller's Calculus midterm?"

I leave him to recuperate. Polley's arranged an agent to drive me home where my parents are waiting for me. My father's angry but doesn't yell at me. They've been told what happened but obviously not all the details. I fill them in on what they don't know. My mom says she was so upset about Ralph but they wouldn't even tell her what hospital he was sent to. I tell her that Speck is doing fine.

"At least it's over then," my father says. "The two aliens— they're dead?"

"Yeah—they had the warehouse rigged. I guess in case they were discovered and to destroy all their evidence. But it's not over yet. It's just starting."

"What do you mean? They got the aliens—what more do they want?"

"It wasn't just about the aliens here. It's about what's happening over there. There's a war on over there."

"Yes—their war, not ours. Why do we have to get involved with their war? I lost one son already to war, I'm not losing another."

"Dad, it's what we chose. If Jack we're here he'd tell you the same thing. You can't decide which war is worth fighting and which isn't. You were so happy when Jack went off—"

"Happy? Is that what you think? Listen, Ryan, I was so terrified the moment he got his orders I couldn't sleep at night. I worried for him every second of every day, and when they drove up in front of our house and told me he was dead I was almost relieved. Not relieved that he was dead, but relieved that finally I can stop being afraid of the worst because the worst has happened. It's done. It's over. I'm not about to start it again with you."

"I never knew that. I wish you had told me, but it doesn't make any difference. I'm sorry, Dad, but I can't live my life for you. I have to live it for me and make my own choices. I know it can get me killed. I hope it doesn't. I don't want to die but I don't want others to die as well and if I can do something, anything, to keep that from happening then I'm going to do it."

"You're right I don't like it," he says. "You'll understand that some day when you become a father."

"I know I will. Can you at least trust me?"

"After what you did today? How can I?"

"I was wrong to sneak out. I know that. If I'd been honest maybe Speckler wouldn't have gotten shot. I promise I'll be nothing but honest from now on."

My mother circles her arm around me. "You don't have to do this alone. You think you have to but you don't. Let the experts do their job."

"They still need me. As long as I have the device that lets me cross over then I have to help. Dad?"

His face is stern, jaw set, reminding me of Violet when she stood up to her uncle. "You're telling me everything, no matter how you think we'll react."

"Absolutely."

A couple of nights later we're driven out to another spot. They have roadblocks set up and a farmhouse has been taken over. I don't ask what happened to the family. Maybe they told them they won a free trip to Hawaii. Maybe they're buried out in the cornfield. I'm sure it's best not to ask questions. Whatever has happened, we're alone out here.

They have lots of equipment set up. Cameras and radiation detection devices and medical devices I guess if I come back with a missing limb or my head on backwards.

The crossing goes smoothly. The headache and nausea is less. Everyone is amazed when I return a few minutes later. After I've been thoroughly checked out the NASA scientists immediately start bombarding me with questions. How does it feel? What do I see? Can I control where I land? I answer them as best as I can.

"If you need further proof I can get video, pictures, when I cross over. The mothership is big enough that I can get a good image of it in the daytime."

"That'll be helpful," the Secretary of Defense says. Her eyes are wide.

The next morning I cross over and get them the video of the mothership and several of the Ravens flying about. They give me a camera with a powerful zoom so I can get as much detail as possible. This is given to the NASA guys to analyze.

A week later, while the honchos are still discussing what to do, I cross over and meet Violet at the library, which has been "closed for renovation." I tell her what's been happening. "And Violet—we got them. The infiltrators. We stopped them."

"How?"

I tell her what happened. She then tells me what's been going on in camp. Hanes has been ruthless. Doyle runs around harassing anyone and everyone. People are starving and winter hasn't fully set in yet. She tells me Tolliver and Brody are still considering taking them down.

"You won't have to now. There's enough food for everyone. Or there will be. I'll start making trips every hour of every day. I can fill this whole library with food and whatever else you need. Tell them all this. Maybe they can convince the Red Coats to join them."

"Maybe some. The young ones. Those who recently joined their ranks. But Hanes and Doyle and the other leaders? They won't give up their luxuries."

I'm determined to help her more than anything. I ask her if she can bring Tolliver and maybe Father Wu with her to be interviewed in order to let our government know what's really happening. Violet says of course and we plan on meeting again tomorrow.

The next day, both men give as much details as they can about the Zs and the Resistance. Father Wu has a list of medical supplies they need most. Both men urge our government for food and basic supplies. "People are starving," Tolliver pleads. "Cold, and malnourished. Most of all, we need weapons. Guns, ammo, explosives. If the Zs mean to blow us to kingdom come before leaving then we aim to put up as much of a fight as possible."

It's a good interview and both men are quite persuasive. The only thing that would have been better is if I could get Tarak on camera. But neither he nor Tanis has been seen or heard since giving me the device. I hope they haven't been captured. If they have it may help speed up the discovery of transuniversal travelling. Who knows, they could already be planning on crossing over with a mass attack. Maybe they've begun to suspect something's wrong since the two Zoktari infiltrators haven't checked in with them.

Violet tells me she needs to be back in camp to help her aunt Alice, who's suddenly come down with the flu. They have very little medicine to treat those who are sick. She promises to come back in three days.

Back in my world, once the videos are screened and scrutinized, everyone is convinced. The president agrees to begin helping the people of Earth 2 as they've begun to be called in an effort now known as Operation Bread Knife. The library is taken over as smoothly as the farmhouse. It's closed down and no one is allowed in. Undercover agents with the highest clearance are stationed all around. No one goes in or out without authorization.

"What's the mayor being told?" I ask Polley.

"Luckily he and the president are golfing buddies," he says.

Every day we experiment with how much I can bring over. We discover that I can carry a medium size backpack, fully loaded. I start bringing food over. Bags of rice, flour, corn meal, salt, packages of military rations, vitamins. They have dark delivery vans pulling into the loading dock of the library, but instead of books they deliver food, guns, medicine. I make trip after trip crossing over with as much as I can until Polley tells me I have to stop and rest.

"You can't keep doing this, Ryan," he says. "Look at yourself. You're exhausted. I don't want you killing yourself."

"I can handle it," I tell him. "My body is getting used to the crossing. I don't have hardly any headaches at all now. Besides, the more I can do the better. I want Violet and her people to have a real Christmas for once."

"That's noble of you kid, but pace yourself is all I'm saying."

"All right. I will. But winter is here and those people don't have much. Many are sick and hungry. And I think it's getting worse for them. Violet said that Hanes is cutting rations. Who knows what else he's doing."

"Hanes? He's the one who guards them? What did you call them—Red Coats?"

"Yeah, Red Coats. They're cowards and bullies. Collaborators trying to save themselves by turning against their own people. I tried to reason with him, but he wouldn't listen."

"The world has always had people like Hanes. Selfish profiteers and vampires who suck the life blood out of people."

"So you see why I have to do this?"

"Okay. Just . . . well, take care of yourself is all. It won't help them if you collapse from exhaustion."

I keep working day and night bringing over supplies. I sleep very little. On the other side, the entire area of the library is now filled with items stacked high. I just hope that Scavengers don't come up here and find all this. Or Zs. When the three days are up I cross over early in the morning. I couldn't sleep at all thinking what Violet will say when she sees it all.

When I cross I catch her looking through all the items.

"Happy New Year," I whisper so I don't startle her.

After a big hug and an even bigger kiss she says, "What is all this?"

"Food, medicine, guns. We did it, Violet. We convinced them. My government. And there's plenty more where this came from. Get the others to help you bring it back. You'll have to make several trips.

I have no time limit since I don't have to worry about being seen when I cross back. We talk some more and I tell her about Speckler and his recovery. He's out of the hospital and doing well. He wants to help but he has to take it easy.

The time comes for me to finally return. "Bring Tolliver and the others to help transport it back," I tell her before I cross back. "Ask them what else I can bring."

213

She does, and the next day when I cross they're all there—Tolliver and Brody and Father Wu and several others. They've already carried out most of the supplies in the library. They've had to be careful, not just with the Zs and Bruzers, but also with their own people. They've set up several locations near camp as a safe spot but the hard part for them is to get word they now have plenty of extra food, clothing, blankets and medicine. Their worried about causing a riot, or worse, of tipping off the Red Coats. If Hanes and Doyle find out then it's all over.

Tolliver shakes my hand and Father Wu gives me a big hug.

"You don't know what this means to us," Tolliver says.

Even Brody is no longer his sarcastic angry self. "Tell them we need more weapons. Grenades. RPGs. Explosives. Lots of explosives." His eyes glitter with the excitement of getting his hands on something more powerful than a kitchen knife or a shocker.

"I'll see what I can do," I say. "But remember, it has to be small enough to fit in my backpack."

"Thank them for us," Father Wu says. "Give them our blessing. This is indeed a happy new year for all of us."

"I will. But really, you both did a great job convincing them. A lot of them were still skeptical about what was happening. They might have just given you food, but not weapons. You convinced them otherwise. What else do you need? More clothing?"

"That would be good. It's getting colder. The children suffer the most. Hats, gloves for them. Scarves. But the food. That is the best thing for them. They can fight the cold when there is real food in their bellies and not just warm broth."

I wonder what has happened with Tarak. Violet tells me he hasn't made contact with them. I don't like that. Almost two weeks have gone by since they gave me the device to return to my own world. What could he be doing? Do they even know that the Zoktari infiltrators are dead? I wish there was some way I could communicate with him.

The winter break is over and finally Speckler and I return to school. After what I've been through in the last two weeks the place seems distant and strange, as if I graduated years ago. I feel older. The daily trials of navigating high school with its petty jealousies and frivolous concerns seem a world away. Who can care about over-hyped dances and stupid school rules when there are aliens bent on our destruction? But both Speckler and I have to make the appearance that everything is normal. Polley spoke to the principal and Mr. C and told them that my leaving the field trip was unavoidable, a family emergency came up that I couldn't talk about but is now resolved. Neither of them was given any more details than that. They didn't like it but what can they do? It was from the FBI. Speckler enjoys the secrecy. He feels like a secret agent.

Everyone quickly finds out that Speckler was shot. How could they not? He has his shirt up on the first day showing off his wound. The story he tells is that he was attacked by muggers who then shot him. His version is that he fought them off and even managed to knock one out. One-Punch Speckler Wally begins to call him. Speck eats it up. I even notice Amy warming up to him. She touches the wound tentatively. He's smiling. Maybe there's hope for them yet.

When the school day is over we rush to the library to continue taking things over. The president hasn't made a decision yet on whether to tell the other leaders about the parallel universe. He'll have to make a decision soon.

After a week of bringing supplies over I find that the supplies from the day before haven't been touched and the library is vacant. They've had several Resistance fighters standing guard just in case a Scavenger or Bruzer happened to show up. I don't like this. It doesn't feel right and I think something is wrong. I go down the stairs to the outside. I can hear explosions in the distance and see flashes of light. There's black smoke in the sky coming from the direction of the camp. I want to run over there but it would take too long. I immediately cross back and find Polley.

"Something's happening," I tell him. "I think their camp is under attack."

"How do you know?"

I tell him what I saw and ask to be driven to the park.

"I have to tell Gost and the others," Polley says.

"We don't have time. If you don't take me I'll cross over right now and run down there, but I have to find out what's going on."

He thinks for a moment. "Okay, let's go."

We drive down to the entrance of Lincoln Park on North Avenue. It's now night, but it's still early and there are plenty of people and cars about. But the park is empty, mostly because there's a foot of snow out and cold as hell. That'll make crossing easier.

"You can't just step out and cross over," Polley says. "Someone will see you."

"I'll cross over here, inside the car."

He looks about. "Wait till it's clear. And are you sure this is a safe spot? On the other side I mean?"

"No. I'm sure someone will probably see me. But it's a chance I'm willing to take."

When there's a moment when no one is walking by I get down low in the car and just before I punch in the code Polley stops me.

"Wait," he says. "Take this, just in case." He takes out his handgun from its shoulder holster and hands it to me. "The safety's off so be careful."

I thank him and put it in my coat pocket. I cross over, dropping down onto the snowy ground.

I was right—they're under attack.

Small ships are flying over the camp shooting indiscriminately. Squads of Bruzers are going through shooting as well. People are screaming, running. Tents are burning. No one notices me in all the confusion. There are bodies everywhere in the snow, including the bodies of Bruzers. I guess the Resistance is putting the guns to some use. The white powder is soaked in blood. My heart races. I have to find Violet.

I start running through the camp trying to avoid getting shot or blasted. I fall in the snow, tripping over the dead and the dying. I pull myself up and continue running till I find Father Wu's tent. There's no one inside. But then I see him—lying in the snow a few feet away. I rush to his side. There's blood on his face and a gaping wound in his abdomen. He's still alive, but barely.

His eyes are open as I bend down and cradle his head. "Ryan?"

"It's me, Father. What's happened?"

"The Red Coats discovered we had the supplies hidden in several tents. They came for it. There was a fight. And then this."

"Where's Violet? Is she still here?"

"They took her," he says. "Bruzers. They grabbed her and took her."

"Where? Where did they take her?"

He points feebly to the sky—to the mothership.

"I'm sorry," he says. "It happened so fast. None of us were prepared. We tried to get people out. Everyone scattered. I don't know how many made it."

He gasps and blood drips from his mouth.

"I can help you," I tell him. "I'll get you out—somewhere safe."

He shakes his head. I can hear him mumble a prayer and then he goes limp in my arms and I know he's dead.

I'm in shock. I stand and look about me. It's all chaos. I don't know where to go or what to do. I need to find Tolliver or Brody. But it's so chaotic I don't know where to go. I turn and see a familiar figure walking towards me. It's Doyle. He's holding shockers in both hands and smiling gleefully. It looks like he's having fun. He sees me and stops.

"You!" he shouts. "Welcome back, boy."

I remove the gun from my pocket and point it at him. His face drops and he stops. "Put that down, boy."

I shake my head. He gets angry and comes for me. I fire. He stops, and looks shocked, amazed that he could be shot. Then he drops to the ground face first and doesn't move.

I begin to move forward to make sure he's dead but then see that several Bruzers have taken notice. A squad moves in my direction. They have guns as well, not shockers that won't work on me. I can't stay so I punch in the code and escape.

I don't notice if anyone saw me materialize out of thin air and I don't care. It's only been a few minutes, but it seems longer. Polley is standing by the car, smoking a cigarette. When he sees me he takes a final drag and drops the butt into the snow.

"Well?" he says.

I shake my head. "They got her."

Polley doesn't say anything as we get into the car and drive off. He takes back the gun, notices it's been fired, but doesn't ask what happened. He knows there will be time later to explain everything. I close my eyes. I wish it would all end. But I don't know how it can. Did I make things worse for them by trying to help? I want to make things better, but how can I? All I can see are bodies and the blood-soaked snow and the face of an angel being taken away.

www.ingramcontent.com/pod-product-compliance
Lightning Source LLC
Chambersburg PA
CBHW060806120626
46557CB00001B/103